U0562300

致敬译界巨匠许渊冲先生

许 渊 冲 译
唐 诗 三 百 首

300 TANG POEMS

译 注

许渊冲

（上册）

中国出版集团

中译出版社

目录 Contents

一、写景抒怀　　Man and Nature

二、咏物寄兴　Nature Poems

三、赠别怀人　　　Farewell Poems

四、故园乡情　　Homeland Poems

五、情爱相思　　Love Poems

六、咏史怀古   Historical Poems

七、边塞军旅　Frontier Poems

八、政治讽喻　　Political and Satirical Poems

九、人格境界   Personality and Character

十、人生感悟　　Reflections and Recollections

一、写景抒怀

．．．．

春江花月夜

张若虚

春江潮水连海平，海上明月共^①潮生。

滟滟^②随波千万里，何处春江无月明。

江流宛转绕芳甸^③，月照花林皆似霰^④。

空里流霜^⑤不觉飞，汀^⑥上白沙看不见。

江天一色无纤尘，皎皎空中孤月轮。

江畔何人初见月？江月何年初照人？

人生代代无穷已，江月年年望相似。

不知江月待何人，但见长江送流水。

白云一片去悠悠，青枫^⑦浦上不胜愁。

谁家今夜扁舟子^⑧？何处相思明月楼？

许渊冲译唐诗三百首

① 共：一起。
② 滟滟：水波闪动的样子。
③ 甸：郊野。
④ 霰（xiàn）：雪珠。
⑤ 流霜：形容月光洁白如霜。古人以为霜和雪一样，都是飞动的。
⑥ 汀：水中小洲。
⑦ 青枫：暗用《楚辞·招魂》中"湛湛江水兮上有枫，目极千里兮伤春心"的意思。
⑧ 扁舟子：指飘荡在外的游子。

The Moon over the River on a Spring Night

Zhang Ruoxu

In spring the river rises as high as the sea,
And with the river's tide uprises the moon bright.
She follows the rolling waves for ten thousand li;
Where'er the river flows, there overflows her light.
The river winds around the fragrant islet where
The blooming flowers in her light all look like snow.
You cannot tell her beams from hoar frost in the air,
Nor from white sand upon Farewell Beach below.
No dust has stained the water blending with the skies;
A lonely wheel-like moon shines brilliant far and wide.
Who by the riverside did first see the moon rise?
When did the moon first see a man by riverside?
Many generations have come and passed away;
From year to year the moons look alike, old and new.
We do not know tonight for whom she sheds her ray,
But hear the river say to its water adieu.
Away, away is sailing a single cloud white;
On Farewell Beach are pining away maples green.
Where is the wanderer sailing his boat tonight?
Who, pining away, on the moonlit rails would lean?

許渊冲译唐诗三百首

可怜楼上月徘徊，应照离人妆镜台。

玉户①帘中卷不去，捣衣砧②上拂还来。

此时相望不相闻，愿逐月华流照君。

鸿雁长飞光不度③，鱼龙潜跃水成文④。

昨夜闲潭梦落花，可怜春半不还家。

江水流春去欲尽，江潭落月复西斜。

斜月沉沉藏海雾，碣石潇湘⑤无限路。

不知乘月几人归，落月摇情满江树。

① 玉户：装饰华丽的窗户，指闺中。
② 捣衣砧：捶衣服用的石板。
③ 度：飞越。
④ 文：同"纹"，波纹。
⑤ 碣石潇湘：泛指天南地北。碣石，山名，原为河北省乐亭县西南的大碣石山，现已沉落海中。潇湘，潇、湘二水在湖南零陵县合流后称作潇湘。

Alas! The moon is lingering over the tower;

It should have seen her dressing table all alone.

She may roll curtains up, but light is in her bower;

She may wash, but moonbeams still remain on the stone.

She sees the moon, but her husband is out of sight;

She would follow the moonbeams to shine on his face.

But message-bearing swans can't fly out of moonlight,

Nor letter-sending fish can leap out of their place.

He dreamed of flowers falling o'er the pool last night;

Alas! Spring has half gone, but he can't homeward go.

The water bearing spring will run away in flight;

The moon over the pool will sink low.

In the mist on the sea the slanting moon will hide;

It's a long way from northern hills to southern streams.

How many can go home by moonlight on the tide?

The setting moon sheds o'er riverside trees but dreams.

This poem describes five of the most beautiful things in nature: spring, river, flowers, moon, night. The poet writes about a beautiful woman among flowers under the moon on a spring night, thinking of her love sailing on the river. Thus the beauty of nature mingles with the love of man.

春晓①

孟浩然

春眠不觉晓，
处处闻啼②鸟。
夜来风雨声，
花落知多少。

① 春晓：春天的早晨。
② 啼：人的啼哭或鸟兽的叫。此处指鸟叫。

A Spring Morning

Meng Haoran

This spring morning in bed I'm lying,

Not to awake till birds are crying.

After one night of wind and showers,

How many are the fallen flowers!

This quatrain reveals the poet's love of spring and his regret of her departure.

晚泊浔阳望庐山

孟浩然

挂席①几千里，
名山都未逢。
泊舟浔阳郭，
始见香炉峰②。
尝读远公③传，
永怀尘外踪。
东林精舍④近，
日暮空闻钟。

① 挂席：指船扬帆行驶。
② 香炉峰：庐山中的名峰。
③ 远公：指晋代高僧慧远。
④ 精舍：特指慧远的禅舍。

Mount Lu Viewed from Xunyang at Dusk

Meng Haoran

For miles and miles I sail and float,

High famed mountains are hard to seek.

By riverside I moor my boat,

Then I perceive the Censer Peak.

Knowing the hermit's life and way,

I love his solitary dell.

His hermitage not far away,

I hear at sunset but the bell.

许渊冲译唐诗三百首

Mount Lu is a high-famed mountain with one of its peaks looking like a censer. The poet gazes on it at dusk from Xunyang, present-day Jiujiang, a town by the riverside, and speaks of his admiration of the hermit who lived in the East Forest Temple at the foot of the mountain hundreds of years ago. The bell rings from the temple makes the poet feel the tranquillity of the hermit's life.

终南^①望余雪

祖 咏

终南阴岭^②秀，
积雪浮云端。
林表^③明霁色^④，
城中增暮寒。

---

① 终南：终南山，在今陕西长安县南五十里，又称秦岭，绵延八百多里，是渭水和
　　汉水的分水岭。
② 阴岭：山的北面为阴。终南山在长安之南，从长安望去，看到的是山北部。
③ 林表：树林的顶部。
④ 霁色：雨雪过后的阳光。

Snow atop the Southern Mountains

Zu Yong

How fair the gloomy mountainside!
Snow-crowned peaks float above the cloud.
The forest's bright in sunset dyed,
With evening cold the town's overflowed.

许
渊
冲
译
唐
诗
三
百
首

This poem is well-known for its description of natural beauties: the snow-crowned peaks mingling with floating cloud, and the gloomy forest on the mountainside brightened as if dyed by the setting sun.

青溪

王 维

言^①入黄花川^②，

每逐^③青溪水。

随山将万转，

趣途^④无百里。

声喧乱石中，

色静深松里。

漾漾泛菱荇^⑤，

澄澄映葭苇。

我心素已闲，

清川澹如此。

请留盘石上，

垂钓将已矣。

① 言：发语词，无义。
② 黄花川：在唐代凤州黄花县境内，今陕西凤县东北黄花镇附近。
③ 逐：循；沿。
④ 趣途：指走过的路途。趣，同"趋"。
⑤ 菱荇：水中草本植物。菱，一年生草本植物，叶浮水面，果实供食用或制淀粉。
　　荇，即荇菜，供药用，白茎，紫叶，浮水上。

The Blue Stream

Wang Wei

I follow the Blue Rill

To the Stream of Yellow Blooms.

It winds from hill to hill

Till far away it looms.

It roars amid pebbles white

And calms down under pines green.

Weeds float on ripples light,

Reeds mirrored like a screen.

Mind's carefree, alone;

The clear stream flows with ease.

I would sit on a stone

To fish whatever I please.

This poem is typical of the poet's description of hills and rills. His mind is as carefree as the clear stream.

许渊冲译唐诗三百首

山居① 秋暝②

王 维

空山新雨后，
天气晚来秋。
明月松间照，
清泉石上流。
竹喧归浣女③，
莲动下渔舟。
随意春芳歇，
王孙④自可留。

① 山居：山中居所。
② 秋暝：秋天的傍晚。
③ 浣女：洗衣服的女子。浣，洗涤。
④ 王孙：泛指，此处指诗人自己。

Autumn Evening in The Mountains

Wang Wei

After fresh rain in mountains bare,

Autumn permeates evening air.

Among pine trees bright moonbeams peer;

Over crystal stones flows water clear.

Bamboos whisper of washer-maids;

Lotus stirs when fishing boat wades.

Though fragrant spring may pass away,

Still here's the place for you to stay.

This poem reveals the poet's love of nature (i. e. pine trees, whispering bamboos, lotus blooms, bright moonbeams, clear water, crystal stones) and man (i. e. washermaids, fishermen).

许渊冲译唐诗三百首

使至塞上 ①

王 维

单车 ② 欲问边，

属国 ③ 过居延 ④ 。

征蓬 ⑤ 出汉塞，

归雁入胡天。

大漠孤烟直，

长河落日圆。

萧关 ⑥ 逢候骑 ⑦ ，

都护 ⑧ 在燕然 ⑨ 。

① 塞上：边塞之上。
② 单车：出使的车仗简单，随从不多。
③ 属国：一种说法是，汉代称那些仍旧保留原有国号的附属国为属国。另一种说法是，属国是官名"典属国"的简称，其职事是与少数民族交往，苏武归国后任此职。唐代则以其代指使臣，本诗指诗人本人。当时诗人以监察御史的身份出塞慰问得胜将士。
④ 居延：汉属居延国，汉末设县，属张掖郡，在今甘肃省古额济纳旗东南。《后汉书·郡国志》："凉州有张掖居延属国。"
⑤ 征蓬：蓬，草名，茎高尺余，叶如柳叶，开小白花，秋枯根拔，风卷而飞，因此又叫飞蓬。蓬草根浅，随风飘行，所以古人以征蓬、飘蓬比喻漂泊的旅人。
⑥ 萧关：一名古陇关，汉朝与匈奴对抗时的要塞。汉文帝十四年，匈奴杀北地都尉入萧关。其地在今宁夏回族自治区固原县东南。
⑦ 候骑：骑马的侦察兵。
⑧ 都护：唐代边疆设置都护府，都护府的长官为都护，这里指崔希逸。
⑨ 燕然：山名，即蒙古国赛音诺颜部境内的杭爱山。汉车骑将军窦宪击破匈奴北单于，追击至燕然山，登山刻石记功而还，后世用于克敌制胜的典故。这里借用之。

On Mission to the Frontier

Wang Wei

A single carriage goes to the frontier;
An envoy crosses northwest mountains high.
Like tumbleweed I leave the fortress drear;
As wild geese I come under Tartarian sky.
In boundless desert lonely smokes rise straight;
Over endless river the sun sinks round.
I meet a cavalier at the camp gate;
In northern fort the general will be found.

In 737 the poet was sent as an envoy to the frontier and he wrote this poem on his way, in which he compares himself to the rootless tumbleweed and the wild goose longing for home. This poem is well-known for the description of "straight" smoke and "round" sun against the background of a "boundless" desert and an "endless" river.

竹里馆[①]

王　维

独坐幽篁[②]里，
弹琴复长啸[③]。
深林人不知，
明月来相照。

---

① 竹里馆：辋川别墅胜景之一。
② 幽篁：幽深茂密的竹林。《楚辞·九歌·山鬼》："余处幽篁兮终不见天。"
③ 啸：撮口发出悠长而清亮的声音。《晋书·阮籍传》载阮籍擅长啸，入苏门山寻
　孙登，惊闻孙登之啸"若鸾凤之音，响乎岩谷"。魏晋以后，成为隐逸高士的一
　种风尚与标志。

The Bamboo Hut

Wang Wei

Sitting among bamboos alone,

I play on lute and croon carefree.

In the deep woods where I'm unknown,

Only the bright moon peeps at me.

This quatrain describes the communion of a solitary lutist with nature, that is, the solitary moon and a solitary bamboo grove.

辛夷坞①

王　维

木末②芙蓉花，
山中发红萼③。
涧户④寂无人，
纷纷开且⑤落。

① 辛夷坞：辋川附近的地名。辛夷，又名木笔，落叶乔木，春季开花，形似莲花。坞，四周高中间低的地方。
② 木末：树梢。
③ 萼：花苞。
④ 涧户：山涧两崖相向，状若门户，即山涧。孔稚珪《北山移文》："涧户摧绝无与归。"一说山涧里的人家，似非。诗中明说"寂无人"，何来人家？
⑤ 且：又。

The Magnolia Dale

Wang Wei

The magnolia-tipped trees,
In mountains burst in flowers.
The mute brook-side house sees,
Them blow and fall in showers.

許
淵
冲
译
唐
诗
三
百
首

This quatrain reveals the poet's sympathy with the magnolia flowers which burst in blossom
and then fall on decline.

蜀道难

李 白

噫吁嚱，危乎高哉！

蜀道之难，难于上青天！

蚕丛及鱼凫[①]，开国何茫然。

尔来四万八千岁，不与秦塞通人烟。

西当太白[②]有鸟道，可以横绝峨眉巅。

地崩山摧壮士死[③]，然后天梯石栈相钩连。

上有六龙[④]回日之高标[⑤]，下有冲波逆折之回川。

黄鹤之飞尚不得过，猿猱欲度愁攀援。

青泥[⑥]何盘盘，百步九折萦岩峦。

[①] 蚕丛及鱼凫：古蜀国国王。
[②] 太白：太乙，秦岭峰名。
[③] 地崩山摧壮士死：《华阳国志·蜀志》：相传秦惠王想征服蜀国，知道蜀王好色，答应送给他五个美女。蜀王派五位壮士去接人。回到梓潼的时候，看见一条大蛇进入穴中，一位壮士抓住了它的尾巴，其余四人也来相助，用力往外拽。不多时，山崩地裂，壮士和美女都被压死。摧：崩塌。
[④] 六龙：神话中替太阳驾车的羲和，每天赶着六条龙在天空从东行到西。
[⑤] 高标：最高峰。
[⑥] 青泥：岭名，为唐入蜀要道。在今陕西省略阳县。《元和郡县志》："悬崖万仞，山多云雨，行者屡逢泥淖，故号青泥岭。"

Hard is the Road to Shu

Li Bai

Oho! Behold! How Steep! How high!

The road to Shu is harder than to climb the sky.

Since the two pioneers

Put the kingdom in order,

Have passed forty-eight thousand years,

And few have tried to pass its border.

There's a bird track o'er Great White Mountain to the west,

Which cuts through Mountain Eyebrows by the crest.

The crest crumbled, five serpent-killing heroes slain,

Along the cliffs a rocky path was hacked then.

Above stand peaks too high for the sun to pass o'er;

Below the torrents run back and forth, churn and roar.

Even the Golden Crane can't fly across;

How to climb over, gibbons are at a loss.

What tortuous mountain path Green Mud Ridge faces!

Around the top we turn nine turns each hundred paces.

扪参历井①仰胁息，以手抚膺坐长叹。

问君西游何时还？畏途巉岩不可攀。

但见悲鸟号古木，雄飞雌从绕林间。

又闻子规②啼夜月，愁空山，

蜀道之难，难于上青天，使人听此凋朱颜。

连峰去天不盈尺，枯松倒挂倚绝壁。

飞湍瀑流争喧豗，砯崖转石万壑雷。

---

① 扪参历井：形容山势高峻，道路险阻。参、井，皆星宿名。参是蜀的分野，井是
秦的分野（古人认为地上某地区与天上某星宿相应，分成若干界域，叫分野）。
② 子规：杜鹃鸟。据《华阳国志·蜀志》，古有蜀王杜宇，号望帝，后禅位出奔，
其时子规鸟鸣。蜀人因思念杜宇，故觉此鸟鸣悲切。

Looking up breathless, I can touch the stars nearby;

Beating my breast, I sink aground with long, long sigh.

When will you come back from this journey to the west?

How can you climb up dangerous path and mountain crest,

Where you can hear on ancient trees but sad birds wail

And see the female birds fly, followed by the male?

And hear home-going cuckoos weep

Beneath the moon in mountains deep?

The road to Shu is harder than to climb the sky,

On hearing this, your cheeks would lose their rosy dye.

Between the sky and peaks there is not a foot's space,

And ancient pines hang, head down, from the cliff's surface.

And cataracts and torrents dash on boulders under,

Roaring like thousands of echoes of thunder.

许
渊
冲
译
唐
诗
三
百
首

其险也如此，嗟尔远道之人，

胡为乎来哉！剑阁^①峥嵘而崔嵬，

一夫当关，万夫莫开。

所守或匪亲，化为狼与豺。

朝避猛虎，夕避长蛇，

磨牙吮血，杀人如麻。

锦城虽云乐，不如早还家。

蜀道之难，难于上青天，侧身西望长咨嗟！

---

① 剑阁：四川省剑阁县北七里大、小剑山间的一座雄关，即剑门关。西晋张载《剑阁铭》："一人荷戟，万夫趑趄。形胜之地，匪亲勿居。"

So dangerous these places are,

Alas! Why should you come here from afar?

Rugged is the path between the cliffs so steep and high,

Guarded by one

And forced by none.

Disloyal guards

Would turn wolves and pards,

Man-eating tigers at day-break

And at dusk blood-sucking long snake.

One may make merry in the Town of Silk, I know,

But I would rather homeward go.

The road to Shu is harder than to climb the sky,

I'd turn and westward look with long, long sigh.

This poem shows not only the hard way to Shu, present-day Sichuan Province, but also the hard way to rising above in society.

金陵城西楼① 月下吟

李 白

金陵夜寂凉风发，

独上高楼望吴越②。

白云映水摇空城③，

白露垂珠滴秋月。

月下沉吟久不归，

古来相接④ 眼中稀。

解道⑤ 澄江净如练，

令人长忆谢玄晖⑥。

---

① 西楼：南京城西孙楚酒楼，因西晋诗人孙楚曾来此登高吟咏而得名。

② 吴越：今江苏苏州至浙江绍兴一带。

③ 空城：指城中寂无声息，像是无人居住的空城。

④ 相接：指精神相通，有心灵上的共鸣。

⑤ 解道：懂得说。

⑥ 谢玄晖：即谢朓，其字玄晖，南齐著名诗人。他的诗《晚登三山还望京邑》中有
云："余霞散成绮，澄江净如练。"

Orally Composed on the Western Tower of Jinling in Moonlight

Li Bai

The cool breeze blows on silent night in Town of Stone,
To view the south I mount the high tower alone.
White clouds and city walls mirrored on ripples swoon;
Dewdrops look like pearls dripping from the autumn moon.
Crooning long, I won't go back; drowned in moon rays;
How few are connoisseurs in my eyes since olden days!
Seeing the river crystal-clear and silver-white,
How I miss the unforgettable poet bright!

許渊冲译唐诗三百首

The poet gives free rein to his imagination in describing the scenery of Jinling or the Town of Stones: clouds could swoon, pearls could drip from the moon, and the poet could be drowned in moonlight. The unforgettable poet refers to Xie Tiao (464—499).

山中

王 维

荆溪[①] 白石出，
天寒红叶[②] 稀。
山路元[③] 无雨，
空翠[④] 湿人衣。

① 荆溪：长水，源出蓝田县。《水经注·渭水》："长水出自杜县白鹿原，西北流，谓之荆溪。"
② 红叶：枫、槭一类的树叶，秋季经霜之后逐渐由绿变红。
③ 元：原来，本来。
④ 空翠：弥漫在空间的浓翠欲滴的山色。谢灵运《过白岸亭》："空翠难强名，渔钓易为曲。"杜甫《大历三年春白帝城放船出瞿塘峡久居夔府将适江陵漂泊有诗凡四十韵》："石苔凌几杖，空翠扑肌肤。"

In the Hills

Wang Wei

White pebbles hear a blue stream glide;
Red leaves are strewn on cold hillside.
Along thc path no rain is seen,
My gown is moist with drizzling green.

This is a colorful picture of the hills: white pebbles, blue stream, red leaves and the drizzling green which can not only be seen but also heard and felt.

峨眉山月歌

李　白

峨眉①山月半轮②秋，
影入平羌③江水流。
夜发清溪④向三峡⑤，
思君不见下渝州。

① 峨眉：峨眉山，在四川峨眉县。
② 半轮：指月形如半个车轮。
③ 平羌：江名，即青衣江。源出四川芦山县，流经乐山县注入岷江。
④ 清溪：驿名，在今四川犍为县。
⑤ 三峡：关于三峡众说纷纭。《峡程记》：三峡者，明月峡、巫山峡、广溪峡。有
　　人解释为三峡俱在巴东，大抵六七百里，巫山之下为巫峡，巫峡之上为广溪峡，
　　巫峡之下为西陵峡。

The Moon over Mount Brow

Li Bai

The crescent moon looks like old Autumn's golden brow;
Its deep reflection flows with limpid water blue.
I'll leave the town on Clear Stream for the Three Gorges now.
O Moon, how I miss you when you are out of view!

许渊冲译唐诗三百首

This quatrain is written when the poet sails on the river between the steep cliffs which prevent him from seeing the moon he saw over Mount Brow in his homeland.

清溪^①行

李　白

清溪清我心，

水色异诸水。

借问新安江^②，

见底何如此?

人行明镜中，

鸟度屏风^③里。

向晚^④猩猩啼，

空悲远游子^⑤。

① 清溪：在安徽池州西北五里，其地在唐时为秋浦县。
② 新安江：浙江的上游，源出安徽黄山。
③ 屏风：比喻重叠的山峦。
④ 向晚：傍晚。
⑤ 远游子：远游他乡的人。此指诗人自己。

Song of the Clear Stream

Li Bai

The Clear Stream clears my heart;

Its water flows apart.

I ask the River New,

"Why transparent are you?"

On mirror bright boats hie;

Between the screens birds fly.

At dusk the monkeys cry;

In vain the wayfarers sigh.

This poem describes the scenery on the Clear Stream and the poet's feeling on leaving it.

035

望庐山^①瀑布

李　白

日照香炉^②生紫烟^③，

遥看瀑布挂前川^④。

飞流直下三千尺，

疑是银河落九天^⑤。

① 庐山：在今江西省九江市南，为著名风景区，历来有"匡庐奇秀甲天下"之称。
② 香炉：庐山上的香炉峰，因形状如香炉又有烟雾缭绕而得名。
③ 紫烟：紫色的烟气（香炉峰峰顶的烟气在阳光照射下呈现出紫色）。
④ 前川：香炉峰前的水流。
⑤ 九天：古代传说天有九重，九天是天的最高层。

The Waterfall in Mount Lu Viewed from Afar

Li Bai

The sunlit Censer Peak exhales incense-like cloud;
Like an upended stream the cataract sounds loud.
Its torrent dashes down three thousand feet from high,
As if the Silver River fell from the blue sky.

This quatrain describes the beauty of the waterfall in Mount Lu with the Censer Peak above it. The poet compares it to the Silver River, Chinese name for the Milky Way.

日暮

杜　甫

牛羊下来久，
各已闭柴门。
风月自清夜，
江山非故园。
石泉流暗壁，
草露滴秋根[1]。
头白灯明里，
何须花烬[2]繁。

---

[1] 秋根：秋天的草根。沈约诗："草根滴露霜"。
[2] 花烬：灯芯结花，民俗中有"预报喜兆"之意。

After Sunset

Du Fu

The sheep and cattle come to rest,
All thatched gates closed east and west.
The gentle breeze and the moon bright,
Remind me of homeland at night.
Among rocks flow fountains unseen;
Autumn drips dewdrops on grass green.
The candle brightens white-haired head.
Why should its flame blaze up so red?

许渊冲译唐诗三百首

This poem was written in 767 when the poet had left his homeland for several years. As he was in a gloomy mood, he did not like the candlelight to brighten the dark corner of his heart. His nostalgia is intensified by the contrast between the outer world and his inner world.

春夜喜雨

杜　甫

好雨知^①时节，

当春乃发生^②。

随风潜入夜，

润物细无声。

野径^③云俱黑，

江船火独明。

晓看红湿处，

花重锦官城^④。

---

① 知：懂得。本诗中可看作适应的意思。
② 发生：萌发。
③ 野径：田野间的小路。
④ 锦官城：四川成都。成都盛产蜀锦，住过主持织锦的官，因此而得名。

Happy Rain on a Spring Night

Du Fu

Good rain knows its time right,

It will fall when comes spring.

With wind it steals in night;

Mute, it wets everything.

Over wild lanes dark cloud spreads;

In boat a lantern looms.

Dawn sees saturated reds;

The town's heavy with blooms.

许渊冲译唐诗三百首

The spring rain personified gladdens the poet for it knows the right time to fall, moistens everything and lasts long. The poet tells us what he hears, sees and thinks on a rainy night.

江村

杜　甫

清江①一曲②抱村流，

长夏③江村事事幽。

自去自来梁上燕，

相亲相近水中鸥。

老妻画纸为棋局，

稚子④敲针作钓钩。

但有故人供禄米，

微躯⑤此外更何求？

① 清江：清澈的江水，指浣花溪。
② 曲：曲折。
③ 长夏：长长的夏日。
④ 稚子：幼小的儿子。
⑤ 微躯：微贱的身体。这是诗人的一种谦词。

The Riverside Village

Du Fu

See the clear river wind by the village and flow!
We pass the long summer by riverside with ease.
The swallows freely come in and freely out go.
The gulls on water snuggle each other as they please.
My wife draws lines on paper to make a chessboard;
My son bends a needle into a fishing hook.
Ill, I need only medicine I can afford.
What else do I want for myself in my humble nook?

许渊冲译唐诗三百首

This poem describes the thatched hall built in 760 and the leisurely life of the poet.

绝句

杜 甫

两个黄鹂[①]鸣翠柳，
一行白鹭[②]上青天。
窗含西岭[③]千秋雪，
门泊东吴[④]万里船。

① 黄鹂：黄莺。
② 白鹭：体形似鹤而略小一点，颈、腿都较长，全身羽毛纯白。
③ 西岭：泛指岷山，在成都西。
④ 东吴：泛指长江下游。

A Quatrain

Du Fu

Two golden orioles sing amid the willows green;
A flock of white egrets fly into the blue sky.
My window frames the snow-crowned western mountain scene;
My door off says to eastward going ships "Goodbye!"

The first couplet of this quatrain is a colorful picture: golden orioles and green willows, white egrets and blue sky. The second couplet presents a vast view of the east and the west, mountain and river, but within the framework of his door and window.

枫桥① 夜泊②

张 继

月落乌啼霜满天，

江枫渔火对愁眠。

姑苏③ 城外寒山寺④，

夜半钟声⑤ 到客船。

① 枫桥：今江苏省苏州市西枫桥镇，原名"封桥"，因张继此诗而改名为"枫桥"。
② 夜泊：夜间把船停靠在岸边。
③ 姑苏：苏州。苏州市西南有姑苏山，因此而得名。
④ 寒山寺：在苏州西十里，枫桥附近，寺建于南朝梁代，原名妙利普明塔院。相传
   唐初著名高僧寒山曾在此居住，因此改名寒山寺。
⑤ 夜半钟声：当时寺院有半夜敲钟的习惯，多见于唐代诗人的吟咏。

Mooring by Maple Bridge at Night

Zhang Ji

The crows at moonset cry, streaking the frosty sky;
Facing dim fishing boats neath maples, sad I lie.
Beyond the city wall, from Temple of Cold Hill
Bells break the ship-borne roamer's dream in midnight still.

许
渊
冲
译
唐
诗
三
百
首

This quatrain gives a gloomy picture of a roamer dreaming of home in a dimly-lit boat. What he sees is moonset, frosty sky, dimly-lit fishing boats, dark maple trees. What he hears is crows' caw and temple bells. The outer gloom intensifies his inner gloom.

江南行

张　潮

茨菰^①叶烂别西湾^②，
莲子花开犹未还^③。
妾梦不离江上水，
人传郎在凤凰山^④。

① 茨菰（cí gū）：慈姑。多年生草本植物，生在水田里，叶子像箭头，开白花。地下有球茎，黄白色或青白色，可以吃。"茨菰叶烂"之时当为秋末冬初。
② 西湾：江边某处。
③ 犹未还：一作"不见还"。
④ 凤凰山：虚指某山。

Song of the Southern Rivershore

Zhang Chao

When leaves fell in decay, you left the western bay,
But you have not come back now lotus blossoms sway.
My dream oft lingers on the stream or by the fountain,
But you are said to be far away in the mountain.

许
渊
冲
译
唐
诗
三
百
首

A merchant's wife on the southern rivershore longs for her husband who left her in autumn but has not come back in summer. She compares her longing to the long river, but her husband is far away in the far-off mountain.

春山夜月

于良史

春山多胜事①，
赏玩夜忘归。
掬②水月在手，
弄花香满衣。
兴③来无远近，
欲去惜芳菲④。
南望鸣钟处，
楼台深翠微⑤。

① 胜事：美景。
② 掬：双手捧。
③ 兴：兴致。
④ 芳菲：指花草。
⑤ 翠微：青翠的山色。

The Vernal Hill in Moonlit Night

Yu Liangshi

How much delight in vernal hill?
Don't go back but enjoy your fill!
Drinking water, you drink moonbeams;
Plucking flowers, you pluck sweet dreams.
Happy, you would forget the hours;
About to go, you can't leave flowers.
Looking south where you hear the bell,
You'll find green bowers in green dell.

许渊冲译唐诗三百首

This poem describes the exquisite delight in the vernal hill where moonbeams dissolve into the handful of water the poet drinks.

兰溪①棹歌②

戴叔伦

凉月③如眉挂柳湾④，
越中⑤山色镜中看。
兰溪三日桃花雨⑥，
半夜鲤鱼来上滩。

---

① 兰溪：在今浙江省兰溪县西南。
② 棹歌：古代的一种船歌。棹（zhào），划（船）。
③ 凉月：新月。
④ 柳湾：柳树环绕的水湾。
⑤ 越中：今浙江省东部地区，春秋时为越国所在地。
⑥ 桃花雨：指桃花开放时下的雨，即春雨。

A Fisherman's Song on the Orchid Stream

Dai Shulun

The eyebrow-like cool moon hangs over Willow Bay,
The southern mountains seem in the mirror to sway.
Three days rain's fallen with peach petals on the stream;
At midnight on the beach leap the fish, carp and bream.

许
渊
冲
译
唐
诗
三
百
首

This short song describes the beauty of the Orchid Stream and the joy of a fisherman.

江南曲

李　益

嫁得瞿塘贾，
朝朝误妾期。
早知潮有信，
嫁与弄潮儿。

A Southern Song

Li Yi

Since I became a merchant's wife,
I've in his absence passed my life.
A sailor comes home with the tide,
I should have been a sailor's bride.

This song reveals the regret of a merchant's wife whose husband has not kept his promise to come home in due time as a sailor who would come back with the tide.

巫山 ① 曲

孟 郊

巴江 ② 上峡重复重，
阳台碧峭十二峰 ③。
荆王 ④ 猎时逢暮雨，
夜卧高丘 ⑤ 梦神女。
轻红 ⑥ 流烟湿艳姿，
行云飞去明星稀。
目极魂断望不见，
猿啼三声泪滴衣。

① 巫山：巫山山脉位于川鄂交界地区，北与大巴山相连，呈东北、西南走向。
② 巴江：流经今四川、湖北境内，发源于石林县城北，从石林大叠水进入宜良县竹
   山乡而汇入南盘江，因其源头盘旋回绕形如"巴"字而得名。
③ 十二峰：位于巫山县东部的长江两岸，江南江北各有六峰。分别为：登龙、圣泉、
   朝云、望霞（神女）、松峦、集仙、净坛、起云、上升、飞凤、翠屏、聚鹤。
④ 荆王：楚王。古称楚地为荆。
⑤ 高丘：神女居处。《高唐赋》神女自述："妾在巫山之阳，高丘之阴。"
⑥ 轻红：淡红色。

Song of the Mountain Goddess

Meng Jiao

Going upstream, I see mountain on mountain high;
The twelve green peaks with Sunny Terrace scrape the sky.
The king in hunting caught by sudden evening shower
Slept there and dreamed of the Goddess in Sunny Bower.
To her charm added the mist-veiled rainbow dress bright;
Away she flew with faded stars and clouds in flight.
However far I stretch my eyes, she can't be found;
Hearing the monkey's wail, in longing tears I'm drowned.

The legend goes that King Xiang of Chu dreamed of the Mountain Goddess and made love with her in the Sunny Bower, and she would come in morning cloud and go away in evening shower. The poet sees the Peak of Goddess and writes this poem.

許渊冲译唐诗三百首

城东早春

杨巨源

诗家^①清景^②在新春,
绿柳才黄半未匀。
若待上林^③花似锦^④,
出门俱是看花人。

许渊冲译唐诗三百首

① 诗家:诗人。
② 清景:清丽的景色。
③ 上林:上林苑,故址在今陕西省西安市西,建于秦代,汉武帝时加以扩充,为汉宫苑。诗中用来代指京城长安。
④ 锦:五色织成的绸绫。

Early Spring East of the Capital

Yang Juyuan

The early spring presents to poets a fresh scene:
The willow twigs half yellow and half tender green.
When the Royal Garden's covered with blooming flowers,
Then it would be the visitors' busiest hours.

许渊冲译唐诗三百首

This quatrain describes the beauty of spring scenery and the joy of visitors.

湘江曲

张　籍

湘水无潮秋水阔，
湘中月落行人发。
送人发，送人归，
白蘋茫茫鹧鸪飞。

Song on River Xiang

Zhang Ji

The River Xiang unruffled in autumn looks wide,

The wayfarer at moonset leaves the riverside.

We see wayfarers come, we see wayfarers go,

Over white duckweed partridges fly to and fro.

In this quatrain the wayfarers are compared to partridges flying to and fro.

春雪

韩 愈

新年都未有芳华，
二月初惊见草芽。
白雪却嫌春色晚，
故穿庭树作飞花。

Spring Snow

Han Yu

On vernal day no flowers were in bloom, alas!
In second moon I'm glad to see the budding grass.
But white snow dislikes the late coming vernal breeze,
It plays the parting flowers flying through the trees.

许渊冲译唐诗三百首

Spring snow is compared to flying flowers in this quatrain.

晚春[①]

韩 愈

草树[②]知春不久归，
百般红紫斗芳菲。
杨花榆荚[③]无才思，
惟解漫天作雪飞。

① 晚春：一作"游城南晚春"。
② 草树：又作"草木"。
③ 榆荚：榆钱，老呈白色，随风飘落。

Late Spring

Han Yu

The trees and grass know that soon spring will go away;
Of red blooms and green leaves they make gorgeous display.
But willow catkins and elm pods are so unwise,
They wish to be flying snow darkening the skies.

Spring snow is compared to flying flowers in this quatrain.

始闻秋风

刘禹锡

昔看黄菊与君别，

今听玄蝉①我却回②。

五夜③飕飗④枕前觉，

一年颜状镜中来。

马思边草拳毛⑤动，

雕⑥盻青云⑦睡眼开。

天地肃清⑧堪四望，

为君扶病上高台。

① 玄蝉：黑色的知了。
② 我却回：指自己退居故乡洛阳。
③ 五夜：五更。
④ 飕飗（sōu liú）：风声。
⑤ 拳毛：卷曲的毛。
⑥ 雕：猛禽。
⑦ 青云：代指高远天空。
⑧ 肃清：肃杀而清爽。

许渊冲译唐诗三百首

Ode to the Autumn Breeze

Liu Yuxi

Gone with yellow chrysanthemums last year,

You come back when cicada's song I hear.

Your soughing wakes me from dreams at midnight,

A year's wrinkles are seen in mirror bright.

Steeds missing frontier grass with bristles rise;

Eagles longing for clouds open sleepy eyes.

I'll gaze my fill into the boundless sky;

Though ill, for you I'll mount the tower high.

许渊冲译唐诗三百首

The poet shows his spirit to go higher and see farther in the melancholy season.

钱塘湖^① 春行

白居易

孤山^② 寺北贾亭^③ 西,

水面初平云脚^④ 低。

几处早莺争暖树^⑤,

谁家新燕^⑥ 啄春泥。

乱花^⑦ 渐欲迷人眼,

浅草才能没马蹄。

最爱湖东行不足^⑧,

绿杨阴里白沙堤^⑨。

① 钱塘湖：杭州西湖。
② 孤山：独立于西湖里湖与外湖之间的一座小山。
③ 贾亭：贾公亭。
④ 云脚：指贴近地面、湖面的云气。
⑤ 暖树：向阳的树木。
⑥ 新燕：指春燕。
⑦ 乱花：纷繁的花。
⑧ 行不足：游赏不尽。
⑨ 白沙堤：白堤。

On Qiantang Lake in Spring

Bai Juyi

West of Jia Pavilion and north of Lonely Hill,

Water brims level with the bank and clouds hang low.

Disputing for sunny trees, early orioles trill,

Pecking vernal mud in, young swallows come and go.

A riot of blooms begins to dazzle the eye,

Amid short grass the horse hoofs can barely be seen.

I love best the east of the lake under the sky,

The bank paved with white sand is shaded by willows green.

Qiantang Lake is later known as the West Lake in Hangzhou, and Jia Pavilion and Lonely Hill are scenic spots to the east or south of the Lake.

杭州春望

白居易

望海楼^① 明照曙霞，

护江堤^② 白踏晴沙。

涛声夜入伍员庙^③，

柳色春藏苏小家^④。

红袖^⑤ 织绫夸柿蒂^⑥，

青旗^⑦ 沽酒趁梨花^⑧。

谁开湖寺^⑨ 西南路^⑩，

草绿裙腰一道斜。

① 望海楼：又名望潮楼，即中和堂东楼，东楼在凤凰山上，离州衙不远，是白居易
   喜爱的去处。作者原注："城东楼名望海楼。"
② 护江堤：杭州东南钱塘江岸筑以防备海潮的长堤。
③ 伍员庙：杭州城内吴山（又称胥山、城隍山）上的"伍员庙"。
④ 苏小家：指舞女所居住的秦楼楚馆。苏小，指南齐时期钱塘名妓苏小小。
⑤ 红袖：指织绫女子。
⑥ 柿蒂：指绫的花纹。
⑦ 青旗：代指酒店。
⑧ 梨花：语意双关。作者原注："其俗，酿酒趁梨花时熟，号为'梨花春'。"
⑨ 湖寺：指孤山寺。
⑩ 西南路：指由断桥向西南通往湖中到孤山的长堤，即白沙堤（简称白堤）。

Spring View in Hangzhou

Bai Juyi

Viewed from the Seaside Tower morning clouds look bright;

Along the riverbank I tread on fine sand white.

The General's Temple hears roaring nocturnal tide;

Spring dwells in the Beauty's Bower green willow hide.

The red sleeves weave brocade broidered with flowers fine;

Blue streamers show amid pear blossoms a shop of wine.

Who opens a southwest lane to the temple scene?

It slants like a silk girdle around a skirt green.

The General refers to Wu Yuan whose wrath against the King of Chu seems to be heard in the roaring tide. The Beauty refers to Su Xiaoxiao who was buried in the West Lake.

许

渊

冲

译

唐

诗

三

百

首

暮江吟

白居易

一道残阳铺水中，
半江瑟瑟^①半江红。
可怜^②九月初三夜，
露似真珠^③月似弓。

---

① 瑟瑟：原指碧色宝石，此处指江面上，残阳照不到之处的情景。因其为碧色，如
碧石，故称瑟瑟。
② 可怜：可爱。
③ 真珠：珍珠。

Sunset and Moonrise on the River

Bai Juyi

The departing sunbeams pave a way on the river;
Half of its waves turn red and the other half shiver.
How I love the third night of the ninth moon aglow!
The dewdrops look like pearls, the crescent like a bow.

許
渊
冲
译
唐
诗
三
百
首

This quatrain describes the poet's love of the beautiful river at sunset and at moonrise.

溪居

柳宗元

久为簪组^①累，
幸此南夷^②谪^③。
闲依农圃邻，
偶似山林客。
晓耕翻露草，
夜榜^④响溪石。
来往不逢人，
长歌楚天^⑤碧。

许渊冲译唐诗三百首

① 簪组：这里是做官的意思。
② 南夷：这里指当时南方的少数民族地区。
③ 谪：被降职或调往偏远地区。
④ 夜榜：夜航。榜，划船。
⑤ 楚天：永州古属楚地。

Living by the Brookside

Liu Zongyuan

Tired of officialdom for long,

I'm glad to be banished southwest.

At leisure I hear farmer's song;

Haply I look like hillside guest.

At dawn I cut grass wet with dew;

My boat comes o'er pebbles at night.

To and fro there's no man in view;

I chant till southern sky turns bright.

許
渊
冲
译
唐
诗
三
百
首

The poet sings of his leisurely life after his banishment to the southwest.

雨后晓行独至愚溪北池

柳宗元

宿云^①散洲渚^②，

晓日明^③村坞^④。

高树临清池，

风惊夜来雨。

予心适^⑤无事，

偶^⑥此成宾主。

① 宿云：因昨夜降雨，故称残云为宿云。
② 洲渚：指水中陆地。
③ 明：照亮。
④ 坞：村外障蔽物。
⑤ 适：恰巧。
⑥ 偶：偶然。一说投合。

The Northern Pool Visited Alone after the Rain at Dawn

Liu Zongyuan

Over the islets disperse clouds of last night,

The rising sun makes poolside village bright.

A tall tree overlooks the water clear;

Raindrops fall, startled by the wind severe.

Unoccupied, my mind is just carefree;

By chance the tree plays host to welcome me.

The poet is as carefree as the tree by the poolside.

雪晴晚望

贾　岛

倚杖望晴雪，

溪云几万重。

樵人 ① 归白屋，

寒日下危峰。

野火烧冈草 ②，

断烟生石松。

却回山寺路，

闻打暮天钟。

---

① 樵人：打柴的人。
② 冈草：山冈上的野草。

Evening View of a Snow Scene

Jia Dao

Cane in hand, I gaze on fine snow;

Cloud on cloud spreads over the creek.

To snow-covered cots woodmen go;

The sun sets on the frowning peak.

In the wildfire burns the grass dried;

Mid rocks and pines smoke and mist rise.

Back to the temple by the hillside,

I hear bells ring in evening skies.

许渊冲译唐诗三百首

This poem is written after the poet's failure in the civil service examinations.

江南春

杜 牧

千里莺啼绿映红，
水村山郭酒旗^①风。
南朝^②四百八十寺，
多少楼台烟雨中。

① 酒旗：俗称"酒望子"，是酒家的标志。
② 南朝：指宋、齐、梁、陈四朝，南朝皇帝大都信奉佛教。

Spring on the Southern Rivershore

Du Mu

Orioles sing for miles amid red blooms and green trees;

By hills and rills wine shop streamers wave in the breeze.

Four hundred eighty splendid temples still remain

Of Southern Dynasties in the mist and rain.

许

渊

冲

译

唐

诗

三

百

首

This quatrain shows the poet's admiration of the splendor of the Southern Rivershore.

清明

杜　牧

清明^① 时节雨纷纷，
路上行人欲断魂^②。
借问酒家何处有，
牧童遥指杏花村。

① 清明：二十四节气之一，在阳历四月五日前后。
② 断魂：伤心的样子。

The Mourning Day

Du Mu

A drizzling rain falls like tears on the Mourning Day;
The mourner's heart is going to break on his way.
Where can a wine shop be found to drown his sad hours?
A cowherd points to a cot amid apricot flowers.

On the Mourning Day early in the third moon, the mourners' tears mingle with the drizzling rain. This picture shows the commotion of man with nature.

商山早行

温庭筠

晨起动征铎①，

客行悲故乡。

鸡声茅店月，

人迹板桥霜。

槲②叶落山路，

枳③花明驿墙④。

因思杜陵⑤梦，

凫⑥雁满回塘⑦。

① 动征铎（duó）：震动出行的铃铛。征铎，车行时悬挂在马颈上的铃铛。铎，大铃。
② 槲（hú）：一种落叶乔木。
③ 枳（zhǐ）：也叫"臭橘"。一种落叶灌木。
④ 驿墙：驿站的墙壁。驿，古时候递送公文的人或来往官员暂住、换马的处所。
⑤ 杜陵：在长安城南，因汉宣帝陵墓所在而得名。这里指长安。作者此时从长安赴
　　襄阳投友，途经商山。
⑥ 凫（fú）：野鸭。
⑦ 回塘：岸边弯曲的湖塘。

Early Departure on Mount Shang

Wen Tingyun

At dawn I rise, with ringing bells my cab goes,
But grieved in thoughts of my home, I feel lost.
As the moon sets over thatched inn, the cock crows;
Footprints are left on wood bridge paved with frost.
The mountain path is covered with oak leaves,
The post-house bright with blooming orange trees.
The dream of my homeland last night still grieves,
A pool of mallards playing with wild geese.

This poem reveals the poet's homesickness by describing the scenery.

宿骆氏亭①寄怀崔雍崔衮②

李商隐

竹坞③无尘水槛④清，
相思迢递隔重城。
秋阴不散霜飞晚，
留得枯荷听雨声。

① 骆氏亭：骆氏人家的园亭。
② 崔雍崔衮（gǔn）：李商隐的表叔兼知遇者崔戎的两个儿子崔雍、崔衮。
③ 竹坞：遍植竹子的凹地。
④ 水槛：临水有栏杆的亭榭，此指骆氏亭。

For the Cui Brothers at Luo's Pavilion

Li Shangyin

In the bamboo grove by the clean poolside I stay;

Separated from you by towns, I miss you far away.

The autumn gloom undispersed and late frost remain;

Only the withered lotus listen to the rain.

许渊冲译唐诗三百首

Passing one rainy night at Luo's Pavilion, the poet thought of the Cui brothers far away and wrote this quatrain which describes his gloomy mood rather than autumn gloom.

天涯

李商隐

春日在天涯，
天涯日又斜。
莺啼如有泪，
为湿最高花。

The End of the Sky

Li Shangyin

Spring is far, far away

Where the sun slants its ray.

If orioles have tear,

Wet highest flowers here!

This quatrain may be said to be an elegy of spring, of the poet's life and of his era. The place is far away and the time late, even a happy bird would be saddened to shed tears on beautiful flowers.

许渊冲译唐诗三百首

二、咏物寄兴
·
·
·

咏蝉

骆宾王

西陆^①蝉声唱，
南冠^②客思深。
那堪^③玄鬓影^④，
来对白头吟^⑤。
露重飞难进，
风多响易沉。
无人信高洁，
谁为表予心？

① 西陆：指秋天。《隋书·天文志》："日循黄道东行，一日一夜行一度，三百六十五日有奇而周天。行东陆谓之春，行南陆谓之夏，行西陆谓之秋，行北陆谓之冬。"
② 南冠：指囚犯。《左传·成公九年》："晋侯观于军府，见钟仪，问之曰：'南冠而系者谁也？'有司对曰：'郑人所献楚囚也。'"钟仪，南方楚国人，戴楚冠，故曰"南冠"。后世遂以之代指囚犯。此诗中诗人以此自喻。
③ 那堪：怎能忍受得了。那，一作"不"。
④ 玄鬓影：指蝉。古代妇女将鬓发梳为蝉翼之状，称蝉鬓，这里以蝉鬓称蝉。崔豹《古今注》："魏文帝宫人莫琼树始制蝉鬓，缥缈如蝉。"玄，黑色。
⑤ 白头吟：白头，诗人自指。当时骆宾王不足四十岁，因身处狱中而以白头自况，极言烦恼之深重。吟，指蝉鸣。又以《白头吟》为古乐府曲调名，相传西汉时司马相如将娶茂陵女为妾，卓文君作《白头吟》以自伤。

许渊冲译唐诗三百首

The Cicada

Luo Binwang

Of autumn the cicada sings;
In prison I'm worn out with care.
How can I bear its blue-black wings
Which remind me of my grey hair?
Heavy with dew, it cannot fly;
Drowned in the wind, its song's not heard
Who would believe its spirit high?
Could I express my grief in word?

Hearing in prison the cicada sing, the poet compares himself to a cicada which cannot fly and whose song cannot be heard.

感遇三十八首（其二）

陈子昂

兰若①生春夏，
芊蔚②何青青！
幽独空林色，
朱蕤③冒紫茎。
迟迟白日晚，
嫋嫋④秋风生。
岁华尽摇落，
芳意竟何成？

① 兰若：兰花和杜若。
② 芊（qiān）蔚：草木茂盛、一片碧绿的样子。《列子·力命》："美哉国乎，郁郁芊芊。"
③ 蕤（ruí）：草木花朵下垂的样子。陆机《文赋》："播芳蕤之馥馥。"张九龄《感遇十二首》（其一）："兰叶春葳蕤。"
④ 嫋嫋：同"袅袅"，轻盈柔美的样子。

The Orchid (II)

Chen Zi'ang

In late spring grows the orchid good,
How luxuriant are its leaves green!
Alone it adorns empty wood
With red blooms and violet stems lean.
Slowly, slowly shortens the day;
Rippling, rippling blows autumn breeze.
By the year's end it fades away.
What has become of it fragrance, please?

许渊冲译唐诗三百首

The poet compares himself to the fragrant orchid which grows in late spring in an empty wood and fades away by the year's end.

咏风

王 勃

肃肃^①凉风生，

加我林壑清。

驱烟寻涧户^②，

卷雾出山楹^③。

去来固^④无迹，

动息如有情。

日落山水静，

为君起松声。

---

① 肃肃：疾速而来的风声。"肃肃"一词，可释为风行疾速的样子，如《诗·召南·小
   星》："肃肃宵征，夙夜在公，实命不同。"另可释为风声，如《后汉书·董祀
   妻传》："胡风春夏起，肃肃入我耳。"
② 涧户：山洞中的陋室，也指家居山涧者的门户。
③ 山楹：山间的房屋。汉庄忌的《哀时命》里有"凿山楹而为室兮，下被衣於水渚"
   的句子。王逸注为"凿山石以为室柱"。楹，厅堂的外柱。
④ 固：诚然；当然。

The Breeze

Wang Bo

Soughing, the cool breeze blows;
My wooded dell clean grows.
It drives smoke off the rill,
Rolls up mist over the hill,
Leaves no trace when we part,
And moves as if moved at heart.
When sunset calms the scene,
Hear the song of pines green.

许渊冲译唐诗三百首

The poet praises the breeze which appeals to our eyes by cleaning the dell and to our ears by making the pines sing their green song.

咏柳①

贺知章

碧玉②妆成一树高，
万条垂下绿丝绦③。
不知细叶谁裁出，
二月春风似剪刀。

---

① 咏柳：一作"柳枝词"。
② 碧玉：形容柳叶碧绿鲜嫩。
③ 丝绦（tāo）：丝带。这里形容柳条。

The Willow

He Zhizhang

The slender beauty's dressed in emerald all about;

A thousand branches droop like fringes made of jade.

But do you know by whom these slim leaves are cut out?

The wind of early spring is sharp as scissor blade.

许渊冲译唐诗三百首

This is a fine picture of the willow in which the imaginative poet compares the tree to a beautiful woman dressed in emerald and its branches to the fringes of her skirt, and its slim leaves cut by the sharp wind as by the scissor blade.

孤雁

杜 甫

孤雁不饮啄，
飞鸣声念群。
谁怜一片影，
相失万重云?
望尽似犹见，
哀多如更闻。
野鸦无意绪，
鸣噪自纷纷。

The Lonely Swan

Du Fu

The lonely swan won't drink nor eat,

But longs to join its flock to fleet.

Who will pity its shadow lonely,

Astray in the clouds, it wails only.

Out of sight, still it seems in view;

Lost in grief, its song's heard anew.

What do insensible birds know?

You hear only caws of the crow.

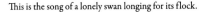

This is the song of a lonely swan longing for its flock.

燕子来舟中作

杜　甫

湖南为客动经春，

燕子衔泥两度新。

旧入故园尝识主，

如今社日[①]远看人。

可怜处处巢居室，

何异飘飘托此身。

暂语船樯还起去，

穿花贴水益沾巾。

---

① 社日：古时农村春分前后祭社神（土地神）和五谷神的日子。

To the Swallow Coming to My Boat

Du Fu

Another spring in boat I stay;

Again swallows peck clods of clay.

You know me in my native land;

Now gazing from afar you stand.

Ah, here and there you build your nest;

Now and again I find no rest.

You greet me and then leave the mast;

My tears stream down to see you past.

This poem presents a contrast between the swallow building its nest and the poet who could not go home.

归雁

钱　起

潇湘①何事等闲②回，
水碧沙明两岸苔③。
二十五弦④弹夜月，
不胜清怨⑤却飞来。

① 潇湘：潇湘二水名，在今湖南境内。
② 等闲：随随便便；轻易。
③ 苔：一种植物，鸟类的食物，雁尤喜食。
④ 二十五弦：指瑟这种乐器。《楚辞·远游》："使湘灵鼓瑟兮。"
⑤ 清怨：此处指曲调凄清哀怨。

To the North-flying Wild Geese

Qian Qi

Why won't you stay on Southern River any more?
Why leave its water clear, sand bright and mossy shore?
You cannot bear the grief revealed in the moonlight
By the Princess' twenty-five strings, so you take flight.

The Princess refers to the daughter of Emperor Yao and wife to Emperor Shun who died on the Southern River, and the Princess played on the twenty-five strings to drown her grief.

鸣筝

李 端

鸣^①筝金粟柱^②，
素手玉房^③前。
欲得周郎顾，
时时误拂弦。

---

① 鸣：弹奏
② 金粟柱：柱，筝上系弦的柱。金粟，柱上的装饰。
③ 玉房：闺房。一说为安在古筝上的垫子。

The Golden Zither

Li Duan

How clear the golden zither rings
When her fair fingers touch its strings!
To draw attention from her lord,
Now and then she strikes a discord.

This quatrain speaks of music and the musician.

许渊冲译唐诗三百首

隋宫燕

李 益

燕语如伤旧国春，
宫花一落已成尘。
自从一闭风光后，
几度飞来不见人。

Swallows in the Ruined Palace

Li Yi

The swallows' twitter seems to grieve over the lost spring;
To dust have returned palace flowers on the wing.
Since the overthrown dynasty closed its splendid scene,
They have come many times but nobody is seen.

许
渊
冲
译
唐
诗
三
百
首

The poet imagines swallows grieve over the ruined palace of the overthrown dynasty.

观祈雨

李　约

桑条无叶土生烟，
箫管① 迎龙水庙② 前。
朱门几处看歌舞，
犹恐春阴咽管弦。

---

① 箫管：这里泛指各种乐器。
② 水庙：龙王庙。

Praying for Rain

Li Yue

No leaves sprout from mulberry trees on drought-scorched earth;
Flutes and pipes are played to evoke the Rain God's mirth.
But the rich see dances and hear songstresses sing;
They only fear rain clouds would damage their lute string.

This quatrain makes a contrast between the poor praying for rain and the rich afraid the rain would spoil their pleasure.

望夫石

王　建

望夫处，江悠悠。

化为石，不回头。

上头日日风复雨，

行人归来石应语。

The Woman Waiting for Her Husband

Wang Jian

Waiting for him alone

Where the river goes by,

She turns into a stone

Gazing with longing eye.

Atop the hill from day to day come wind and rain;

The stone should speak to see her husband come again.

The legend goes that a woman waiting for the return of her husband turned into a stone statue by the riverside. Thus the stone becomes a symbol of lovesickness.

牡丹

薛　涛

去春零落暮春时，

泪湿红笺怨别离。

常恐便同巫峡^①散，

因何重有武陵期^②？

传情每向馨香得，

不语还应彼此知。

只欲栏边安枕席，

夜深闲共说相思。

① 巫峡：指宋玉《高唐赋》中楚襄王梦中与巫山神女相会的故事。
② 武陵期：指陶渊明《桃花源记》中的武陵渔人误入桃花源的故事和刘晨、阮肇天台山遇仙女的故事。据《幽明录》载，东汉时，刘、阮二人入天台山采药，曾因饥渴，登山食桃，就溪饮水，于溪边遇到两位仙女，相爱成婚。半年以后，二人思家求归。直到出山，才知道已经过去三百多年了。古典诗歌中常用天台山故事来比拟这种由于轻易和情人分别而产生的追悔之情。

To the Peony Flower

Xue Tao

Petal by petal you fell in late spring last year;
Since you are gone, my paper's wet with tear on tear.
I am afraid you'd vanish like cloud in a dream.
How can I wish to see you on Peach Blossom Stream?
Your fragrance sweet reveals you have a loving heart;
Your silence shows we know each other far apart.
By the side of your balustrade I'd only sleep;
To tell you how I long for you when night is deep.

许渊冲译唐诗三百首

This poems shows how deep the poetess loves the flower.

杨柳枝词

白居易

一树春风千万枝，
嫩于金色软于丝。
永丰^①西角荒园里，
尽日无人属阿谁?

① 永丰：唐代京都洛阳坊名。

Song of Willow Branch

Bai Juyi

A tree of million branches sways in breeze of spring,

More tender, more soft than golden silk string by string.

But in west corner of a garden in decay,

Who would come to admire its beauty all the day?

This quatrain reveals the poet's sympathy for a willow tree in a decayed garden.

惜牡丹花

白居易

惆怅阶前红牡丹，
晚来唯有两枝残。
明朝风起应吹尽，
夜惜衰红^①把火看。

① 红：这里代指牡丹花。

The Last Look at the Peonies at Night

Bai Juyi

I'm saddened by the courtyard peonies brilliant red,
At dusk only two of them are left on their bed.
I am afraid they can't survive the morning blast,
By lantern light I take a look at the long, long last.

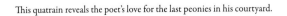

This quatrain reveals the poet's love for the last peonies in his courtyard.

大林寺①桃花

白居易

人间②四月芳菲③尽，
山寺桃花始盛开。
长恨春归无觅处，
不知转入此中来。

① 大林寺：位于今庐山香炉峰上，牯岭附近。庐山有三座大林寺，这里的大林寺是
上大林寺，是晋代僧昙诜创建。
② 人间：这里指平原的村落。
③ 芳菲：这里指花草繁茂、芳香。

Peach Blossoms in the Temple of Great Forest

Bai Juyi

All flowers in late spring have fallen far and wide,
But peach blossoms are full-blown on this mountainside.
I oft regret spring's gone without leaving its trace;
I do not know how it's come up to adorn this place.

The poet expresses his joy at seeing peach blossoms in Mount Lu when other flowers are all fallen in late spring.

白云泉

白居易

天平山①上白云泉②，

云自无心水自闲。

何必奔冲山下去，

更添波浪向人间！

---

① 天平山：位于苏州城西二十里左右，因为山势高峻，峭拔入云，故又称白云山。
此山后来在宋代时被赐给范仲淹及其后人，所以又称为赐山、范坟山。天平山有
三绝，分别为怪石、清泉、红枫。白云亭和白云泉就在此山上。
② 白云泉：位于苏州城西天平山上，被称为"吴中第一水"。上天平山的路有三段，
称为"三白云"，下白云处有白云亭，亭侧就是白云泉。泉水清洌而晶莹，据说
用白云泉的水沏泡的茶，香味四溢，远近闻名。

White Cloud Fountain

Bai Juyi

Behold the White Cloud Fountain on the sky-blue Mountain!
White clouds enjoy pleasure while water enjoys leisure.
Why should the torrent dash down from the mountain high
And overflow the human world with waves far and nigh?

This quatrain shows the poet's love of freedom.

菊花

元 稹

秋丛绕舍似陶家[①]，

遍绕篱边日渐斜。

不是花中偏爱菊，

此花开尽更无花。

[①] 陶家：这里指陶渊明家。陶渊明，东晋诗人，写有"三径就荒，松菊犹存""采菊东篱下，悠然见南山"等名句，所以后代常常将陶渊明与菊花相连，表现一种隐士的高洁。

Chrysanthemums

Yuan Zhen

Around the cottage like Tao's autumn flowers grow;
Along the hedge I stroll until the sun slants low.
Not that I favor partially the chrysanthemum,
But it is the last flower after which none will bloom.

Tao refers to the poet Tao Yuanming, well-known for his love of chrysanthemums.

杨生青花紫石砚歌

李　贺

端州^①石工巧如神，踏天磨刀割紫云^②。

傭刓^③抱水含满唇^④，暗洒苌弘^⑤冷血痕。

纱帷昼暖墨花春，轻沤漂沫松麝薰^⑥。

干腻薄重立脚匀，数寸光秋无日昏^⑦。

圆毫^⑧促点声静新：孔砚^⑨宽硕何足云！

---

① 端州：就是今广州肇庆，这里盛产砚石，被称为端砚。唐代书法家柳公权评各家砚石时，将端砚列为第一。紫色端砚尤其被世人称颂，因为它石质坚实、细润，不损害笔毫，而且雕工精美。砚中的青花是指砚台贮水处的赤黄点，世人称为"鸲鹆（qú yù）眼"。青花本是砚石上的青筋，但是当它入水时，就像有萍藻在浮动，所以被世人珍视。

② 紫云：这里指紫花砚石。

③ 傭刓：傭（yōng），指将砚石料磨至平整；刓（wán），指在砚石料上雕刻。

④ 唇：这里指紫砚的贮水处。

⑤ 苌（cháng）弘：古代关于苌弘有两说。一说他是东周时的内史大夫，据说是孔子的老师；另一说她是周敬王夫人。《庄子·外物》载：苌弘因为忠诚被贬到蜀地，死去后留下的血三年化为碧。不论苌弘是哪位，苌弘化碧的典故都是一种含冤的象征。这里苌弘则只是借用来指碧色。

⑥ 松麝薰：这里指松烟和麝香烧制的优等墨。

⑦ 日昏：这里指砚台中的墨没有昏暗之处。

⑧ 圆毫：这里指饱蘸墨水的笔毫圆润。

⑨ 孔砚：这里指尼山石砚。孔子名丘，字仲尼，后人把他的出生地称为尼山，有人取尼山石为砚，以表达对孔子的尊重，但是尼山砚质料不好，用起来也不舒服。

The Violet Inkstand of Master Yang

Li He

The mason of Duanzhou has marvel-doing hands,

Whetting his knife to carve blue clouds, aloft he stands.

He grinds the stone in order to make an inkwell;

Violet flowers look dim like cold blood shed pell-mell.

Black flowers seem like spring at noon behind the screen;

The pine-soot ink steeped in water smells like musk keen.

Smooth, water-proof, flat and heavy, it stands steadfast;

Like autumn bright its color, rain or shine, will last.

Your brush will make no noise when on paper you write.

Could the inkstone of Confucius give such delight?

The poet glorifies the mason who carves violet clouds on the inkstand.

早雁

杜 牧

金河①秋半虏②弦开，

云外惊飞四散哀。

仙掌③月明孤影过，

长门④灯暗数声来。

须知胡骑纷纷在，

岂逐春风一一回。

莫厌潇湘⑤少人处，

水多菰米⑥岸莓苔⑦。

① 金河：今大黑河，在今内蒙古自治区呼和浩特市南面。这里泛指北方少数民族地区。
② 虏：回纥，当时经常侵扰唐朝边疆。
③ 仙掌：汉武帝在建章宫内立铜人，金铜仙人双手捧露盘，供汉帝取甘露以求长生。
④ 长门：宫名，汉武帝陈皇后失宠后所居宫殿。这里用仙掌和长门代指长安的皇宫。
⑤ 潇湘：水名，在今湖南省，泛指湖南一带。
⑥ 菰（gū）米：一种水生植物，嫩茎叫茭白，果实称菰米，都可以食用。
⑦ 莓苔：青苔。

To the Early Wild Geese

Du Mu

The foe shoot arrows on frontier in autumn day;
The startled grieved wild geese disperse and fly away.
The statue sees their shadows pass beneath the moon bright;
The lonely palace hears their cries in candlelight.
You know the foe would run their horses therefore long.
Could you go back one and all when spring sings its song?
Don't say few live on Southern rivers up and down!
With water plants the Southern shores are overgrown.

The poet compares the refugees to the wild geese flying from north to south, for they also fled from the northern frontier occupied by the foe to the southern rivershore.

霜月

李商隐

初闻征雁已无蝉,
百尺楼高水接天。
青女^①素娥^②俱耐冷,
月中霜里斗婵娟^③。

---

① 青女:指青宵玉女。主管霜雪的女神。
② 素娥:指月宫的嫦娥。
③ 婵娟:古代大概有三种意思。一是形容姿态曼妙优雅(唐孟郊《婵娟篇》有"花婵娟,泛春泉;竹婵娟,笼晓烟");二是指美女、美人(唐方干《赠赵崇侍御》有"却教鹦鹉呼桃叶,便遣婵娟唱竹枝");三是形容月色明媚或指明月(唐刘长卿《湘妃》有"婵娟湘江月,千载空蛾眉")。这里的"婵娟"是指青女、素娥的美丽容貌。

Frost and Moon

Li Shangyin

No cicadas trill when I first hear wild geese cry;
The high tower overlooks water blending with the sky.
The Moon Goddess and her Maid of Frost are cold-proof;
They vie in beauty in moonlight over frosty roof.

Seeing the bright moon and frost, the poet imagines the Moon Goddess and her Maid of Frost are vying in beauty.

蝉

李商隐

本以高难饱，

徒劳恨费声。

五更疏欲断，

一树碧无情。

薄宦^① 梗犹泛^②，

故园芜已平^③。

烦君^④ 最相警，

我亦举家清^⑤。

① 薄宦：这里指小的地方官。
② 梗犹泛：这里指转徙为官，没有安定之所。《战国策·齐策》载：桃梗人与西岸土人（用土做的木偶）辩论，桃梗人嘲笑土人经不住水淹，西岸土人则反驳说："我被水淹没，最多还原成西岸的土；而你如果被水冲走，就不知道会被水带到哪里。"后来就用"泛梗"来表现一种转徙无定的生活状态。
③ 故园芜已平：化用陶渊明《归去来兮辞》中的"田园将芜胡不归"。
④ 君：这里指蝉。
⑤ 清：这里指清贫。

To the Cicada

Li Shangyin

High, you can't eat your fill;
In vain you wail and trill.
At dawn you hush your song;
The tree is green for long.
I drift as water flows;
And waste my garden grows.
Thank you for warning due,
I am as poor as you.

The poet compares himself to the poor, hungry cicada.

落花

李商隐

高阁客竟去，
小园花乱飞。
参差连曲陌[1]，
迢递[2]送斜晖。
肠断未忍扫，
眼穿仍欲归。
芳心向春尽，
所得是沾衣。

---

[1] 曲陌：弯弯曲曲的田间小路。古人称路"南北为阡，东西为陌"。
[2] 迢递：这里指遥远的样子。

Falling Flowers

Li Shangyin

The guest has left my tower high,
My garden flowers pell-mell fly.
Here and there over the winding way
They say goodbye to parting day.
I won't sweep them with broken heart,
But wish they would not fall apart.
Their love with spring won't disappear,
Each dewdrop turns into a tear.

The poet describes his gloomy mood on seeing the falling flowers.

柳 ①

李商隐

曾逐东风②拂舞筵，

乐游春苑③断肠天。

如何肯到清秋日，

已带斜阳又带蝉。

---

① 柳：这里应指曲江柳。长安城南曲江盛产柳树，而且与乐游苑相邻，是京城士女游览之所。

② 东风：这里指春天之风。古人把四方与四季相对应：春对东，夏对南，秋对西，冬对北。

③ 乐游春苑：乐游苑，又称乐游原。位于今西安城南大雁塔东北的高地，本来为汉宣帝时的乐游庙。乐游苑是长安城最高处，登苑可眺望全城，每到三月三日（上巳）、九月九日（重阳），京城士女多至此登赏，诗人也著有众多吟咏乐游苑的诗篇，李商隐就有一首《登乐游原》。

To the Willow Tree

Li Shangyin

Having caressed the dancers in the vernal breeze,
You're ravished amid the merry-making trees.
How can you wait until clear autumn days are done
To shrill like poor cicadas in the setting sun?

The poet compares himself to the willow ravishing in spring and waiting in autumn.

鹦鹉

罗　隐

莫恨雕笼^① 翠羽残，
江南地暖陇西^② 寒。
劝君^③ 不用分明语，
语得分明出转难。

① 雕笼：这里指雕刻精美的鸟笼。
② 陇西：指陇山，就是六盘山南段的别称，一直延伸到陕西、甘肃边境以西，传说
是鹦鹉的产地，所以鹦鹉又被称为"陇客"。
③ 君：这里指鹦鹉。

To the Parrot

Luo Yin

Do not complain of golden cage and wings cut short;

The southern land is far warmer than the northwest.

Don't clearly speak if you listen to my exhort;

You will offend if clearly your complaint's expressed.

This is a satire against clear complaint for fear of offence.

黄河

罗　隐

莫把阿胶①向此倾，

此中天意固难明。

解通银汉②应须曲，

才出昆仑③便不清。

高祖誓功衣带小④，

仙人占斗客槎⑤轻。

三千年⑥后知谁在，

何必劳君报太平？

---

① 阿（ē）胶：由驴皮熬制而成，具有药用价值。古时，阿胶以山东东阿县阿井水煎成，所以被称为阿胶。一般呈块状，入水即溶，阿胶水近乎透明。

② 银汉：这里指银河。

③ 昆仑：这里指昆仑山。郦道元《水经注》已经辨明"黄河发源于昆仑"一说，与昆仑的实际位置并不相符。但是诗人们仍然相信这种说法，李白就有"黄河西来绝昆仑，咆哮万里触龙门"的诗句。

④ 高祖誓功衣带小：这里使用了汉高祖的典故，当年汉高祖刘邦平定天下，大封功臣时曾发下重誓——"使河如带，泰山若砺"，汉代对功臣的分封才会失效。

⑤ 客槎（chá）：指登天的工具。汉代张骞曾经坐着木筏，误闯银河，当时的名士严君平夜观天象，说有"客星"闯入牵牛、织女星座，所以后人就称张骞所乘的木筏为"客槎"。

⑥ 三千年：东晋王嘉《拾遗记·高辛》记载："黄河千年一清，至圣之君以为大瑞。"这里用黄河三千年一清夸张地表述时代的更替。

The Yellow River

Luo Yin

Don't try to make the muddy Yellow River clean!
Could Heaven mirrored in the waves be clearly seen?
How could a winding stream go up the Milky Way?
Just out of Mount Kunlun, it is muddy like clay.
In vain the emperor swore to narrow it down;
Could a raft reach the Polar Star wearing a crown?
Who knows if it will clear up after three thousand years?
Why should you worry if clear or not it appears?

The poet satirizes the imperial government as the muddy Yellow River which could not be made clean, for it was muddy from its source.

許渊冲译唐诗三百首

金钱花 [1]

罗 隐

占得佳名绕树芳，
依依相伴向秋光。
若教此物堪收贮，
应被豪门尽劚将 [2]。

---

[1] 金钱花：旋覆花，夏秋之间开花，花色金黄，花朵圆而覆下，中央呈筒状，形如
铜钱，娇美可爱，所以又被称为金钱花。

[2] 劚将：这里指把金钱花砍下来。劚，读作（zhú），是砍的意思。

To the Coinlike Golden Flower

Luo Yin

You grow around a tree with a name bright,
You cling together steeped in autumn light.
If your flowers could be stored up like gold,
The rich would pluck you down since days of old.

This quatrain is a satire against man's greed for gold.

柳

罗　隐

瀋岸^① 晴来送别频，
相偎相倚不胜^② 春。
自家飞絮犹无定，
争解垂丝绊路人？

① 瀋岸：这里指瀋水两岸。长安东郊有瀋水、瀋桥、瀋柳三大景观，隋唐之际瀋桥
　 两岸已是杨柳含烟、瀋岸春色的风景名胜之地，古人常在这里送别行人，所以有
　 "杨柳含烟瀋岸春，年年攀折为行人"的诗句。
② 胜："尽"的意思。

To the Willow

Luo Yin

By riverside you see lovers part on fine day;
They cling together but they cannot make spring stay.
Your catkins waft in the breeze when your branches sway,
Could you retain those who are going far away?

The poet regrets neither he nor the willow could retain parting lovers.

蜂

罗　隐

不论平地与山尖，
无限风光尽被占。
采得百花成蜜后，
为谁辛苦为谁甜？

To the Bee

Luo Yin

On the plain or atop the hill,

Of beauty you enjoy your fill.

You gather honey from flowers sweet.

For whom are you busy and fleet?

The poet complains of the labor lost of the bee.

白莲

陆龟蒙

素蘤^①多蒙别艳欺，
此花端合在瑶池^②。
无情有恨何人觉？
月晓风清欲堕时。

① 蘤（huā）：古代"花"字。
② 瑶池：古代传说中昆仑山上的池名，是西王母所居住的地方，《史记》和《穆天子传》均有记载。这里用"瑶池"来指仙境。

White Lotus

Lu Guimeng

White lotus blooms are often outweighed by red flowers;

They'd rather be transplanted before lunar bowers.

Heartless they seem, but they have deep grief no one knows.

See them fall in moonlight when the morning wind blows.

The poet describes the pure spirit of the white lotus blooms.

题菊花

黄　巢

飒飒西风^①满院栽，

蕊寒香冷蝶难来。

他年我若为青帝^②，

报与桃花一处开。

---

① 西风：这里指秋风，因为古人用四个方向来比说四个季节：东为春，南为夏，西为秋，北为冬。

② 青帝：古代指司春之神。

To the Chrysanthemum

Huang Chao

In soughing western wind you blossom far and nigh;
Your fragrance is too cold to invite butterfly.
Some day if I as Lord of Spring come into power,
I'd order you to bloom together with peach flower.

The poet was the leader of peasant uprising by the end of the Tang Dynasty.

菊花

黄　巢

待到秋来九月八①，
我花②开后百花杀。
冲天香阵③透长安，
满城尽带黄金甲④。

① 九月八：农历九月八日，九月九日是重阳节，古代有赏菊、喝菊花酒的风俗。
② 我花：这里指菊花。
③ 香阵：这里指菊花的芬芳。
④ 黄金甲：这里指菊花的形状与颜色像黄金制成的盔甲。

The Chrysanthemum

Huang Chao

When autumn comes, the Mountain-climbing Day is nigh;

My flower blows when other blooms come to an end.

In battle array its fragrance rises sky-high,

The capital with its golden armor will blend.

許
渊
冲
译
唐
诗
三
百
首

The poet speaks as if he were the lord of chrysanthemums in golden armor. The Mountain-climbing Day is the ninth day of the ninth moon according to lunar calendar.

云

来 鹊 [1]

千形万象 [2] 竟还空 [3]，

映水藏山片复重。

无限旱苗枯欲尽，

悠悠闲处作奇峰。

---

[1] 来鹊：应为"来鹏"。据陈伯海主编的《唐诗汇评》中记载，《全唐诗》中来鹊
名下的一卷诗，除《圣政纪颂并序》是来鹊所作外，全部都是来鹏所作。参见陈
伯海主编《唐诗汇评（下）》，第 2776 页，浙江教育出版社，1995 年。

[2] 千形万象：这里指夏云的形态不断变化。

[3] 空：这里指没有降下甘霖，而不是其他诗歌中的"空当""空灵"之"空"。

To the Cloud

Lai Hu

You have a thousand shapes in flakes or piles in vain;
Hidden in mountains or on water you remain.
The drought is so severe that all seedlings would die.
Why won't you come down but leisurely tower high?

The poet complains that clouds won't turn into rain to combat the drought.

子规①

吴　融

举国繁华委逝川，

羽毛飘荡一年年。

他山叫处花②成血③，

旧苑春来草似烟。

雨暗不离浓绿树，

月斜长吊欲明天。

湘江日暮声凄切，

愁杀行人归去船。

① 子规：指子规鸟，又称秭归鸟。相传子规鸟为屈原妹妹屈幺姑的精灵所化，每年农历五月，此鸟啼叫"我哥回呦！我哥回呦！"以提醒人们做粽子、修龙舟，准备迎接端午佳节，祭祀屈原。子规又称杜鹃鸟，传说古代蜀国国王杜宇归隐，让位给他的丞相开明，当时正好是二月，即子规鸟啼叫的季节，蜀人怀念杜宇，所以就称子规鸟为杜鹃。
② 花：这里指杜鹃花，又叫映山红。
③ 成血：这里是指杜鹃花名称的由来。传说当年杜宇离开蜀国，但是不忘他的子民，常常化作杜鹃鸟飞回蜀国，他每啼叫一声，就会从喉咙里喷出一口鲜血；第二年杜鹃鸟飞过之处，就会开出鲜红的杜鹃花。后来诗人常用杜鹃啼血的典故表现凄凉悲哀的情绪。

To the Cuckoo

Wu Rong

You see your splendor gone with the wind disappear;
You waft with resplendent feather from year to year.
Your tears have dyed the flowers red in alien hill;
But when spring comes to your garden, grass looks green still.
Among the leaves, trees dark in rain long you stay;
At moonset you wail and wait for the dawning day.
On Southern River you sadden the setting sun.
Why should you drown in grief the boat of roaming son?

The legend goes that the King of Shu lost his kingdom and turned after his death into a cuckoo which would cry till its tears turned into blood.

菊

郑 谷

王孙^① 莫把比蓬蒿，
九日^② 枝枝近鬓毛。
露湿秋香满池岸，
由来不羡瓦松^③ 高。

① 王孙：这里指贵族公子。
② 九日：这里指九月九日重阳节。
③ 瓦松：这里指长在屋檐上的一种植物。初唐崇文馆学士崔融《瓦松赋》自序中说：
   "崇文馆瓦松者，产于屋溜之上……俗以其形似松，生必依瓦，故曰瓦松。"

To the Chrysanthemum

Zheng Gu

Do not compare your leaves with tumbleweed in hue!

On Mountain-climbing Day our head's adorned with you.

When poolside shores are sweet with your blooms wet with dew,

None envy pine-like plants high on the eaves in view.

许渊冲译唐诗三百首

The poet says that the chrysanthemum is incomparable.

鹧鸪①

郑 谷

暖戏烟芜锦翼齐，

品流应得近山鸡。

雨昏青草湖②边过，

花落黄陵庙③里啼。

游子乍闻征袖湿，

佳人才唱④翠眉低。

相呼相应湘江阔，

苦竹丛深日向西。

① 鹧鸪：产于我国南部，形似雌雉，体大如鸠。古人称它的鸣叫声为"钩辀格磔"，民间以为其叫声极像"行不得也哥哥"，所以古人常借其声以抒写逐客留人之情。
② 青草湖：据盛弘之《荆州记》记载，青草湖就是古巴丘湖，在洞庭湖东南，后来青草湖也就成为洞庭湖的通称。
③ 黄陵庙：位于湘阴县北洞庭湖畔。传说帝舜南巡，死于苍梧，娥皇、女英二妃溺死于湘江，后人就在湘水岸边立祠堂以表纪念，这祠堂就是黄陵庙。
④ 唱：这里是指唱《鹧鸪曲》。据《韵语阳秋》记载，《鹧鸪曲》是效仿鹧鸪声而成之曲，是晚唐新声。

To the Partridges

Zheng Gu

Over warm misty grassland wing to wing you fly.

As fair and good as pheasants in the mountain high.

When Grass-green Lake is darkened in rain, you pass by;

When flowers fall on the Imperial Tomb, you cry.

A roamer would wet his sleeves with tears on hearing your song;

His wife'd sing after you with lowered eyebrows long.

You echo each other on Southern River wide;

The sun sets on the bamboo grove by the Tombside.

许渊冲译唐诗三百首

The partridge seems to cry in Chinese: "Don't go, brother!" The Imperial Tomb refers to the tomb of Emperor Shun who died by the side of the Grass-green Lake and whose wife came to shed tears on the bamboos by the tombside till they were specked.

海棠

郑 谷

春风用意匀颜色，

销得^① 携觞^② 与赋诗。

秾^③ 丽最宜新著雨，

娇娆全在欲开时。

莫愁^④ 粉黛临窗懒，

梁广^⑤ 丹青点笔迟。

朝醉暮吟看不足，

羡他蝴蝶宿深枝。

① 销得：这里是值得的意思。
② 觞（shāng）：古代称酒杯。
③ 秾（nóng）：草木茂盛。
④ 莫愁：古代一个洛阳女子的名字。
⑤ 梁广：中唐著名的花鸟画家。李群玉《长沙元门寺张员外壁画》称："世人只爱
黄花鸟，无处不知梁广名。"

To the Crabapple Flower

Zheng Gu

The vernal breeze has brightened your color so fine;

You stir my mind to write a verse before good wine.

With rain impearled on you, more beautiful you grow;

You're all the more bewitching when about to blow.

The fair forgets to powder her face before you;

The painter hesitates to draw your picture new.

Nor verse nor wine's enough to show delight in me;

I envy butterflies perching deep in your tree.

許
渊
冲
译
唐
诗
三
百
首

The artist's attitude reveals the beauty of the crabapple flower.

小松

杜荀鹤

自小刺头①深草里，
而今渐觉出蓬蒿②。
时人不识凌云木③，
直待凌云始道高。

---

① 刺头：这里指刚发出芽的小松树，顶着有刺的松塔。
② 蓬蒿：指蓬草和蒿草，一般长得比较高。
③ 凌云木：这里指有凌云之高的松树。

The Young Pine

Du Xunhe

While young, the pine tree thrusts its head amid tall grass;

Now by and by we find it outgrow weed in mass.

People don't realize it will grow to scrape the sky;

Seeing it tower in cloud, then they know it's high.

The poet satirizes people's lack of foresight.

许 渊 冲 译 唐 诗 三 百 首

垂柳

唐彦谦

绊惹^① 春风别有情，

世间谁敢斗轻盈?

楚王^② 江畔^③ 无端种，

饿损纤腰^④ 学不成。

---

① 绊惹：这里是逗引的意思。

② 楚王：指楚灵王。

③ 江畔：楚王栽柳之所应该为长江江畔。《中朝故事》载：唐代曲江江畔多柳，号
称"柳衙"。因此，这里的江畔可以理解为长安附近的曲江。

④ 饿损纤腰：指楚灵王喜欢纤腰的人。郢都的人们都用少食的办法想让自己瘦下来，
所以后代有用"楚腰"来形容女子的体态妖娆。杜牧《遣怀》诗中就有"落魄江
湖载酒行，楚腰纤细掌中轻"句。

The Weeping Willow

Tang Yanqian

Flirting with vernal breeze, the willow sways so tender.

Who in the world can vie with it but the waist slender?

It is planted at random by the riverside.

How many maids fond of its leaves of hunger died?

The poet satirizes the maidens trying to make their waist as slender as willow branch.

早梅

齐 己

万木冻欲折，

孤根暖独回。

前村深雪里，

昨夜一枝开。

风递幽香出，

禽窥素艳①来。

明年如应律②，

先发望春台③。

① 素艳：这里指早梅的色彩素净而又娇艳。
② 律：原来指古代校正乐音标准的管状仪器，并且分有十二律；又因为古人用十二
律的名称对应一年的十二个月，所以律又指节气。此处"应律"就是指应该有一
个明媚的春季。
③ 春台：这里代指主持考试的礼部。

To the Early Mume Blossoms

Qi Ji

Frozen are all the trees;
Your warm root will not freeze.
In the village's deep snow
Last night your branch did blow.
Fragrance oozed in wind light;
Birds peep at you still white.
If you blossom next year,
You will foretell spring's near.

The poet shows he is as pure and cold-proof as the mume blossom.

三、赠别怀人·····

于易水^①送人一绝

骆宾王

此地别燕丹^②，
壮士发冲冠。
昔时人已没，
今日水犹寒。

---

① 易水：水名。在今河北易县，战国时属燕（yān）国。战国末年燕太子丹曾在此
  地为壮士荆轲送行。
② 燕丹：指战国时期燕国太子，名丹。

Farewell on River Yi

Luo Binwang

The hero left his friend
With angry hair on end.
The martyr's now no more,
The waves cold as of yore.

The hero and martyr refers to Jing Ke who left his friends on River Yi and planned to kill the king of Qin but failed.

留别王维

孟浩然

寂寂①竟何待，

朝朝空自归。

欲寻芳草②去，

惜与故人违。

当路③谁相假，

知音世所稀。

只应守寂寞，

还掩故园扉。

---

① 寂寂：落寞。
② 芳草：古代比喻忠贞志士，高尚情操。
③ 当路：当政者。

Parting from Wang Wei

Meng Haoran

Lonely, lonely, what is there to hope for?
Day by day I come back without an end.
I would seek fragrant grass in native shore.
How I regret to part with my old friend!
I'm one whom those in high place would elude,
For there are few connoisseurs in the state.
I can but keep myself in solitude
And go back to close my old garden gate.

The poet will leave the capital after his failure in the civil service examinations.

许渊冲译唐诗三百首

送杜少府① 之任蜀州②

王　勃

城阙③ 辅三秦④，

风烟望五津⑤。

与君离别意，

同是宦游人⑥。

海内⑦ 存知己，

天涯若比邻⑧。

无为在歧路，

儿女⑨ 共沾巾。

① 少府：唐人称县令为明府，县尉为少府，与官署名之少府不同。杜少府，其人不详。
② 蜀州：一作蜀川，唐代州名，武则天垂拱年间始置之，治所在今四川省崇庆县。
③ 城阙：指京城长安的城郭宫阙，泛指当时长安附近京畿之地，是送别的地方。
④ 三秦：今陕西一带，本是秦国旧地，项羽灭秦后，分为雍、塞、翟三国。
⑤ 五津：岷江的五个津渡。岷江自灌县到犍为县一段有五个渡口，即白华津、万里津、江首津、涉头津、江南津，是杜少府即将赴任的地方，这里泛指蜀地。
⑥ 宦游人：为仕宦而远游四方的人。
⑦ 海内：四海之内。
⑧ 比邻：近邻。古代五家相连为比。《周礼·地官·大司徒》："令五家为比，使之相保。"唐制，四家为邻。
⑨ 儿女：感情脆弱的孩子。《后汉书·来歙传》："故呼巨卿，欲相属以军事，而反效儿女涕泣乎！"

176

Farewell to Prefect Du

Wang Bo

You'll leave the town walled far and wide
For mist-veiled land by riverside.
I feel on parting sad and drear
For both of us are strangers here.
If you have friends who know your heart,
Distance cannot keep you apart.
At crossroads where we bid adieu,
Do not shed tears as women do!

The poet consoles his friend by saying that distance cannot keep bosom friends apart.

送别杜审言 ①

宋之问

卧病人事绝，

嗟②君万里行。

河桥不相送，

江树远含情。

别路追孙楚③，

维舟吊屈平④。

可惜龙泉剑，

流落在丰城。

---

① 杜审言：初唐诗人，字必简，杜甫的祖父，洛州巩县（今属河南）人。他的诗以
浑厚见长，精于律诗，尤工五律，少时与李峤、崔融、苏味道齐名，称"文章四友"，
晚年与同时期的沈佺期、宋之问齐名，并多有唱和。传有《杜审言集》宋刻一卷。

② 嗟（jiē）：感叹词，叹息。

③ 孙楚：西晋诗人，字子荆，太原中都（今山西平遥西北）人。史称其"才藻卓绝，
爽迈不群"。魏末，孙楚已经四十多岁，才入仕为镇东将军石苞的参军，后为晋
扶风王司马骏征西参军，晋惠帝初为冯翊太守。死时七十多岁。有《孙楚集》
十二卷，今佚。

④ 屈平：战国时期楚国伟大的诗人屈原，名平，字原。屈原才华卓绝，遭谗被逐，
流落沅湘，自沉汨罗江而死。有《离骚》《九歌》《九章》等不朽名作，后世统
称"楚辞"。西汉贾谊贬长沙王太傅时，途经湘水，感怀身世，曾作《吊屈原赋》。

Farewell to Du Shenyan

Song Zhiwen

Ill, visited by none each day,
I sigh for you'll go far away.
I cannot bid farewell to you.
Let riverside tree say adieu!
A hero may not serve till old;
A poet's drowned in river cold.
The precious sword of Dragon's Fountain
Might still shine bright though in deep mountain.

The "poet" here refers to Qu Yuan who drowned himself in River Miluo in 278 BC.

送杜十四①之②江南

孟浩然

荆吴③相接水为乡，
君去春江④正淼茫⑤。
日暮征帆何处泊⑥？
天涯⑦一望断人肠。

① 杜十四：杜晃，诗人的朋友。
② 之：往。
③ 荆吴：这里泛指江南。荆是古代楚国的别称，在今湖北、湖南一带。吴，古国名，
在今江苏、浙江一带。
④ 春江：泛指江南一带春来水满的江河。
⑤ 淼茫：烟波辽阔的样子。
⑥ 泊：靠岸停留。
⑦ 天涯：天边。

Seeing Du Fourteenth off to the East

Meng Haoran

The east and west are joined by boundless water clear;
On the endless spring river goes the boat you steer.
Where will you moor it at sunset far, far apart?
Can I not gaze far, far away with broken heart!

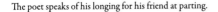

The poet speaks of his longing for his friend at parting.

送刘昱

李 颀

八月寒苇花,

秋江浪头白。

北风吹五两^①,

谁是浔阳^②客。

鸬鹚山^③头微雨晴,

扬州郭里暮潮生。

行人夜宿金陵^④渚,

试听沙边有雁声。

① 五两:指古代的候风器,用五两鸡毛系于高竿顶上而成。

② 浔阳:九江,在镇江的西南方。

③ 鸬鹚山:当在镇江一带,其地现已不可考。

④ 金陵:今南京。

Farewell to Liu Yu

Li Qi

In the eighth moon the weed cold grows,

The autumn waves surge with white crest.

The mast shivers as north wind blows;

Why should my guest go to the west?

The rain no longer drizzles on hilltop;

Out of the door rises the evening tide.

At night along the beach my friend should stop.

Hear lonely wild goose cry by riverside!

This is a dreary picture of parting in autumn.

送魏万之京

李　颀

朝闻游子唱离歌，

昨夜微霜初渡河。

鸿雁不堪愁里听，

云山 [①] 况是客中过。

关城 [②] 树色催寒近，

御苑 [③] 砧声向晚多。

莫见长安行乐处，

空令岁月易蹉跎。

[①] 云山：指令人向往的风景。

[②] 关城：指从洛阳西去要经过的古函谷关与潼关。

[③] 御苑：特指长安城内御苑清华的景致。

Seeing Wei Wan off to the Capital

Li Qi

At dawn I hear the roamer's farewell song;

Last night a thin frost crossed the river long.

Are you not grieved to hear the wild geese cry?

Can you bear clouds and mountains passing by?

Yellow leaves hasten the cold to come near.

Could washerwomen's song reach their men's ear?

Don't make merry in the capital town

And waste the prime of your life up and down!

The poet advises his friend to think more of the hardship than of the pleasure in the capital.

許
渊
冲
译
唐
诗
三
百
首

送魏二

王昌龄

醉别江楼①橘柚香，
江风引雨入舟凉。
忆君遥在潇湘②月，
愁听清猿梦里长。

① 江楼：靠江的高楼。
② 潇湘：潇水在零陵县与湘水汇合，称潇湘。

Farewell to Wei the Second

Wang Changling

Drunk, we leave the wine shop sweetened with orange blooms;
The breeze brings in your boat the rain casting cold glooms.
When steeped in moonlight far away in Southern streams,
You would be grieved to hear monkeys' wail in your dreams.

This quatrain is written when the poet is banished from the capital.

芙蓉楼① 送辛渐②

王昌龄

寒雨③ 连江④ 夜入吴⑤，

平明⑥ 送客⑦ 楚山⑧ 孤。

洛阳亲友如相问，

一片冰心在玉壶。

① 芙蓉楼：故址在今江苏省镇江市的西北角。
② 辛渐：诗人的朋友。这首诗是诗人在芙蓉楼送别辛渐去洛阳时所作。
③ 寒雨：秋雨。
④ 连江：满江，形容雨水很大。
⑤ 夜入吴：夜晚秋雨入镇江。镇江属吴地，故说"夜入吴"。
⑥ 平明：天刚亮。
⑦ 客：指辛渐。
⑧ 楚山：指辛渐即将行经的楚地。

Farewell to Xin Jian at Lotus Tower

Wang Changling

A cold rain dissolved in East Stream invades the night;
At dawn you'll leave the lonely Southern hills in haze.
If my friends in the North should ask if I'm all right,
Tell them I'm free from blame as ice in crystal vase.

The poet speaks of his innocence at parting with his friend.

送别

王　维

下马饮君酒，
问君何所之。
君言不得意，
归卧南山陲。
但去莫复问，
白云无尽时。

At Parting

Wang Wei

Dismounted, I drink with you
And ask what you've in view.
"I can't do what I will;
So I'll do what I will;
I'll ask you no more, friend,
Let clouds drift without end!"

This poet speaks of their love of freedom at their parting.

送梓州李使君^①

王 维

万壑树参天，

千山响杜鹃。

山中一夜雨，

树杪^②百重泉。

汉女^③输橦布^④，

巴^⑤人讼芋田^⑥。

文翁翻^⑦教授，

不敢倚先贤^⑧。

① 李使君：指东川节度使、遂州刺史李叔明，上元二年移镇梓州。
② 树杪（miǎo）：树梢。
③ 汉女：古时曾称嘉陵江为"西汉水"，故有此称。
④ 橦（tóng）布：橦木花织成的布，即木棉布，为梓州特产。
⑤ 巴：古国名，故都在今重庆。
⑥ 芋田：蜀中产芋，当时为主粮之一。
⑦ 翻：彻底改变。
⑧ 先贤：去世的有才德的人。这里指汉景帝时蜀郡守文翁。

Seeing Li off to Zizhou

Wang Wei

The trees in your valley scrape the sky,

You'll hear in your hills cuckoo's cry.

If it rained at night in your mountain,

You'd see your tree tips hung like fountain.

Your women weave to make a suit;

You'd try to solve people's dispute.

The sage before you opened schools;

Like him you should carry out rules.

The poet describes Zizhou and advises his friend to be a good magistrate there.

送元二^①使^②安西^③

王　维

渭城^④朝雨浥^⑤轻尘，

客舍青青柳色新。

劝君更尽一杯酒，

西出阳关^⑥无故人。

① 元二：生平不详。
② 使：出使。
③ 安西：唐代的安西都护府，治所在今新疆库车县境内。
④ 渭城：秦代首都咸阳，汉代改为渭城，在今陕西西安市西北、渭水北岸。
⑤ 浥（yì）：湿润。
⑥ 阳关：在今甘肃敦煌县西南，因在玉门关南，故称阳关。

Seeing Yuan the Second off to the Northwest Frontier

Wang Wei

No dust is raised on the road wet with morning rain;

The willows by the hotel look so fresh and green.

I invite you to drink a cup of wine again;

West of the Sunny Pass no more friends will be seen.

许
渊
冲
译
唐
诗
三
百
首

This is a most popular farewell song often sung at parting.

送秘书晁监还日本国

王　维

积水①不可极，

安知沧海东！

九州何处远？

万里若乘空。

向国唯看日②，

归帆但信风③。

鳌④身映天黑，

鱼眼射波红⑤。

乡树扶桑⑥外，

主人孤岛中。

别离方异域，

音信若为⑦通！

---

① 积水：指海。《荀子·儒效》："积土而为山，积水而为海。"

② 向国唯看日：古人认为日本国地近东方日出处，故云。

③ 信风：任风，随风飘荡。

④ 鳌：海中大龟。

⑤ 鱼眼射波红：《古今注》："鲸鱼者，海鱼也……眼为明月珠。"此处暗用其说。

⑥ 扶桑：《山海经》《淮南子》等书所载神话，传说东方有扶桑木，是日出处。

⑦ 若为：如何能；怎能。

Seeing Secretary Chao Back to Japan

Wang Wei

The sea is far and wide.

Who knows the other side?

How far is it away?

A thousand miles, you say.

Look at the sun, O please!

Your sail should trust the breeze.

Turtles bear the dark sky;

Giant fish raise waves high.

When you are in your isle,

There're trees from mile to mile.

Though we're separated for long,

Would you send me your song?

The poet imagines how his Japanese friend would cross the sea and go to his homeland.

闻王昌龄左迁①龙标②遥有此寄

李　白

杨花落尽子规啼，

闻道龙标过五溪③。

我寄愁心与明月，

随君直到夜郎④西。

To Wang Changling Banished to the West

Li Bai

All willow-down has fallen and sad cuckoos cry
To hear you banished southwestward beyond Five Streams.
I would confide no sorrow to the moon on high
For it will follow you west of the Land of Dreams.

The only thing that could join the poet and his banished friend together is the moon.

赠汪伦 ①

李 白

李白乘舟将欲行，
忽闻岸上踏歌 ② 声。
桃花潭 ③ 水深千尺，
不及汪伦送我情。

---

① 汪伦：李白在桃花潭结识的朋友，性格豪爽。
② 踏歌：一边唱歌，一边用脚踏地打着拍子。
③ 桃花潭：水潭名，在今安徽泾县西南。

许渊冲译唐诗三百首

To Wang Lun

Li Bai

I, Li Bai, sit in a boat about to go,

When suddenly on shore your farewell songs overflow.

However deep the Lake of Peach Blossoms may be,

It's not so deep, O Wang Lun, as your love for me.

This is the poet's most popular farewell song.

许渊冲译唐诗三百首

灞陵行[1] 送别

李 白

送君灞陵亭，

灞水流浩浩。

上有无花之古树，

下有伤心之春草。

我向秦人问路歧[2]，

云是王粲[3]南登之古道。

古道连绵走西京，

紫阙[4]落日浮云生。

正当今夕断肠处，

骊歌[5]愁绝不忍听。

---

① 行：古诗体裁之一。
② 路歧：歧路；岔道。
③ 王粲：字仲宣，东汉末年人，建安七子之一。曾因避董卓之乱，离开长安，南投
   荆州刘表。
④ 紫阙：皇帝居住的宫殿。
⑤ 骊歌：《骊驹之歌》的简称。《骊驹之歌》是一首古老的歌曲，内容是关于离别
   的。骊驹是一种马和驴所生的骡子。

Farewell at the Old Pavilion

Li Bai

We part at the Pavilion Old;

The river flows its water cold.

Above we see trees not in bloom.

Below the vernal grass in gloom.

I ask a wanderer if we go astray;

He says an ancient poet took this way.

The way extends to the west capital,

Where floating clouds at sunset veil the palace hall.

Heart-broken here and now I part with you.

How can we bear to hear songs of adieu?

许渊冲译唐诗三百首

The poet parts with his friend at the Old Pavilion by the riverside where was buried Emperor Wen of the Han Dynasty.

黄鹤楼 ① 送孟浩然之广陵 ②

李　白

故人 ③ 西辞 ④ 黄鹤楼，
烟花 ⑤ 三月下 ⑥ 扬州。
孤帆远影碧空尽，
唯见长江天际流。

---

① 黄鹤楼：旧址在今湖北省武汉市蛇山黄鹄矶上，是古代游览胜地。
② 广陵：今江苏省扬州市。
③ 故人：指孟浩然。
④ 西辞：因黄鹤楼在广陵之西，孟浩然由西去东，所以说"西辞"。
⑤ 烟花：指春天鲜花盛开，迷蒙、绚烂的景色。
⑥ 下：顺流东下。

Seeing Meng Haoran off at Yellow Crane Tower

Li Bai

My friend has left the west where the Yellow Crane towers
For River Town green with willows and red with flowers.
His lessening sail is lost in the boundless blue sky,
Where I see but the endless River rolling by.

Meng leaves for the most beautiful town at the most beautiful time of the year.

鲁郡①东石门②送杜二甫③

李 白

醉别复④几日，

登临遍池台⑤。

何时石门路，

重有金樽⑥开。

秋波落泗水⑦，

海色明徂徕⑧。

飞蓬⑨各自远，

且尽手中杯。

① 鲁郡：今山东省曲阜市。
② 石门：山名，在鲁郡东北。
③ 杜二甫：杜甫在同族兄弟中排行第二，因有此称。如白居易称元稹"元九"。
④ 复：还有。
⑤ 池台：池塘楼阁。
⑥ 金樽：金属的酒杯。
⑦ 泗水：水名，在今山东中部，源出泗水县东蒙山南麓，西流经曲阜、兖州，折南至济宁市东南入运河。
⑧ 徂徕：山名，在今山东泰安市东南。
⑨ 飞蓬：飘荡无定的蓬草。

Farewell to Du Fu at Stone Gate

Li Bai

Before we part we've drunk for many days
And visited all the scenic spots and ways.
When at the Stone Gate shall we meet and drain
Our brimming golden cups of wine again?
The autumn waves of River Si still flow;
The seaside mountains stand in morning glow.
You'll go away as thistledown will fly.
So let us fill our cups and drink them dry.

This is a farewell song written by the romantic poet to the realistic poet.

宣州谢朓楼 ① 饯别校书叔云 ②

李 白

弃我去者，
昨日之日不可留。
乱我心者，
今日之日多烦忧。
长风万里送秋雁，
对此可以酣高楼。
蓬莱 ③ 文章建安骨 ④，
中间小谢 ⑤ 又清发。
俱怀逸兴壮思飞，
欲上青天揽明月。
抽刀断水水更流，
举杯消愁愁更愁。
人生在世不称意，
明朝散发 ⑥ 弄扁舟 ⑦。

① 谢朓楼：南齐诗人谢朓做宣城太守时建，又称谢公楼、北楼，唐末改名叠嶂楼。
② 校书叔云：李白曾为秘书省校书郎，唐人同姓者常相互攀连亲戚，李云当较李白
　 长一辈，但不一定是近亲。
③ 蓬莱：传说中的海外三仙山之一，据传为仙府藏书所在，汉时称中央政府的著述
　 藏书处东观为蓬莱山，"蓬莱文章"指汉代文章。
④ 建安骨：汉献帝建安时代的诗文慷慨多气，史称建安风骨。
⑤ 小谢：谢朓，与其先辈谢灵运分别称大、小谢。
⑥ 散发：古人平时都是用簪子束发，并戴上帽子。散发则是不束发、不戴帽，指避
　 世隐居。《后汉书·袁闳传》："常（锢）事将作，闳遂散发绝世。"
⑦ 扁舟：小船。越亡吴后，范蠡"乘扁舟浮于江湖"，后世就以弄扁舟喻避世隐遁。

Farewell to Uncle Yun, Imperial Librarian, at Xie Tiao's Pavilion in Xuancheng

Li Bai

What left me yesterday

Can be retained no more;

What troubles me today

Is the times for which I feel sore.

In autumn wind for miles and miles the wild geese fly.

Let's drink in face of this in the pavilion high!

Your writing's forcible like ancient poets while

Mine is in Junior Xie's clear and spirited style.

Both of us have an ideal high;

We would reach the moon in the sky.

Cut running water with a sword, it will faster flow;

Drink wine to drown your sorrow, it will heavier grow.

If we despair of all human affairs,

Let us roam in a boat with loosened hairs!

The poet complains to his uncle they could not fulfill their ideal in times of trouble.

送友人入蜀

李　白

见说蚕丛①路，

崎岖不易行。

山从人面起，

云傍马头生。

芳树笼秦栈②，

春流绕蜀城。

升沉③应已定，

不必问君平④。

---

① 蚕丛：帝喾（kù）之后，始封于蜀的国王。即蜀为古蚕丛国。
② 秦栈：秦时入蜀的栈道。
③ 升沉：指宦海沉浮。
④ 君平：西汉人严遵，字君平，善于占卜，隐居不仕，曾于成都市上卖卜。

To a Friend Parting for Shu

Li Bai

Rugged is the road, I hear,

Built by the pioneer.

In front steep mountains rise;

Beside my horse cloud flies.

Over plank way trees hang down;

Spring water girds the town.

Decided our rise and fall.

Do not bother at all!

This verse is descriptive as well as lyrical.

别董大 ①

高　适

千里黄云白日曛②，
北风吹雁雪纷纷。
莫愁前路无知己，
天下谁人不识君。

① 董大：董庭兰，唐代著名音乐家。
② 曛：曛黄，夕阳西沉时的黄昏景象。

Farewell to a Lutist

Gao Shi

Yellow clouds spread for miles and miles have veiled the day;

The north wind blows down snow and wild geese fly away.

Fear not you've no admirers as you go along.

There is no connoisseur on earth but loves your song.

The poet believes that there is no connoisseur but loves the lutist's song.

别韦参军

高 适

二十解书剑 ①，西游长安城。

举头望君门，屈指 ② 取公卿。

国风冲融迈三五，朝廷欢乐弥寰宇。

白璧皆言赐近臣，布衣不得干明主。

归来洛阳无负郭 ③，东过梁宋非吾土。

兔苑为农岁不登 ④，雁池垂钓心长苦。

世人遇我同众人，唯君于我最相亲。

且喜百年有交态，未尝一日辞家贫。

弹棋 ⑤ 击筑 ⑥ 白日晚，纵酒高歌杨柳春。

欢娱未尽分散去，使我惆怅惊心神。

丈夫不作儿女别，临歧涕泪沾衣巾。

① 解书剑：会读书击剑。
② 屈指：计算时日。
③ 负郭：近城的田，最为肥美。
④ 岁不登：收成不好。
⑤ 弹棋：古时两人对局棋，二十四子，红黑各半。
⑥ 筑：状如筝的乐器，十三弦，以竹击。

Farewell to Wei, a Military Officer

Gao Shi

I came at twenty with my sword and books
And visited the west capital town.
I gazed at your mansion with longing looks
And thought it easy to attain renown.
The emperor surpassed the ancient kings,
Music and rites were performed up and down.
He lavished on his favorites jade rings,
But unknown talents can't come near the Crown.
What could I do but come back to my land?
Going east, I could not do what I wish.
I cannot earn a living by the hand,
Nor would I with a hook and line catch fish.
For the world, like a common people I appear;
But for you, I am dear and near as a compeer.
From year to year I thank you for your friendly way;
You've not refused a helping hand, not for a day.
We play chess and on lute till day fades into night;
We drink and croon in spring with willows in delight.
We'll separate when our joy has not come to an end.
How can my heart not be grieved to part with my friend?
But men at parting should not grieve as women do,
So shed no tears at crossroads when we bid adieu!

The poet is recommended by Wei to take part in the civil service examinations.

送灵澈上人 ①

刘长卿

苍苍竹林寺,
杳杳②钟声晚。
荷笠③带夕阳,
青山独归远。

---

① 灵澈上人:中唐时期一位著名诗僧,俗姓杨,出家后号灵澈,字源澄,会稽(今
浙江绍兴)人。
② 杳杳:深远处。
③ 荷笠:背着斗笠。荷,负、背。

Seeing off a Recluse

Liu Changqing

Green, green the temple amid bamboos,

Late, late bell rings out the evening.

Alone, he's lost in mountains blue,

With sunset his hat is carrying.

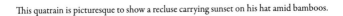

This quatrain is picturesque to show a recluse carrying sunset on his hat amid bamboos.

许渊冲译唐诗三百首

别严士元

刘长卿

春风倚棹① 阖闾城②，
水国③ 春寒阴复晴。
细雨湿衣看不见，
闲花落地听无声。
日斜江上孤帆影，
草绿湖南万里情。
君去若逢相识问，
青袍④ 今已误儒生⑤。

① 倚棹（zhào）：停船。棹，划船工具，常用以代指船。
② 阖闾（hé lú）城：苏州城，相传是春秋时吴王阖闾所建。
③ 水国：水乡。
④ 青袍：青色的官服，唐代品级最低的官着青色。
⑤ 儒生：诗人自称。

Farewell to Yan Shiyuan

Liu Changqing

In vernal breeze outside town walls we stop our oar;
The cloudy weather turns fine on chilly river shore.
Our gowns are wet with drizzling rain although unseen;
The flowers fall at leisure unheard by ears keen.
Your lonely sail sets off at sunset on the stream;
The grass will green for miles the southern shore in dream.
If you meet with some friends who inquire after me,
Tell them the blue-gowned petty official's carefree.

The poet describes the scenes and discloses his mind to his friend.

悲陈陶

杜　甫

孟冬十郡良家子，
血作陈陶泽中水。
野旷天清无战声，
四万义军同日死。
群胡归来血洗箭，
仍唱胡歌饮都市。
都人回面向北啼，
日夜更望官军至。

Lament on the Defeat at Chentao

Du Fu

In early winter noble sons of household good
Blended with water in Chentao mires their pure blood.
No more war cry under the sky on the vast plain,
In one day forty thousand loyal warriors slain.
The enemy came back with blood-stained arrows long;
They drank in market place and shouted barbarous song.
Our countrymen turned north their faces bathed in tears;
Day and night they expect the royal cavaliers.

The poet weeps over the forty thousand men slain by the rebels in Chentao and expects in vain the recovery of the lost land by the royal forces.

许
渊
冲
译
唐
诗
三
百
首

春日忆李白

杜　甫

白也诗无敌，
飘然思不群。
清新庾开府[1]，
俊逸鲍参军[2]。
渭北[3]春天树，
江东[4]日暮云。
何时一樽酒，
重与细论文[5]。

[1] 庾开府：庾信，南北朝著名诗人。因其曾在北周为骠骑大将军、开府仪同三司，故称庾开府。
[2] 鲍参军：鲍照，刘宋时曾为荆州前军参军。也是南北朝著名诗人。
[3] 渭北：渭水北岸，借指长安一带，当时杜甫也在此地。
[4] 江东：指今江苏省南部和浙江省北部一带，当时李白在此地。
[5] 论文：论诗。六朝以来，通称诗为文。

Thinking of Li Bai on a Spring Day

Du Fu

Li Bai is unrivalled in verse;

He towers in the universe.

Fresher than Yu on northern shore;

Brighter than Bao, poet of yore.

I long for him as longing tree;

At sunset will he think of me?

When may we drink a cup of wine

And talk about prose and verse fine?

Du Fu in the north thinks of Li Bai in the south and compares him to two poets of yore.

轮台歌奉送封大夫^①出师西征

岑 参

轮台城头夜吹角，轮台城北旄头^②落。

羽书^③昨夜过渠黎^④，单于^⑤已在金山西。

戍楼西望烟尘黑，汉军^⑥屯在轮台北。

上将拥旄^⑦西出征，平明吹笛大军行。

四边伐鼓雪海涌，三军大呼阴山^⑧动。

虏塞兵气连云屯，战场白骨缠草根。

剑河风急雪片阔，沙口石冻马蹄脱。

亚相^⑨勤王甘苦辛，誓将报主静边尘^⑩。

古来青史谁不见，今见功名胜古人。

① 封大夫：封常清，当时任安西、北庭节度使。
② 旄（máo）头：星名，即昴星，二十八宿之一。《史记·天官书》中记载："昴为旄头，胡星也。"古人认为旄头跳跃预示胡兵大起，而旄头落则预示着胡兵覆灭。
③ 羽书：军用紧急文书，有急事通报时用鸟羽插之，表示速疾。
④ 渠黎：渠犁，地名，在今新疆吉木萨尔县和米泉县之间。
⑤ 单于（chán yú）：汉代时匈奴称其君主为单于，这里借指唐代西域少数民族首领。
⑥ 汉军：指唐朝军队。唐诗中多以汉代唐。
⑦ 旄：古代出征的大将或出使的使臣，都以旌节为凭信，为皇帝所赐，是军权的象征。旌节用金属或竹子做成，而以牦牛尾装饰在端部，称旄。
⑧ 阴山：地名，在今内蒙古自治区境内，泛指边城。
⑨ 亚相：这里指封常清，封常清以节度使摄御史大夫，次于丞相，故称亚相。
⑩ 静边尘：使边患平定。

224

Song of Wheel Tower in Farewell to General Feng on His Western Expedition

Cen Shen

At night the horn blows on Wheel Tower walls;
The Tartar Star north of Wheel Tower falls.
Feathered dispatch passed southeast of the town:
West of Mount Gold Tartar chiefs settled down.
From the lookout we see dust raised by horses;
North of Wheel Tower camp the royal forces.
Our general with flags will westwards go;
At dawn the army march when bugles blow.
Frozen waves surge when drams are booming out;
The Shady Mountain trembles at soldiers' shout.
Over Tartar forts clouds shiver at war cry;
On battleground white bones with grass roots lie.
Over Sword Stream swirling wind drives clouds on flake;
On frozen stone at Sand Mouth horsehoofs break.
Deputy commander, you bear all pain;
You swear to pacify, the border plain.
Have you not read the history of yore?
We love not ancients less, but moderns more.

The poet imagines a battle between the Tartar forces and the royal army led by General Feng.

送李副使^①赴碛西^②官军

岑 参

火山^③六月应更热，
赤亭道^④口行人绝。
知君惯度祁连城^⑤，
岂能愁见轮台^⑥月。
脱鞍暂入酒家垆^⑦，
送君万里西击胡。
功名只向马上取，
真是英雄一丈夫。

① 李副使：名不详。副使，官名，唐制，于节度使下设副使一人协理军中事务。
② 碛（qì）西：指安西。《唐会要》卷七八："安西四镇节度使，开元十二年以后，
   或称碛西节度，或称四镇节度。"安西即今天新疆维吾尔自治区库车县附近地区。
③ 火山：今新疆吐鲁番盆地中的火焰山。
④ 赤亭道：位于火山附近，在今新疆鄯善县境内。
⑤ 祁（qí）连城：今甘肃张掖东南，位于燕支山西侧，为唐代使西必经之地。
⑥ 轮台：唐代庭州有轮台县，这里指的是汉置古轮台（今新疆轮台县东南），李副
   使赴碛西必经此地。
⑦ 垆（lú）：酒店安置酒瓮的土墩子，后成为酒店的代称。

Seeing General Li off to the West

Cen Shen

Fiery Mountain in sixth moon hotter than before,

No people pass by Red Pavilion any more.

I know you're used to hardship on the west frontier;

Oh, could the moon over Wheel Tower make you drear?

Unsaddle your horse, drink and drown in wine your woe;

I'll see you go for miles and miles to beat the foe.

You will win rank and fame only on battle steed;

A real hero must have done heroic deed.

This quatrain reveals a wife's fear of being deserted.

古别离

孟 郊

欲别牵郎衣，
郎今到何处?
不恨归来迟，
莫向临邛去!

Leave Me Not

Meng Jiao

I hold your robe lest you should go.
"Where are you going, dear, today?
Your late return brings me less woe
Than your heart being stolen away."

许
渊
冲
译
唐
诗
三
百
首

This quatrain reveals a wife's fear of being deserted,

再授连州至衡阳 ① 酬柳柳州 ② 赠别

刘禹锡

去国 ③ 十年同赴召，

渡湘千里又分歧 ④ 。

重临事异黄丞相 ⑤ ，

三黜 ⑥ 名惭柳士师 ⑦ 。

归目并随回雁尽，

愁肠正遇断猿时。

桂江东过连山下，

相望长吟有所思。

① 连州、衡阳：连州，今广东连县。衡阳，指唐代横州治所。
② 酬柳柳州：酬，答谢之意，在这里指答复柳宗元《衡阳与梦得分路赠别》一诗。柳柳州指柳宗元，当时被贬为柳州刺史。
③ 去国：就是离开京都的意思。去，离开。国，指长安。
④ 分歧：分路赴任，柳宗元由水路至柳州，刘禹锡由陆路至连州。歧，岔路、分手之地。
⑤ 黄丞相：指汉代的黄霸，字次公，淮阳阳夏人，曾两次任颍川太守。
⑥ 黜（chù）：贬；罢免。
⑦ 柳士师：指柳下惠，春秋鲁国人，居处曰柳下，死后谥号惠。士师，狱官，主察狱讼之事。

Farewell to Liu Zongyuan in Exile

Liu Yuxi

Recalled together after an exile of ten years,

Again we're banished for long miles and say adieu.

We reappear but unlike our noble compeers;

Thrice in exile I feel I'm unworthy of you.

We watch returning wild geese till they're out of sight;

We're sad to hear the monkey wail with broken heart.

The Western River flows far from the Southern height.

Longing for each other, can we be kept apart?

许渊冲译唐诗三百首

The poet was banished to the south and his friend to the west for ten years, both were recalled and again banished together, but the poet said he was unworthy of his friend for he was not so straightforward.

送友人

薛 涛

水国^①蒹葭^②夜有霜，

月寒山色共苍苍^③。

谁言千里自今夕，

离梦杳^④如关塞长。

① 水国：水乡，在诗里指巴山蜀水一带。
② 蒹葭（jiān jiā）：蒹，指没有长穗的芦苇。葭，指初生的芦苇。
③ 苍苍：在这里指一种深青色。
④ 杳（yǎo）：指远得没有尽头。

Farewell to a Friend

Xue Tao

Waterside reeds are covered with hoarfrost at night;

The green mountains are drowned in the cold blue moonlight.

Who says a thousand miles will separate us today?

My dream will follow you though you are far away.

The poetess shows her love by saying distance cannot separate friends in dreams.

許淵冲译唐诗三百首

赋得^① 古原^② 草送别

白居易

许渊冲译唐诗三百首

离离^③原上草，

一岁一枯荣。

野火烧不尽，

春风吹又生。

远芳^④侵古道，

晴翠^⑤接荒城。

又送王孙^⑥去，

萋萋^⑦满别情。

① 赋得：凡是指定、限定的诗题，按惯例要在题目上加"赋得"二字。
② 古原：古原野。也有人认为是乐游原，是汉宣帝修建的游览地，在陕西长安城南。
③ 离离：青草茂盛的样子。
④ 远芳：春草的芳香播散得很远。
⑤ 晴翠：阳光下翠绿的野草。
⑥ 王孙：本指贵族子弟，后来成为对他人的尊称。这里指即将远游的友人。
⑦ 萋萋：青草长得茂盛的样子。

Grass on the Ancient Plain in Farewell to a Friend

Bai Juyi

Wild grasses spread over ancient plain;
With spring and fall they come and go.
Fire tries to burn them up in vain;
They rise again when spring winds blow.
Their fragrance overruns the way;
Their green invades the ruined town.
To see my friend going away,
My sorrow grows like grass overgrown.

The poet compares his friendship to the overgrown grass on the ancient plain.

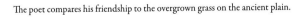

舟中读元九^①诗

白居易

把君诗卷灯前读，
诗尽灯残天未明。
眼痛灭灯犹暗坐，
逆风吹浪打船声。

---

① 元九：元稹，字微之，因在族中排行第九，因此称元九。是白居易的挚友。

Reading Yuan Zhen's Poems in a Boat

Bai Juyi

I read your book of poetry by the lamplight,
And finish it when oil burns low at dead of night.
Eyes sore, I blow the light out and sit in the dark;
The waves brought up by adverse wind beat on the bark.

The poet and his friend are in exile, so he feels waves rise in his heart as on the river.

酬^①乐天频梦微之^②

元 稹

山水万重^③书断绝，
念君怜我梦相闻。
我今因病魂颠倒，
唯梦闲人不梦君。

① 酬：应和；酬答。
① 酬：应和；酬答。
② 微之：元稹，字微之。
③ 山水万重：形容路途非常遥远。

Dream and No Dream

Yuan Zhen

Letters can't pass over thousands of mountains and streams.
How much I thank you for you have sent me your dreams.
I'm sorry that in illness I can't tell old friends from new;
I dream of indifferent people, but not you.

The poet who has not dreamed of his friend sends him as much friendship as his friend who has.

許
渊
冲
译
唐
诗
三
百
首

重赠^① 乐天

元 稹

休遣^② 玲珑^③ 唱我诗，
我诗多是别君词。
明朝又向江头别，
月落潮平是去时。

---

① 重赠：这首诗是为送别白居易而写的。在此之前元稹已写过一首《赠乐天》的诗，
　　因此叫"重赠"。
② 休遣：别让。
③ 玲珑：原诗题下作者自注云："乐人商玲珑能歌，歌予数十诗。"商玲珑是白居
　　易身边的乐工，善于歌唱。

240

Parting Again with Bai Juyi

Yuan Zhen

Don't let the songstress sing my songs anew!
Most of them are farewell poems for you.
Tomorrow again we'll part by riverside,
Alas! At moonset when outflows the tide.

寄扬州韩绰 [①] 判官 [②]

杜 牧

青山隐隐水迢迢 [③]，
秋尽江南草未凋 [④]。
二十四桥 [⑤] 明月夜，
玉人 [⑥] 何处教吹箫。

---

① 韩绰（chuò）：生平事迹不详。从杜牧的另一首《哭韩绰》诗来看，当是杜牧的
   友人，后同在京城为官，二人有很深厚的友谊。
② 判官：唐代的一种官职，负责在节度使、观察使府中掌管文书事务。
③ 迢迢：一作"遥遥"。遥远。
④ 草未凋：一作"草木凋"。
⑤ 二十四桥：宋代沈括《梦溪笔谈·补笔谈》并举其桥名，说二十四座桥，即唐代
   扬州城的二十四座小桥（沈氏实列举二十三座）；清代李斗在其《扬州画舫录·卷
   十五》中，则说二十四桥，即吴家砖桥，一名红药桥。
⑥ 玉人：美人，此处指韩绰。

For Han Chuo, Judge of Yangzhou

Du Mu

The dreaming green hills stretch as far as the blue streams;
At autumn's end grass seems still green on southern shore.
Twenty-four fairies on the bridge steeped in moonbeams,
Are they still playing on the flute now as before?

This is a beautiful description of an autumn scene in Yangzhou.

宣州送裴坦[①]判官往舒州[②]，时牧欲赴官归京

杜　牧

日暖泥融雪半消，

行人芳草马声骄。

九华山[③]路云遮寺，

清弋江[④]村柳拂桥。

君意如鸿高的的[⑤]，

我心悬旆[⑥]正摇摇[⑦]。

同来不得同归去，

故国逢春一寂寥。

[①] 裴坦：字知进，中进士后任宣州判官，与杜牧同事。
[②] 舒州：春秋时称皖国，唐武德四年（621年）改隋同安郡为舒州，至德二年（757年）改为盛唐郡，旋复名。《唐书·地理志》中的"淮南道舒州同安郡"，在今安徽省潜山一带。
[③] 九华山：中国佛教四大名山之一，号称"佛国仙城"。在今安徽省青阳县西南，是裴坦此行往赴舒州的必经之地。
[④] 清弋江：一名青弋江。《元和郡县志》："宣州宣城县清弋水，州西九十九里。"《方舆纪要》："宁国府宣城县青弋江，府西六十里，源出泾县及池州府之石埭县，又太平县及府西南境诸川皆汇入焉。"
[⑤] 的的：这里形容心情舒畅。
[⑥] 悬旆（pèi）：比喻心中不定，犹如风中飘舞的旗子。
[⑦] 摇摇：心神无主，忐忑不安的样子。《史记·苏秦传》："心摇摇然如悬旆，而无所终薄。"

Farewell to Pei Tan, Judge of Xuancheng, upon Going Back to the Capital

Du Mu

The snow in warming sun has half melted away;

You who will go on fragrant grass hear your horse neigh.

Over the mountain path clouds veil the temple drear;

The willow tips caress the bridge on River Clear.

Your ideal will fly up as high as the wild geese;

My mind still flutters like a streamer in the breeze.

Coming together, I cannot go back with you.

How lonely I'd feel at home when spring comes anew!

This poem depicts the scenery in the first half and the poet's mind in the second.

别离

陆龟蒙

丈夫非无泪，

不洒离别间。

杖剑①对尊②酒，

耻为游子颜。

蝮蛇③一螫④手，

壮士即解腕⑤。

所志在功名，

离别何足叹。

① 杖剑："仗剑"，持剑之意。杖，持、拿着。
② 尊：一种酒器。又作"樽""罇"。
③ 蝮蛇：我国剧毒蛇类的一种。
④ 螫（shì）：有毒腺的虫子刺人叫作螫。《史记·田儋列传》："蝮螫手则斩手，螫足则斩足。"
⑤ 解腕：斩断手腕。

Parting

Lu Guimeng

A hero may shed tears,

Not when parting with peers.

Sword in hand, he drinks wine,

Unlike roamer who pine.

When bitten by the snake,

He would have his wrist break.

With his career at heart,

He won't regret to part.

This poem talks about heroic parting.

送日本国僧敬龙①归

韦 庄

扶桑②已在渺茫③中，

家在扶桑东更东。

此去与师谁共到，

一船明月一帆风。

① 敬龙：日本僧人的名字。诗中的"师"也是指此人。
② 扶桑：《梁书·东夷传》中记载："扶桑在大汉国东二万余里，地在中国之东，其土多扶桑木，故以为名。"《十洲记》中也称："扶桑在碧海中，树长数千丈，一千余围，两干同根，更相依倚，日所出处。"一般以扶桑为东海古国，后来称日本为扶桑。
③ 渺茫：遥远空荡的样子。

Farewell to a Japanese Monk

Wei Zhuang

The land of mulberry is in the boundless sea;

Your home's farther east to the land of mulberry.

Who would arrive with you at the land of your dreams?

A sail unfurled in wind, a boat steeped in moonbeams.

Japan was called the land of mulberry.

送友游吴越

杜荀鹤

去越从吴过，
吴疆与越连。
有园多种桔，
无水不生莲。
夜市桥边火，
春风寺外船。
此中偏重客，
君去必经年。

Seeing a Friend off to the South

Du Xunhe

You go from north to south,
From land to river mouth.
Oranges in gardens loom;
Lotus on water bloom.
The night fair's bright as day;
Outside temples boats stay.
Welcome from far and near
Would make you stay a year.

This is a beautiful description of the Southern Rivershore.

山中 [1]

王　勃

长江悲已滞 [2]，

万里念将归。

况属 [3] 高风 [4] 晚，

山山黄叶飞。

---

[1] 山中：高步瀛在《唐宋诗举要》卷八中说，此诗"疑咸亨二年（671年）寓巴蜀时作"。

[2] 滞：停滞。

[3] 况属：碰巧遇到。况，何况。属，一作"复"。

[4] 高风：秋高气爽时的风，即秋风。

In the Mountains

Wang Bo

The Long River grieves over my long stay,

For my home is a thousand miles away.

Now blows the evening wind so high;

From mountain to mountain yellow leaves fly.

The poet staying in the mountains thinks of his home far away when autumn leaves fall.

四、故园乡情
· · ·

题大庾岭①北驿②

宋之问

阳月③南飞雁，

传闻至此回④。

我行殊未已⑤，

何日复归来？

江静潮初落，

林昏瘴⑥不开。

明朝望乡处，

应见陇头梅⑦。

① 大庾（yǔ）岭：五岭之一。在今江西省大庾县境内，唐时是通向岭南的要道。
② 驿：驿舍、亭驿的简称。古代官办的交通站，邮递人员与官员来往可于此停宿。北驿就是大庾岭北面的驿站。
③ 阳月：阴历十月。《尔雅》："十月为阳。"故称十月为"阳月"。
④ 至此回：古代相传到了冬天，北雁南飞，到了大庾岭这个地方便止息下来折回。
⑤ 殊未已：还没有停止。殊，还。
⑥ 瘴（zhàng）：瘴气。旧指南方山林间的热空气，从前人们认为湿热蒸汽能使人得疟疾等传染病。
⑦ 陇头梅：岭头梅。大庾岭地处亚热带，十月即见梅花。旧时岭上多梅，故又称"梅岭"。沈德潜在《唐诗别裁集》中说："陇头疑是岭头。"据南朝宋盛弘之《荆州记》记载，陆凯和范晔相善，自江南寄梅花一枝，诣长安，与晔，并赠诗曰："折梅逢驿使，寄与陇头人。江南无所有，聊赠一枝春。"诗中的"陇头梅"，当即用其事，形容思乡更切。

At the Northern Post of the Peak of Mumes

Song Zhiwen

In the tenth moon wild geese south fly;
They will turn back at this peak high.
But I must farther southward go.
When may I come back? Do you know?
The river's calm when ebbs the tide;
Dense fog darkens the forest wide.
Tomorrow looking for my homeland,
I can only see mume trees stand.

It was believed that the south-going wild geese would not pass the Peak of Mumes. The banished poet thinks he is not so fortunate as the wild geese for he must go farther south.

回乡偶①书二首（其一）

贺知章

少小离家老大回，
乡音无改鬓毛衰②。
儿童相见不相识，
笑问客从何处来。

① 偶：偶然；不经意。
② 鬓毛衰：指人的年纪大了，鬓发稀疏脱落。

Home-coming (I)

He Zhizhang

I left home young and not till old do I come back,

Unchanged my accent, my hair no longer black.

The children whom I meet do not know who am I,

"Where do you come from, sir?" they ask with beaming eye.

许
渊
冲
译
唐
诗
三
百
首

回乡偶书二首（其二）

贺知章

离别家乡岁月多，
近来人事半消磨。
唯有门前镜湖水，
春风不改旧时波。

Home-coming (II)

He Zhizhang

Since I left my homeland so many years have passed;

So much has faded away and so little can last.

Only in Mirror Lake before my oldened door

The vernal wind still ripples waves now as before.

许渊冲译唐诗三百首

渡汉江 ①

宋之问

岭外 ② 音书断，

经冬复历春。

近乡情更怯，

不敢问来人。

许渊冲译唐诗三百首

① 汉江：水名，是长江的一条支流，这里指襄阳附近的一段汉水。
② 岭外：这里指五岭以南的地区。五岭由大庾岭、越城岭、骑田岭、萌诸岭、都庞岭组成，是位于广东、广西和江西、湖南交界处的一座山脉，是长江与珠江的分水岭。

Crossing River Han

Song Zhiwen

I longed for news on the frontier
From day to day, from year to year.
Now nearing home, timid I grow,
I dare not ask what I would know.

许渊冲译唐诗三百首

This quatrain describes the contradictory mind of the banished poet.

九月九日忆山东①兄弟

王　维

独在异乡为异客，
每逢佳节倍思亲。
遥知兄弟登高②处，
遍插茱萸③少一人。

① 山东：指华山以东。
② 登高：古代风俗，重阳节要登高饮酒。
③ 茱萸：一种有香味的植物。《太平御览》引《风土记》云："俗于此日……折茱萸以插头，言辟热气而御初寒。"

Thinking of My Brothers on Mountain-climbing Day

Wang Wei

Alone, a lonely stranger in a foreign land,

I doubly pine for my kinsfolk on holiday.

I know my brothers would, with dogwood spray in hand,

Climb up the mountain and miss me so far away.

许渊冲译唐诗三百首

It was believed in China that to climb up mountains and carry dogwood spray on the ninth day of the ninth lunar month could drive evil spirits away.

杂诗[①]（其二）

王　维

君自故乡来，

应知故乡事。

来日[②]绮窗[③]前，

寒梅[④]著花[⑤]未。

---

① 杂诗：写随时产生的零星感想和琐事，不定题目的诗。
② 来日：指动身前来的那天。
③ 绮窗：雕刻花纹的窗子。绮，有花纹的丝织品。
④ 寒梅：冬天开的梅花。
⑤ 著花：开花，开放。

Our Native Place (II)

Wang Wei

You come from native place,

What happened there you'd know.

Did mume blossoms in face

Of my gauze window blow?

The poet shows his love of his native place by asking a trifling question.

静夜思

李 白

床前明月光，
疑是地上霜。
举头望明月，
低头思故乡。

许渊冲译唐诗三百首

Thoughts on a Tranquil Night

Li Bai

Before my bed a pool of light—
O can it be frost on the ground?
Looking up, I find the moon bright;
Bowing, in homesickness I'm drowned.

Seeing a pool of moonlight, the poet is drowned in the pool of homesickness.

寄东鲁^①二稚子

李 白

吴地^②桑叶绿，吴蚕已三眠^③。

我家寄东鲁，谁种龟阴田^④？

春事已不及，江行复茫然^⑤。

南风吹归心，飞堕酒楼^⑥前。

楼东一株桃，枝叶拂青烟。

此树我所种，别来向三年。

桃今与楼齐，我行尚未旋^⑦。

娇女字平阳，折花倚桃边。

折花不见我，泪下如流泉。

---

① 东鲁：指山东任城（今山东济宁）。
② 吴地：指江苏一带。
③ 三眠：蚕蜕皮，辄卧不食，古人谓眠。这里三眠指入春很久了。
④ 龟阴：龟山的北面，在山东新泰市西南，济宁近处。
⑤ "江行"句：江行，乘船回去。茫然，行踪不定。
⑥ 酒楼：指李白在任城的酒楼。
⑦ 未旋：没有回去。

For My Two Children in East Lu

Li Bai

Mulberry leaves in Southern land are green;

The silkworms thrice in sleep must have been.

In Eastern Lu my family stays still.

Who'd help to sow our fields north of Lu Hill?

It's now too late to do farm work of spring.

What then am I to do while traveling?

The southern wind is blowing without stop;

My heart flies back to my old familiar wine-shop.

East of the shop there's a peach tree oft missed;

Its branches must be waving in bluish mist.

It is the tree I planted three years ago;

If it has grown to reach the eaves, I don't know.

I have not been at home for three long years;

I can imagine my daughter appears

Beside the tree and plucks a flower pink,

Without seeing me, she must have, I think,

Shed copious tears.

小儿名伯禽，与姊亦齐肩。

双行桃树下，抚背复谁怜?

念此失次第^①，肝肠日忧煎。

裂素写远意^②，因之汶阳川^③。

① 失次第：形容内心烦忧的样子。
② "裂素"句：素，白绢。远意，对远方亲人的思念。
③ 汶阳川：汶河，今山东省境内。

My younger son has grown

Up to his sister's shoulders.

Beneath full-blown

Peach tree they stand side by side.

But who's there

To pat them on the back?

I feel, whene'er

I think of this, so painful that I write

And send to them this poem on silk white.

The poet shows his paternal love for his son and daughter in East Lu (Shandong).

春夜洛城[1] 闻笛

李 白

谁家[2] 玉笛暗飞声，
散入春风满洛城。
此夜曲中闻折柳[3]，
何人不起故园情[4]。

① 洛城：洛阳城。今河南省洛阳市。
② 谁家：哪一个。
③ 折柳：乐府横吹曲《折杨柳》，内容多抒发离别之情。
④ 故园情：怀念家乡的感情。

Hearing the Flute on a Spring Night in Luoyang

Li Bai

From whose house has come the song of jade flute unseen?

It fills the town of Luoyang, spread by wind of spring.

Tonight I hear the farewell song of Willow Green.

To whom the tune will not nostalgic feeling bring?

许渊冲译唐诗三百首

It was a Chinese custom to break a twig of willow and present it to the parting friend, so the willow song has become a farewell song. On hearing it, the poet thinks of home.

除夜①作

高　适

旅馆寒灯独不眠，
客②心何事转凄然③。
故乡今夜思千里，
霜鬓④明朝又一年。

---

① 除夜：指除夕，即每年农历最后一天的夜晚。
② 客：在异乡漂流的人。
③ 凄然：凄凉悲伤的样子。
④ 霜鬓：斑白的鬓发，代指年老。

Written on New Year's Eve

Gao Shi

Sleepless alone at an inn by cold lamplight,

Why should a roamer feel so sad and drear?

Thinking of my home far away tonight,

I'll have more frosty hair in the new year.

许渊冲译唐诗三百首

The poet is homesick on (lunar) Near Year's Eve when the family should get together.

月夜

杜　甫

今夜鄜州①月，

闺中②只独看。

遥怜小儿女，

未解忆长安。

香雾云鬟③湿，

清辉玉臂寒。

何时倚虚幌④，

双照泪痕干。

① 鄜（fū）州：今陕西省富县。
② 闺中：此指妻子。
③ 云鬟：形容女子头发蓬松的样子。
④ 虚幌：轻薄透明的帷帐。

A Moonlit Night

Du Fu

On the moon over Fuzhou which shines bright,

Alone you would gaze in your room tonight.

I'm grieved to think our little children dear

Too young to yearn for their old father here.

Your cloudlike hair is moist with dew, it seems;

Your jade-white arms would feel the cold moonbeams.

O when can we stand by the window side,

Watching the moon with our tear traces dried?

As a refugee, the poet writes this poem to his wife far away in Qiang Village at Fuzhou.

春望

杜　甫

国破^①山河在，
城春草木深。
感时花溅泪，
恨别鸟惊心。
烽火^②连三月，
家书抵^③万金。
白头搔更短，
浑^④欲不胜簪^⑤。

① 国破：指国都长安被叛军占领。
② 烽火：战火。
③ 抵：值。
④ 浑：简直。
⑤ 不胜簪：不能别上发簪。

Spring View

Du Fu

On war-torn land streams flow and mountains stand;

In vernal town grass and weeds are overgrown.

Grieved over the years, flowers make us shed tears;

Hating to part, hearing birds breaks our heart.

The beacon fire has gone higher and higher;

Words from household are worth their weight in gold.

I cannot bear to scratch my grizzled hair;

It grows too thin to hold a light hairpin.

许渊冲译唐诗三百首

This poem with inner rhymes shows the poet's love of his country and his family.

羌村三首（其一）

杜　甫

峥嵘①赤云西，

日脚下平地。

柴门鸟雀噪，

归客千里至。

妻孥②怪我在，

惊定还拭泪。

世乱遭飘荡，

生还偶然遂③。

邻人满墙头，

感叹亦歔欷④。

夜阑⑤更秉烛，

相对如梦寐。

① 峥嵘：山高峻的样子，这里形容天空中云层重叠。
② 妻孥（nú）：妻子和儿女。
③ 遂：如愿。
④ 歔欷（xū xī）：感叹的样子。
⑤ 夜阑：夜深。

Coming Back to Qiang Village (I)

Du Fu

Like rugged hills hangs gilt-edged cloud;

The sunset sheds departing ray.

The wicket gate with birds is loud,

When I come back from far away.

At my appearance starts my wife;

Then calming down, she melts in tears.

Happy, I come back still in life,

While people drift in bitter years.

My neighbors look over the wall;

They sigh and from their eyes tears stream.

When night comes, candles light the hall;

We sit face to face as in dream.

This poem describes the reunion of the poet's family at Qiang Village.

月夜忆舍弟

杜 甫

戍鼓[①]断人行，

边秋[②]一雁声。

露从今夜白，

月是故乡明。

有弟皆分散，

无家问死生。

寄书长[③]不达，

况乃未休兵。

① 戍鼓：戍楼上的更鼓。
② 边秋：秋天的边境。
③ 长：一直，老是。

Thinking of My Brothers on a Moonlit Night

Du Fu

War drums break people's journey drear;

A swan honks on autumn frontier.

Dew turns into frost since tonight;

The moon viewed from home is more bright.

I've brothers scattered here and there;

For our life or death none would care.

Letters can't reach where I intend;

Alas! The war's not come to an end.

许渊冲译唐诗三百首

The poet sighs for his brothers cannot get together in time of war.

逢入京使 [①]

岑 参

故园[②] 东望路漫漫[③]，
双袖龙钟[④] 泪不干。
马上相逢无纸笔，
凭[⑤] 君传语报平安。

① 入京使：回京城的使者。
② 故园：家乡。
③ 漫漫：遥远的样子。
④ 龙钟：沾湿的样子。
⑤ 凭：烦；请。

许渊冲译唐诗三百首

On Meeting a Messenger Going to the Capital

Cen Shen

I look eastward, long, long my homeward way appears;
My old arms tremble and my sleeves are wet with tears.
Meeting you on horseback, with what brush can I write?
I can but ask you to tell my kin I'm all right.

许渊冲译唐诗三百首

The quatrain is a short message the poet asks the messenger to send home.

行军^①九日^②思长安故园

岑 参

强^③欲^④登高^⑤去，

无人送酒来。

遥怜^⑥故园菊，

应傍^⑦战场^⑧开。

① 行军：行营。
② 九日：指农历九月九日重阳节。
③ 强：勉强。
④ 欲：准备；打算。
⑤ 登高：古人在九月九日重阳节，有登高赏菊、佩戴茱萸、饮菊花酒的习俗。
⑥ 怜：怜爱；想念。
⑦ 傍：挨着。
⑧ 战场：彼时京城长安被安史叛军所占据，沦为了战场。

Thinking of Home While Marching on Mountain-climbing Day

Cen Shen

Up the mountain I'd force myself to go,
But nobody would bring me wine around.
Chrysanthemums of my homeland should blow
To beautify the far-off battleground.

许渊冲译唐诗三百首

The poet would drink and enjoy chrysanthemums at home on Mountain-climbing Day.

归雁 ①

钱　起

潇湘 ② 何事 ③ 等闲 ④ 回?

水碧沙明两岸苔。

二十五弦 ⑤ 弹夜月,

不胜 ⑥ 清怨却 ⑦ 飞来。

① 归雁: 指北归的大雁。
② 潇湘: 潇水和湘江在今湖南永州芝山区北合流后的统称, 位于洞庭湖的南面。
③ 何事: 何故; 什么原因。
④ 等闲: 无端; 轻易; 随便。
⑤ 二十五弦: 指弦乐器瑟。《史记·封禅书》载: 或曰: "太帝使素女鼓五十弦瑟, 悲, 帝禁不止, 故破其瑟为二十五弦。"
⑥ 不胜: 忍受不了。
⑦ 却: 仍; 还。

To the Returning Wild Geese

Qian Qi

Why will you stay on South River no more
With blue water, bright sand and mossy shore?
The moonbeams play on twenty-five sad strings.
Can you not bear the grief the zither brings?

許
渊
冲
译
唐
诗
三
百
首

The poet imagines the wild geese fly north for they cannot bear the grief of the princess who plays on a zither of twenty-five strings at the emperor's death by the riverside.

喜外弟^① 卢纶见宿^②

司空曙

静夜四无邻，

荒居^③旧业^④贫。

雨中黄叶树，

灯下白头人。

以^⑤我独沉^⑥久，

愧君相见频^⑦。

平生自有分，

况是蔡家亲^⑧。

① 外弟：指表弟。古代称呼姑姑、舅舅、姨的比自己小的儿子为外弟。
② 见宿：住宿。
③ 荒居：指在荒郊野外居住。
④ 旧业：指家中旧有的产业。
⑤ 以：因为。
⑥ 沉：沉沦，这里指保持沉默，不评说时事。
⑦ 频：屡次；多次。
⑧ 蔡家亲：指姑舅表亲。

许渊冲译唐诗三百首

My Cousin Lu Lun's Visit

Sikong Shu

I feel lonely on quiet night,

A poor scholar in a sad plight.

A yellow-leafed tree in the rain,

By lamplight but white hairs remain.

Alone I have sunk low for long,

Still you would come to hear my song.

It's fate for us to meet or part,

But we are cousins dear at heart.

The poor poet is happy at his cousin's visit.

夏夜宿表兄话旧 ①

窦叔向

许
渊
冲
译
唐
诗
三
百
首

夜合花 ② 开香满庭，

夜深微雨醉初醒。

远书 ③ 珍重何曾达 ④，

旧事 ⑤ 凄凉不可听。

去日 ⑥ 儿童皆长大，

昔年 ⑦ 亲友半凋零 ⑧。

明朝又是孤舟别，

愁见河桥酒幔 ⑨ 青。

① 话旧：叙谈过去的事情。
② 夜合花：夜来香，又名"夜香花"。
③ 远书：指寄给远方亲朋的书信。
④ 何曾达：什么时候曾送到过。
⑤ 旧事：指过去的事情。
⑥ 去日：昔日。指过去两人分别之时。
⑦ 昔年：当年。
⑧ 凋零：凋谢零落。这里指亲友去世。
⑨ 酒幔：酒旗。又叫"酒帘"，俗称"望子"。

Talking with My Cousin One Summer Night

Dou Shuxiang

The courtyard's fragrant with flowers blowing at night;
When night is deep, we wake from wine in drizzling rain.
We've not received from far away letters we write;
It's hard to talk about the bygone days with pain.
The children of the past have all grown tall and high;
Half of our friends and kinsmen are gone and departed
Tomorrow when my lonely boat bids you goodbye,
Can we, seeing the streamers, not be broken-hearted?

The poet, appreciated by the premier, was transferred after the premier's dismissal.

题^①稚川^②山水

戴叔伦

松下茅亭五月凉，
汀^③沙云树晚苍苍。
行人^④无限秋风思，
隔水青山似故乡。

① 题：题写；书写。
② 稚川：地名。
③ 汀：水边的平地。
④ 行人：在外浪游的人。

A Scenery like His Homeland

Dai Shulun

Summer is cool beneath thatched roof under the pine,

Clouds cast a gloom over the trees and the sand fine.

In autumn breeze the roamer will sink in a dream.

How like his homeland look hills beyond the stream?

許渊冲译唐诗三百首

The poet does not describe the scenery so much as his own feeling.

淮上^①喜会梁川^②故人

韦应物

江汉^③曾为客，

相逢每醉还。

浮云一别后^④，

流水十年间。

欢笑情如旧，

萧疏鬓已斑^⑤。

何因不归去?

淮上有秋山。

① 淮上：淮水边。
② 梁川：今陕西南郑县东。
③ 江汉：指今湖北一带。
④ 浮云一别后：指人生聚散无常，如浮云不定。李白《送友人》："浮云游子意"。
⑤ 斑：指头发斑白。

298

Meeting with Friends on River Huai

Wei Yingwu

We met on River Huai;
Not till drunk did we go.
We went as clouds float by;
In ten years waves still flow.
We laugh as in old days,
Though our hair has turned white.
Why don't I go away?
I love autumn hills bright.

Meet or part, the river will ever flow and the poet will ever love his homeland.

淮上^①即事寄广陵亲故

韦应物

前舟已眇眇，

欲度^②谁相待。

秋山起暮钟，

楚雨连沧海。

风波离思满，

宿昔容鬓改。

独鸟下东南，

广陵^③何处在。

① 淮上：淮阴。
② 度：同"渡"。
③ 广陵：今江苏扬州。

For Kinsfolk and Friends at Guangling

Wei Yingwu

Gone is the ferry boat.

Who'll carry me afloat?

At dusk uphill bell rings;

Over seaside rain sings.

Grief saddens the waves cold;

My face and hair look old.

Southeast flies a lone bird;

Your voices can't be heard.

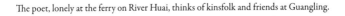

The poet, lonely at the ferry on River Huai, thinks of kinsfolk and friends at Guangling.

寒食^①寄京师诸弟

韦应物

雨中禁火^②空斋冷，
江上流莺^③独坐听。
把酒看花想诸弟，
杜陵^④寒食草青青。

---

① 寒食：《荆楚岁时记》云："冬至后一百五日谓之寒食。"
② 禁火：古代寒食节"禁火三日"（《荆楚岁时记》）。
③ 流莺：莺声圆啭如流。
④ 杜陵：汉宣帝陵，在西安府城东南十五里。韦应物是杜陵人，以此代指对家乡的思念。

For My Brothers in the Capital on Cold Food Day

Wei Yingwu

No fire is made in empty room on rainy days;

I hear alone the riverside orioles' lays.

Drinking, I gaze on flowers and miss my brothers dear;

On Cold Food Day homeland grass grows green and drear.

In ancient China the Cold Food Day fell three days ahead of the Mourning Day, that is, the fourth or fifth day in the third lunar month. No fire was made on Cold Food Day because an ancient sage burned himself in the mountains, so people would eat cold food in mourning for him.

闻雁

韦应物

故园^①眇^②何处，
归思方悠^③哉。
淮南^④秋雨夜，
高斋闻雁来。

① 故园：故乡。
② 眇：同"渺"，形容距离很远。
③ 悠：长。
④ 淮南：淮水之南。时诗人任滁州刺史，滁州在唐代属于淮南道（今安徽省滁县）。

On Hearing Homing Wild Geese

Wei Yingwu

My native land's far, far away,

My nostalgia grows day by day.

Alone on rainy autumn night

I hear homing wild geese in flight.

The poet longs for his home on hearing the home going wild geese.

喜见外弟^① 又言别

李　益

十年^② 离乱^③ 后，

长大^④ 一相逢。

问姓惊初见，

称名忆旧容^⑤。

别来沧海事^⑥，

语罢暮天钟^⑦。

明日巴陵^⑧ 道，

秋山又几重。

① 外弟：指表弟。古代称呼姑姑、舅舅、姨的比自己小的儿子为外弟。
② 十年：指唐代天宝十四年（755 年）至宝应二年（763 年）之间的"安史之乱"。
　"十年"是举其成数而言之。
③ 离乱：指诗人与表弟因安史之乱而造成的分离。
④ 长大：指成人。
⑤ 旧容：过去的容貌。
⑥ 沧海事：指变化剧烈、巨大的世事。
⑦ 暮天钟：指傍晚时候的钟声。
⑧ 巴陵：地名，巴陵县（今湖南岳阳）。

许渊冲译唐诗三百首

Meeting and Parting with My Cousin

Li Yi

We parted young for ten long years;

Not till grown up do we meet again.

At first I think a stranger appears;

Your name reminds me of your face then.

We talk of changes night and day

Until we hear the evening bell.

Tomorrow you'll go southward way

Over autumn hills, O farewell!

The poet parted with his young cousin in time of war and met with him ten years later when they were grown up.

游子吟

孟　郊

慈母手中线，
游子身上衣。
临行密密缝，
意恐迟迟归。
谁言寸草①心，
报得三春晖②。

① 寸草：小草，比喻游子。
② 三春晖：三春，指春天的孟春、仲春、季春。三春晖比喻母爱如春天的阳光。

Song of the Parting Son

Meng Jiao

From the threads a mother's hand weaves,

A gown for parting son is made.

Sewn stitch by stitch before he leaves,

For fear his return be delayed.

Such kindness as young grass receives

From the warm sun can't be repaid.

This is a well-known song showing the mother's love for her son.

309

左迁①至蓝关②示侄孙湘

韩　愈

一封朝奏九重天③，

夕贬潮州路④八千。

欲为圣明除弊事，

肯将衰朽惜残年⑤。

云横秦岭⑥家何在，

雪拥蓝关马不前。

知汝⑦远来应有意，

好收吾骨瘴江⑧边。

---

① 左迁：指被贬。
② 蓝关：蓝田关，在今陕西蓝田县南。
③ 九重天：借指皇帝。
④ 潮州路：指潮阳郡，今广东潮阳。
⑤ 肯将衰朽惜残年：肯，岂肯、怎么能够。将，因为。惜残年，顾惜老年的生命。
⑥ 秦岭：秦岭山脉，在蓝田县东南。
⑦ 汝：你，指代韩湘。
⑧ 瘴江：指潮州附近的韩江，是有名的瘴疠之地。

许渊冲译唐诗三百首

Written for My Grandnephew at the Blue Pass

Han Yu

To the Celestial Court a proposal was made,
And I am banished eight thousand li away.
To undo the misdeeds I would have given aid,
Dare I have spared myself with powers in decay?
The Ridge veiled in barred clouds, where can my home be seen?
The Blue Pass clad in snow, my horse won't forward go.
You have come from afar and I know what you mean:
Not to leave my bones there where miasmic waves flow.

许渊冲译唐诗三百首

The old poet was banished for his anti-Buddhist proposal.

邯郸[①] 冬至[②] 夜思家

白居易

许渊冲译唐诗三百首

邯郸驿里逢冬至，

抱膝灯前影伴身。

想得家中夜深坐，

还应[③] 说着远行人。

---

① 邯郸：唐代县名，属河北道磁州。今为河北省邯郸市。

② 冬至：农历二十四节气之一，在阴历十二月二十二日或二十三日。古代冬至日有
隆重的节日活动。

③ 还应：还可能。

Thinking of Home on Winter Solstice Night at Handan

Bai Juyi

At roadside inn I pass the Winter Solstice Day
Clasping my knees, with my shadow in company.
I think, till dead of night my family would stay,
And talk about the poor lonely wayfaring me.

许渊冲译唐诗三百首

While young, the poet thought of home at a lonely inn on Winter Solstice Day, which was as important as New Year's Day during the Tang Dynasty.

望驿台^①

白居易

靖安宅^②里当窗柳，

望驿台前扑地花^③。

两处春光同日尽，

居人思客客思家。

① 望驿台：在今四川省广元县西南。
② 靖安宅：白居易挚友元稹的住宅，在长安城朱雀门街东第二街靖安坊内。
③ 扑地花：花飘落坠地。

For Roaming Yuan Zhen

Bai Juyi

Your wife gazes at yellowing willows at home;
You on flowers falling on the ground while you roam.
Spring comes to end in two places on the same day;
You think of home and she of you far, far away.

Yuan and his wife long for each other on seeing falling flowers and yellow leaves.

自河南经乱^①，关内阻饥^②，兄弟离散，各在一处。因望月有感，聊书所怀，寄上浮梁大兄^③、於潜七兄^④、乌江十五兄^⑤，兼示符离^⑥及下邽^⑦弟妹

白居易

时难^⑧年荒^⑨世业^⑩空，弟兄羁旅^⑪各西东。

田园寥落^⑫干戈^⑬后，骨肉流离道路中。

吊影^⑭分为千里雁，辞根^⑮散作九秋蓬^⑯。

共看明月应垂泪，一夜乡心^⑰五处^⑱同。

① 河南经乱：贞元十五年（799年）春，宣武节度使董晋死后，部下举兵叛乱。三月，彰义节度使吴少诚又叛。这两次战乱，都在当时河南境内。
② 关内阻饥：贞元十四、十五年，长安周围旱灾严重。阻饥，艰难饥荒。
③ 浮梁大兄：诗人的大哥白幼文，于贞元十五年任浮梁县主簿。
④ 於潜七兄：诗人叔父的大儿子，曾任於潜县尉。
⑤ 乌江十五兄：诗人的堂兄，曾任乌江县主簿。
⑥ 符离：今安徽省宿县。诗人父亲在彭城为官，将家安在符离，所以符离是诗人青年时期的故乡。
⑦ 下邽：今陕西省渭南县，也是诗人的老家。
⑧ 时难：指"河南经乱"。
⑨ 年荒：指"关内阻饥"。
⑩ 世业：祖宗留下的产业。
⑪ 羁旅：流落异乡。
⑫ 寥落：荒芜。
⑬ 干戈：指战乱。
⑭ 吊影：指形影相吊、孤单寂寞的样子。
⑮ 辞根：树叶离开根部，比喻兄弟背井离乡。
⑯ 九秋蓬：秋风中的飞蓬，比喻兄弟迁徙，行踪不定。
⑰ 乡心：思念故乡之心。
⑱ 五处：指题目中所提到的那五个地方。

许渊冲译唐诗三百首

Thinking of My Brothers and Sisters Scattered Here and There, I Write this Poem for Them by the Light of the Moon

Bai Juyi

Hard times with famine spread ruins in our home town;
My brothers go their way east or west, up and down.
Battles have left the fields and gardens desolate;
By roadside wander families wars separate.
Like far-off wild geese over lonely shadows we weep,
As scattered rootless tumbleweed in autumn deep.
We should shed yearning tears to view the moon apart;
Though in five places, we have the same homesick heart.

许

渊

冲

译

唐

诗

三

百

首

The poet shows his love for his brothers and sisters scattered in five places in wartime.

别舍弟宗一 ①

柳宗元

零落残魂 ② 倍黯然 ③，

双垂别泪越江 ④ 边。

一身去国六千里，

万死 ⑤ 投荒 ⑥ 十二年。

桂岭 ⑦ 瘴 ⑧ 来云似墨，

洞庭 ⑨ 春尽水如天。

欲知此后相思梦，

长在荆门 ⑩ 郢 ⑪ 树烟。

---

① 舍弟宗一：指诗人的堂弟柳宗一。
② 残魂：残余的魂魄。
③ 黯（àn）然：心情沮丧的样子。
④ 越江：粤江。这里指代柳江。
⑤ 万死：经历了无数的艰难和磨砺。
⑥ 投荒：指被贬到边远地区。
⑦ 桂岭：在今广西贺县东北。这里指柳州一带的山岭。
⑧ 瘴：瘴气。
⑨ 洞庭：洞庭湖，是柳宗一去江陵的必经之地。
⑩ 荆门：荆门山，今在湖北省宜都县西北。
⑪ 郢（yǐng）：春秋时期楚国的都城，在今湖北省江陵市西北，这也是柳宗一必经之地。

Farewell to My Younger Brother

Liu Zongyuan

Lonely, I feel more gloomy when I part with you;

Standing by riverside, we shed tears of adieu.

I am banished from home thousands of miles away;

Not dead for twelve long years, in the west land I stay.

Miasmic clouds darken the southern mountains high;

When spring ends on East lake, water blends with the sky.

From now on I would think of you and you of me;

I'd haunt in dreams our native land from tree to tree.

The poet reveals his homesickness while parting with his younger brother.

与浩初上人^① 同看山寄京华^② 亲故

柳宗元

海畔^③ 尖山似剑铓^④，

秋来处处割愁肠。

若为^⑤ 化得身千亿，

散上峰头望故乡。

① 上人：和尚的尊称。
② 京华：京城。
③ 海畔：畔，边。柳州在南方，距海较近，故称海畔。
④ 剑铓：剑锋，剑的顶部尖锐部分。
⑤ 若为：怎能。

许渊冲译唐诗三百首

Rocky Hills Viewed Together with Abbot Haochu

Liu Zongyuan

The seaside rocky hills look sharp like sword or dart;
They thrust out when autumn comes to cut and break my heart.
If I could be transformed into rocks, I would stand
Atop a thousand peaks to watch for my homeland.

The poet wishes to be transformed into a rock to watch for his homeland far away.

幼女词

施肩吾

幼女^①才六岁，
未知巧与拙。
向夜^②在堂前，
学人拜新月^③。

① 幼女：小女儿。
② 向夜：指傍晚。
③ 新月：农历每个月初的月亮。这里指七月初七的月亮。

Song of My Youngest Daughter

Shi Jianwu

My youngest daughter's six years old;
She cannot tell clumsy from clever.
At night on crossing the threshold,
She prays the moon to shine forever.

许

渊

冲

译

唐

诗

三

百

首

This quatrain describes the fond hope of the poet's six-year-old daughter.

望夫^①词

施肩吾

手爇^② 寒灯向影频^③，
回文机^④ 上暗生尘^⑤。
自家夫婿^⑥ 无消息^⑦，
却^⑧ 恨桥头卖卜人^⑨。

① 望夫：盼望丈夫归来。
② 爇（ruò）：点燃；焚烧。
③ 频：屡次；多次。
④ 回文机：织回文锦的织布机。
⑤ 暗生尘：灰尘覆盖，暗示已经很久没有织布了。
⑥ 夫婿：指丈夫。
⑦ 消息：指音信。
⑧ 却：回头；转向。
⑨ 卖卜人：指算命先生。

Longing for Her Husband

Shi Jianwu

Often looking back to her shadow by cold lamplight,

She only sees the dusty loom drowned in dark night.

Having never received news from her husband dear,

She blames the fortune-teller to say he'd appear.

许渊冲译唐诗三百首

The unreasonable blame shows the wife is eager to see her husband's return.

旅次①朔方②

刘 皂

客③舍④并州⑤数十霜⑥，

归心日夜忆咸阳⑦。

无端⑧又⑨渡桑干水⑩，

却望并州是故乡。

① 旅次：指寄居在外。次，临时住宿。
② 朔方：地名，指灵州，即今甘肃灵武附近，这里泛指北方。
③ 客：指在外地浪游的人。
④ 舍：居住。
⑤ 并州：古地名，在唐代又称太原府，其辖地在今山西中部一带。
⑥ 十霜：十年。因为每年秋冬季节都要下霜，所以用"霜"来代"年"。
⑦ 咸阳：地名，诗人的家乡所在地。
⑧ 无端：没有什么原因。
⑨ 又：再。
⑩ 桑干水：河名，今名桑干河。即今永定河的上游，发源于今山西北部，流入今河北官厅水库。

Farther North

Liu Zao

Ten long, long winters in northern town I did stay;
My heart cried out for my southern home night and day.
Now as I cross the river, farther north I roam;
My heart cries out for northern town as for my home.

This quatrain describes well a roamer's psychology.

示弟

李 贺

别弟三年后，

还家一日余。

醁醽^①今夕酒，

缃帙^②去时书^③。

病骨^④犹^⑤能在，

人间底事^⑥无。

何须^⑦问牛马^⑧，

抛掷任枭卢^⑨。

---

① 醁醽（lù líng）：酒名。用渌水和郫湖水酿制的酒，味道甜美，所以叫"酥醒酒"，也叫"醁醽酒"。

② 缃帙：古代以浅黄色的绢帛做成的用来包书的封皮。缃（xiāng），浅黄色。

③ 去时书：离家时带走的书。

④ 病骨：指自己生病的身体。

⑤ 犹：还。

⑥ 底事：何事；啥事。

⑦ 何须：没有必要。

⑧ 牛马：牛，此处是指古代的一种赌博用具，上面画有"牛犊"图案。马，是因"牛"连类而及之。

⑨ 枭卢：此处是指古代赌博中的两种胜采名称。卢最好，枭次之。

For My Younger Brother

Li He

I left three years ago;

Again I'm in my nooks.

Tonight green wine aglow,

I forget yellow books.

Ill, I survive at last.

What won't happen on earth?

Glad that the die is cast,

I'm free from care or mirth.

许渊冲译唐诗三百首

The poet writes this poem after his failure at civil service examinations.

夜雨寄北①

李商隐

君问归期未有期，
巴山②夜雨涨秋池。
何当③共剪西窗烛，
却话④巴山夜雨时。

① 夜雨寄北：又题作"夜雨寄内"。
② 巴山：四川大巴山的简称，这里指四川一带。
③ 何当：何时。
④ 却话：再说。

Written on a Rainy Night to My Wife in the North

Li Shangyin

You ask me when I can return, but I don't know;
It rains in western hills and autumn pools overflow.
When can we trim by window side the candlelight
And talk about the western hills in rainy night?

This poet answers his wife's question first by a picture and then by another question.

正月崇让宅 ①

李商隐

密锁重关掩绿苔，
廊深阁迥此徘徊。
先知风起月含晕 ②，
尚自露寒花未开。
蝙拂帘旌 ③ 终展转，
鼠翻窗网 ④ 小惊猜。
背灯独共馀香语，
不觉犹歌《起夜来》⑤。

---

① 崇让宅：洛阳崇阳坊有河阳节度使王茂元的住宅。
② 月含晕：月色朦胧。
③ 帘旌：帘上端的布横沿。
④ 窗网：古代将窗扇刻成网形，故云。
⑤《起夜来》：乐府曲调。

Our Old Abode—Elegy on My Deceased Wife

Li Shangyin

Doors locked, curtains drawn down, on the mossy ground,

In winding corridor alone I stroll around.

By lunar halo the rising wind is foretold.

How can the flowers bloom when drenched in dew cold?

I toss in bed when curtain's hit by a bat;

I am surprised to hear in the net squeak a rat.

Alone I talk with your shadow by the lamplight.

How can I help singing with you "Rising at Night"?

The poet describes the dreary old adode after his wife's death.

秋寄从兄^①贾岛

无 可

暝^②虫喧^③暮色，

默思坐西林^④。

听雨寒更^⑤彻^⑥，

开门落叶深。

昔因京邑病^⑦，

并起洞庭心^⑧。

亦是吾兄事，

迟回共^⑨至今。

① 从兄：堂房亲属，堂哥，伯父或叔父家比自己大的儿子。
② 暝：一作"暗"。日落，天黑。
③ 喧：叫。
④ 西林：古寺名。位于江西庐山。
⑤ 更：夜里的计时单位，一夜分为五更，每更约两小时。
⑥ 彻：一作"尽"。贯通。
⑦ 京邑病：指贾岛进京科考，失利之后的忧愤心理。
⑧ 洞庭心：归隐的想法。
⑨ 共：一作"直"。共同。

Written in Autumn for My Cousin Jia Dao

Wu Ke

The crickets' chirp breaks twilight late;

In the West Wood I meditate.

I hear a shower cold which grieves,

But outdoors I see fallen leaves.

The capital's weal and woe wake

Our dream to float on Dongting Lake.

Sink or swim, you will go your way;

You won't come back but go astray,

The poet, a monk, advises his cousin who was once a monk too, to float on the lake after his failure in the civil service examinations and not to go astray once more.

骄儿诗

李商隐

衮师[①]我骄儿，美秀乃无匹[②]。

文葆未周晬[③]，固已知六七。

四岁知姓名，眼不视梨栗。

交朋颇窥观[④]，谓是丹穴物[⑤]。

前朝[⑥]尚器貌，流品方第一[⑦]。

不然神仙姿，不尔燕鹤骨[⑧]。

安得此相谓，欲慰衰朽质[⑨]。

青春妍和月，朋戏浑[⑩]甥侄。

绕堂复穿林，沸若金鼎溢[⑪]。

① 衮师：诗人儿子的名字。
② 无匹：无比。
③ 文葆未周晬：文葆，包裹婴儿的绣花小被。周晬（zuì），周岁。
④ 窥观：暗中观察。
⑤ 丹穴物：指凤凰。
⑥ 前朝：魏晋南北朝。
⑦ 流品方第一：流品，姿态仪表。方，比。
⑧ 燕鹤骨：富贵之相。
⑨ 衰朽质：衰弱多病的人。
⑩ 浑：混杂。
⑪ 金鼎溢：比喻喧闹无比。

Song of My Proud Son

Li Shangyin

I am proud of my son,
He is second to none.
Come down one year from Heaven,
He could tell six from seven.
Knowing his name at four,
No pears would he adore.
My friends would come and say
He is no common clay.
His appearance admired
Leaves nothing to be desired.
An immortal would fain
Say he's swallow or crane.
What my friends say, all told,
Would comfort a man old.
In vernal night or day
With his cousins he'd play.
They pass from hall to hall,
Boisterous one and all.

门有长者来，造次①请先出。

客前问所须，含意不吐实②。

归来学客面，闹败秉爷笏③。

或谑张飞胡④，或笑邓艾吃⑤。

豪鹰毛崰屴⑥，猛马气佶傈⑦。

截得青筼筜⑧，骑走恣唐突⑨。

忽复学参军，按声唤苍鹘⑩。

又复纱灯旁，稽首礼夜佛⑪。

仰鞭胃⑫蛛网，俯首饮花蜜。

① 造次：匆忙。
② 不吐实：不说真话。
③ 闹败秉爷笏：败，指小孩冲门而入。秉爷笏（hù），拿着父亲上朝时的手板。
④ 张飞胡：三国蜀国将领张飞的胡须。
⑤ 或笑邓艾吃：邓艾，三国魏国的将领。吃，说话口吃。
⑥ 崰屴（zè lì）：高耸的样子。
⑦ 佶傈（jí lì）：健壮的样子。
⑧ 筼筜（yún dāng）：竹子。
⑨ 恣唐突：任意横冲直撞。
⑩ 苍鹘：唐代参军戏中的配角。
⑪ 稽首礼夜佛：稽首，叩头。礼，拜。
⑫ 胃（juàn）：挂。

When guests come to see me,
He would come out with glee.
When asked what he need,
He'd veil the truth, indeed.
He mimics one guest's face
In haste and without grace,
Another bearded guest
Stammering without rest.
Like an eagle in flight
Or a strong steed in fight,
He rides a hobby horse
Running with all its force.
He jeers at officers
Blaming their messengers.
By lamplight he makes vows
And to Buddha he bows.
He sweeps webs with his whip,
And honey he would sip.

欲争蛱蝶轻，未谢柳絮疾。

阶前逢阿姊，六甲①颇输失。

凝走弄香奁②，拔脱金屈戌③。

抱持多反侧，威怒不可律④。

曲躬牵窗网，略唾⑤拭琴漆。

有时看临书⑥，挺立不动膝。

古锦请裁衣⑦，玉轴⑧亦欲乞。

请爷书春胜⑨，春胜宜春日。

芭蕉斜卷笺⑩，辛夷低过笔⑪。

爷昔好读书，恳苦自著述⑫。

① 六甲：古代一种类似下棋的游戏。
② 凝走弄香奁：凝走，硬走。香奁（lián），妇女的梳妆匣。
③ 金屈戌：指梳妆台上的铜扣环。
④ 律：约束。
⑤ 略（kā）唾：吐唾沫。
⑥ 临书：写字。
⑦ 裁衣：裁剪衣服。
⑧ 玉轴：饰玉的卷轴。
⑨ 春胜：立春那天挂在花枝上的彩绸小旗。
⑩ 笺：笺纸。
⑪ 辛夷低过笔：辛夷，人们常常称为木笔花。过笔，递笔。
⑫ 恳苦自著述：恳苦，勤苦。著述，写作。

As light as butterflies,
With willow down he vies.
Meeting his sister dear,
He plays games without fear.
He takes her toilet box
And breaks the golden locks.
Lying on ground, he'd stay;
Threatened, he'd not obey.
He draws the window screen,
Spits and wipes the lute clean.
Sometimes watching me write,
He stands unmoved upright.
Of brocade he makes cover;
Of books he seems a lover.
Asking me to write "spring",
Of spring day he would sing.
Banana's paper white,
Its bud a brush to write.
Then I was fond of books,

憔悴①欲四十，无肉畏蚤虱②。

儿慎勿学爷，读书求甲乙③。

穰苴④司马法，张良黄石术⑤。

便为帝王师，不假更纤悉⑥。

况今西与北，羌戎⑦正狂悖⑧。

诛赦两末成，将养⑨如痼疾⑩。

儿当速成大，探雏入虎穴。

当为万户侯，勿守一经帙⑪。

① 憔悴：面容清瘦的样子。
② 蚤虱（zǎo shī）：跳蚤和虱子。
③ 甲乙：古代科举考试录取分为甲、乙两第。
④ 穰苴（ráng jū）：春秋时齐国的名将，著有《司马法》。
⑤ 张良黄石术：张良，汉高祖的谋臣。黄石术，传说张良得到老人黄石公的兵书。
⑥ 不假更纤悉：假，依靠。纤悉，细微之事。
⑦ 羌戎：西北的少数民族。
⑧ 狂悖（bèi）：指很猖獗。
⑨ 将养：养息。
⑩ 痼疾：难治之病。
⑪ 经帙：经书。

Studying long in my nooks,

At forty lean and wise,

I fear nor bug nor lice.

Do not learn to win fame

Like me without a name

Try to learn from the sages

Of the different ages!

You'd be master of kings,

Carefree from trifling things.

The foe in the northwest

Are producing unrest.

Nor war nor peace can cure;

They're hard disease, for sure.

Grow up, be man of men.

Kill the foe in the den!

Son, be a hero brave

And not a scholar grave.

The poet describes in detail the son he is proud of and he lays his hope on.

许

渊

冲

译

唐

诗

三

百

首

上
册
终

致敬译界巨匠许渊冲先生

许 渊 冲 译
唐 诗 三 百 首

300 TANG POEMS

译 注

许渊冲

（下册）

中国出版集团
中译出版社

目录

Contents

一、写景抒怀　　Man and Nature

二、咏物寄兴 Nature Poems

三、赠别怀人   Farewell Poems

四、故园乡情　Homeland Poems

五、情爱相思   Love Poems

六、咏史怀古　　Historical Poems

七、边塞军旅　　　Frontier Poems

八、政治讽喻　　Political and Satirical Poems

九、人格境界　　Personality and Character

十、人生感悟　　　Reflections and Recollections

五、情爱相思
· · ·

相思 ①

王　维

红豆②生南国，

春来发几枝?

愿③君多④采撷⑤，

此物最相思。

① 唐范摅《云溪友议》："明皇幸岷山，百官皆窜辱……唯李龟年奔迫江潭……龟年曾于湘中采访使筵上唱'红豆生南国，春来发几枝。劝君多采撷，此物最相思'，又唱'清风明月苦相思，荡子从戎十载余。征人去日殷勤嘱。归雁来时数附书'。此词皆王右丞所制，至今梨园唱焉。歌阕，合座莫不望行幸而惨然。"据此，安史之乱以前当已有此诗。此诗以家常语道出人间相思寄意之事，遂广为人们传诵。
② 红豆：相思木所结子，产于亚热带地区，古人又称其为相思子。唐李匡乂《资暇集》卷下："豆有圆而红，其首乌者，举世呼为相思子，即红豆之异名也。"李时珍《本草纲目》卷三十五："相思子生岭南，树高丈余，白色，其叶似槐，其花似皂荚，其荚似扁豆，其子大如小豆，半截红色，半截黑色，彼人以嵌首饰。"梁武帝《欢闻歌》："南有相思木，含影复同心。"
③ 愿：一作"劝"。
④ 多：一作"休"。
⑤ 撷（xié）：采摘。

Love Seeds

Wang Wei

The red beans grow in southern land.

How many load in spring the trees?

Gather them till full is your hand;

They would revive fond memories.

The red beans are called love seeds.

春思

李　白

燕①草如碧丝，
秦②桑低绿枝。
当君怀归日，
是妾断肠时。
春风不相识，
何事入罗帏③?

① 燕：指今河北北部，当年是戍边之地。
② 秦：今陕西一带，系征夫们的家乡。
③ 罗帏：丝织的帘帐。

A Faithful Wife Longing for Her Husband in Spring

Li Bai

Northern grass looks like green silk thread;

Western mulberries bend their head.

When you think of your home on your part,

Already broken is my heart.

Vernal wind, intruder unseen,

O how dare you part my bed screen!

The wife is so faithful to her husband that she would not allow the vernal wind to part her bed screen.

远别离

李　白

远别离，

古有皇英之二女，

乃在洞庭之南，

潇湘之浦。

海水直下万里深，

谁人不言此离苦？

日惨惨兮云冥冥，

猩猩啼烟兮鬼啸雨。

我纵言之将何补？

皇穹窃恐不照余之忠诚，

雷凭凭兮欲吼怒。

尧舜当之亦禅禹。

君失臣兮龙为鱼，

权归臣兮鼠变虎。

Sorrow of Separation Severed for Aye

Li Bai

From the two princesses of ancient day,

Emperor Shun was buried south of the lake,

Where the two rivers meet awake,

And flow for miles and miles into the sea.

From the sorrow of separation who is free?

The sun is gloomy, veiled by dark cloud;

In mist and rain the monkeys wail and ghosts cry aloud.

Of what avail is all that I say?

The Royal Dome knows not my loyalty;

Its thunder roars against me.

Even emperors to successors should give way.

When the king's not supported, the dragon turns into fish;

The rats in power become tigers as they with.

或云：尧幽囚，
舜野死。
九疑联绵皆相似，
重瞳孤坟竟何是？
帝子泣兮绿云间，
随风波兮去无还。
恸哭兮远望，
见苍梧之深山。
苍梧山崩湘水绝，
竹上之泪乃可灭。

Emperor Yao was put in jail:

Emperor Shun died in the field to no avail.

Alike the Nine Mysterious Peaks look.

Where to find Emperor Shun's lonely tomb?

The princesses wept among the cloud green;

They gazed from afar and shed tears;

Now only the deep green mountain appears.

Only when mountains crumble and rivers go dry

Would the tear-specked bamboos vanish from the eye.

许
渊
冲
译
唐
诗
三
百
首

The legend goes that the two princesses were daughters of Emperor Yao and wives to Emperor Shun who died by the side of Dongting Lake and was buried at the foot of the Nine Mysterious Peaks. The princesses wept over the death of Emperor Shun and their tears specked the bamboos.

长干①行

李 白

妾发初覆额，
折花门前剧②。
郎骑竹马来，
绕床③弄青梅。
同居长干里，
两小无嫌猜。
十四为君妇，
羞颜未尝开。
低头向暗壁，
千唤不一回。
十五始展眉，
愿同尘与灰。
常存抱柱④信，
岂上望夫台⑤。

① 长干：古建康（南京）里巷名。
② 剧（jù）：游戏。
③ 床：井栏，后院水井的围栏。
④ 抱柱：《庄子·杂篇·盗跖》："尾生与女子期（约会）于梁（桥）下，女子不来，水至不去，抱梁柱而死。"
⑤ 望夫台：在忠州（今重庆市忠县）南数十里。

许渊冲译唐诗三百首

Ballad of a Trader's Wife

Li Bai

My forehead barely covered by my hair,

Outdoors I plucked and played with flowers fair.

On hobby horse he came upon the scene;

Around the well we played with mumes still green.

We lived close neighbors on Riverside Lane,

Carefree and innocent, we children twain.

At fourteen years old I became his bride;

I often turned my bashful face aside.

Hanging my head, I'd look on the dark wall;

I would not answer his call upon call.

I was fifteen when I composed my brows;

To mix my dust with his were my dear vows.

Rather than break faith, he declared he'd die.

Who knew I'd live alone in tower high?

十六君远行，

瞿塘滟滪堆。

五月不可触，

猿声天上哀。

门前迟行迹，

一一生绿苔。

苔深不能扫，

落叶秋风早。

八月蝴蝶黄，

双飞西园草。

感此伤妾心，

坐愁红颜老。

早晚下三巴[①]，

预将书报家。

相迎不道远，

直至长风沙[②]。

① 三巴：巴东、巴郡、巴西。汉献帝时分巴地为三郡。是今天重庆、夔州、合州一带。
② 长风沙：在今安徽省安庆市东长江边上。

I was sixteen when he went far away,

Passing Three Gorges studded with rocks grey,

Where ships were wrecked when spring flood ran high,

Where gibbons' wails seemed coming from the sky.

Green moss now overgrows before our door;

His footprints, hidden, can be seen no more.

Moss can't be swept away, so thick it grows,

And leaves fall early when the west wind blows.

In yellow autumn butterflies would pass

Two by two in west garden over the grass.

The sight would break my heart and I'm afraid,

Sitting alone, my rosy cheeks would fade.

"O when are you to leave the western land?

Do not forget to tell me beforehand!

I'll walk to meet you and would not call it far

Even to go to Long Wind Beach where you are."

This ballad describes the love of a merchant's wife for her husband.

长相思

李　白

长相思，在长安。

络纬^①秋啼金井阑^②，

微霜凄凄簟^③色寒。

孤灯不明思欲绝，

卷帷望月空长叹。

美人如花隔云端！

上有青冥^④之高天，

下有渌水^⑤之波澜。

天长路远魂飞苦，

梦魂不到关山难。

长相思，摧心肝。

① 络纬：虫名，又名蟋蟀、纺织娘、促织。
② 金井阑：井上的栏杆。意思是井栏的木石美丽，价值如金玉。
③ 簟（diàn）：竹席。
④ 青冥：青色天空。《楚辞》："据青冥而攄虹兮。"
⑤ 渌（lù）水：清澈的水。

Endless Longing

Li Bai

I long for one in all at royal capital.

The autumn cricket wails beside the golden rails.

Light frost mingled with dew, my mat looks cold in hue.

My lonely lamp burns dull, of longing I would die;

Rolling up screens to view the moon, in vain I sigh.

Above, the boundless heaven spreads its canopy screen;

Below, the endless river rolls its billows green.

My soul can't fly over sky so vast nor streams so wide;

In dreams I can't go through mountain pass to her side.

We are so far apart; the longing breaks my heart.

许渊冲译唐诗三百首

The poet describes a woman's love for her lord in the capital. By tradition, the Beauty in a classical Chinese poem may refer to the sovereign. So it is said this poem reveals the poet's loyalty to the emperor.

闺情①

李　端

月落星稀天欲明，
孤灯未灭梦难成。
披衣更向门前望，
不忿②朝来鹊喜声。

① 闺情：古典诗歌中有一类内容多为描写女子思念丈夫或情人，以及女子对爱情的
　向往，这些都称为"闺情"或"闺怨"。大多是男性诗人模仿女子的语气，有时
　也有所寄托。
② 不忿：不满；恼怒。

A Wife Longing for Her Husband

Li Duan

The stars are sparse when sinks the moon before daybreak;
The lonely lamplight not yet quenched, she lies awake.
Not dressed up, opening the door with longing eyes,
She complains of the false news announced by magpies.

许渊冲译唐诗三百首

It was believed in China that magpies would announce happy news, i. e., the return of the husband.

写情

李　益

水纹①珍簟②思悠悠,

千里佳期③一夕休。

从此无心爱良夜,

任他明月下西楼。

① 水纹：席子上的花纹像水的波纹，因此称水纹。
② 珍簟（diàn）：贵重的竹席。
③ 佳期：本指好时光，引申为男女约会的好时机。

A Date

Li Yi

On bamboo mat I long for you without a break,

Coming from afar, you don't keep the date you make.

From now on, I won't care for any lovely night;

In vain on the west tower may the moon shine bright.

许
渊
冲
译
唐
诗
三
百
首

The poet describes a woman waiting for her lover who has not kept his promise.

江南曲

于 鹄

偶向江边采白蘋，

还随女伴赛江神①。

众中不敢分明语，

暗掷金钱②卜远人。

---

① 赛江神：旧俗用仪仗、鼓乐、杂戏迎江神，祈求降福，谓之"迎神赛会"，"赛江神"即是其中之一。

② 掷金钱：一种占卜方法，以抛掷金钱的向背推断吉凶。

Song of the Southern Shore

Yu Hu

By riverside I pick white duckweed in company;

And watch the divine procession carelessly.

As I dare not show that for my husband I yearn,

I cast a coin aside to know when he'll return.

This poem describes a woman eager to see the return of her husband.

古别离

孟 郊

欲别牵郎衣,

郎今到何处?

不恨归来迟,

莫向临邛 ① 去。

---

① 临邛(qióng):四川邛崃,相传为西汉司马相如和卓文君相识之地。

Leave Me Not

Meng Jiao

I hold your robe lest you should go.
Where are you, dear, going today?
Your late return brings me less woe
Than your heart being stolen away.

The poet describes a woman afraid that her lover would change mind.

古怨别

孟　郊

飒飒^①秋风生，

愁人怨离别。

含情两相向，

欲语气先咽^②。

心曲^③千万端，

悲来却难说。

别后唯所思，

天涯共明月。

---

① 飒飒：形容秋风的声音。

② 气先咽：因为伤心，气塞声断讲不出话来。

③ 心曲：心事。

Complaint of Parting

Meng Jiao

The soughing autumn wind is blowing;

Grieved, I complain my man is going.

We face each other eye to eye;

Before I speak, I sob and sigh.

My heart is like a winding stream,

How can I tell my dreary dream?

When I miss him after we part,

We can but share moonlight apart.

许渊冲译唐诗三百首

This poem describes a woman complaining of the separation from her lord.

题都城南庄

崔　护

去年今日此门中，
人面桃花相映红。
人面不知何处去，
桃花依旧笑春风。

许渊冲译唐诗三百首

Written in a Village South of the Capital

Cui Hu

In this house on this day last year a pink face vied
In beauty with the pink peach blossoms side by side.
I do not know today where the pink face has gone;
In vernal breeze still smile pink peach blossoms full blown.

许渊冲译唐诗三百首

This quatrain is written in memory of a beauty the poet met with in the preceding year.

新嫁娘词三首（其三）

王　建

三日入厨下，
洗手作羹汤。
未谙①姑②食性，
先遣小姑③尝。

① 谙：熟悉。
② 姑：婆婆。
③ 小姑：丈夫的妹妹。

A Bride (III)

Wang Jian

Married three days, I go shy-faced
To cook a soup with hands still fair.
To meet my mother-in-law's taste,
I send to her daughter the first share.

This quatrain describes the psychology of a young bride.

秋思赠远二首（其一）

王　涯

当年只自守空帷，
梦里关山觉别离。
不见乡书传雁足^①，
唯看新月吐蛾眉^②。

① 雁足：古代传说大雁和鱼均可传递书信。
② 蛾眉：像蚕蛾触须似的弯而长的眉毛，形容女子容貌美丽。

Autumn Thoughts for My Wife (I)

Wang Ya

In bygone years alone in empty room did I stay
To dream of the mountains of homeland far away.
Seeing no wild geese bringing me your letter now,
I only find the new moon like your arching brow.

许渊冲译唐诗三百首

秋思赠远二首（其二）

王　涯

厌攀杨柳临清阁，
闲采芙蕖^①傍碧潭。
走马台^②边人不见，
拂云堆^③畔战初酣。

① 芙蕖（fú qú）：荷花，又称莲花、芙蓉。
② 走马台：走马章台，又称章台。汉代长安章台下有街名走马章台街，《汉书·张敞传》："然敞无威仪，时罢朝会，过走马章台街，使御史驱，自以便面拊马。又为妇画眉，长安中传张京兆眉抚。"
③ 拂云堆：地名，在朔方，本诗中代指征战之地。

Autumn Thoughts for My Wife (II)

Wang Ya

When tired of breaking willow branch before my bower,

I pluck at leisure by poolside the lotus flower.

I cannot find your face when I ride on my horse,

But hear the cloud echo war cries of combat force.

The poet in garrison on the frontier longs for his wife far away at home.

竹枝词二首（其一）

刘禹锡

杨柳青青江水平，
闻郎江上唱歌声。
东边日出西边雨，
道是^①无晴^②却^③有晴。

---

① 道是：说是。
② 晴："情"的同音字，用来暗喻感情的"情"。
③ 却：一作"还"。

Bamboo Branch Songs (I)

Liu Yuxi

Between the green willows the river flows along;

My gallant in a boat is heard to sing a song.

The west is veiled in rain, the east enjoys sunshine,

My gallant is as deep in love as the day is fine.

竹枝词二首（其二）

刘禹锡

山桃红花满上头^①，
蜀江^②春水拍山流。
花红易衰似郎意，
水流无限似侬^③愁。

① 上头：山上头。
② 蜀江：泛指四川省境内的河流。
③ 侬：我。女子自称。

Bamboo Branch Songs (II)

Liu Yuxi

The mountain's red with peach blossoms above;

The shore is washed by spring waves below.

Red blossoms fade fast as my gallant's love;

The river like my sorrow will ever flow.

These two quatrains describe a woman's complaint of her gallant.

长恨歌

白居易

汉皇^①重色思倾国^②，御宇^③多年求不得。

杨家有女^④初长成，养在深闺人未识。

天生丽质难自弃，一朝选在君王侧。

回眸^⑤一笑百媚生，六宫^⑥粉黛^⑦无颜色。

春寒赐浴华清池^⑧，温泉水滑洗凝脂^⑨。

侍儿扶起娇无力，始是新承恩泽^⑩时。

云鬓^⑪花颜金步摇^⑫，芙蓉帐暖度春宵。

春宵^⑬苦短^⑭日高起，从此君王不早朝^⑮。

① 汉皇：指唐玄宗。
② 倾国：形容女子极其美貌。
③ 御宇：治理天下。
④ 杨家有女：指杨玉环，蒲州永乐人。幼时养在叔父家。
⑤ 眸：本指瞳仁，泛指眼睛。
⑥ 六宫：本专指皇后寝宫，后泛指妃嫔居处。
⑦ 粉黛：代指美女。
⑧ 华清池：华清宫温泉，在今陕西临潼。
⑨ 凝脂：指白嫩光泽的肌肤。
⑩ 新承恩泽：初受宠爱。
⑪ 云鬓：形容女子鬓发轻盈飘逸。
⑫ 金步摇：金制垂珠头钗，行则摇动。
⑬ 春宵：春夜。
⑭ 苦短：暗示欢愉无厌，故嫌夜短。
⑮ 早朝：早晨上朝听政。

The Everlasting Longing

Bai Juyi

The beauty-loving monarch longed year after year

To find a beautiful lady without a peer.

A maiden of the Yangs to womanhood just grown,

In inner chambers bred, to the world was unknown.

Endowed with natural beauty too hard to hide,

She was chosen one day to be the monarch's bride.

Turning her head, she smiled so sweet and full of grace

That she outshone in six palaces the fairest face.

She bathed in glassy water of Warm-fountain Pool

Which laved and smoothed her creamy skin when spring was cool

Without her maids' support, she was too tired to move,

And this was when she first received the monarch's love,

Flower-like face and cloud-like hair, golden-headdressed.

In lotus-adorned curtain she spent the night blessed.

She slept till the sun rose high for the blessed night was short,

From then on the monarch held no longer morning court.

承欢侍宴无闲暇，春从春游夜专夜①。

后宫②佳丽③三千④人，三千宠爱在一身⑤。

金屋⑥妆成娇侍夜，玉楼宴罢醉和春⑦。

姊妹弟兄皆列土，可怜⑧光彩生门户。

遂令天下父母心，不重生男重生女。

骊宫⑨高处入青云，仙乐⑩风飘处处闻。

缓歌慢舞⑪凝丝竹⑫，尽日君王看不足⑬。

渔阳鼙鼓动地来，惊破霓裳羽衣曲⑭。

九重城阙烟尘生⑮，千乘万骑西南行。

① 夜专夜：一夜连着一夜，整日整夜。
② 后宫：后妃所居宫室。
③ 佳丽：美女。
④ 三千：极言其多。
⑤ 一身：指杨贵妃一人。
⑥ 金屋：用汉武帝"金屋藏娇"典。指杨贵妃所居之处。
⑦ 醉和春：指酒与情同醉。
⑧ 可怜：可美。
⑨ 骊宫：指骊山华清宫。
⑩ 仙乐：形容乐声美妙，非人间能闻。
⑪ 缓歌慢舞：轻歌曼舞。
⑫ 凝丝竹：指歌舞紧扣乐声。丝竹，弦乐和管乐的合称。
⑬ 看不足：看不厌。
⑭ 霓裳羽衣曲：舞曲名。
⑮ "九重"句：九重城阙，指京城长安。烟尘，烽烟尘土，指战火。

In revels as in feasts she shared her lord's delight,

His companion on trips and his mistress at night.

In inner palace dwelt three thousand ladies fair,

On her alone was lavished royal love and care.

Her beauty served the night when dressed up in Golden Bower,

She was drunk with wine and spring at banquet in Jade Tower.

Her sisters and brothers all received rank and fief,

And honors showered on her household, to the grief

Of fathers and mothers who would rather give birth

To a fair maiden than to any son on earth,

The lofty palace towered high into the cloud;

With divine music borne on the breeze the air was loud.

Seeing slow dance and hearing fluted or stringed song,

The emperor was never tired the whole day long.

But rebels beat their war drums, making the earth quake

And "Song of Rainbow Skirt and Coat of Feathers" break,

A cloud of dust was raised o'er city walls nine-fold;

Thousands of chariots and horsemen southwestward rolled.

翠华^①摇摇行复止，西出都门百余里。

六军^②不发无奈何，宛转^③蛾眉^④马前死。

花钿^⑤委地^⑥无人收，翠翘^⑦金雀^⑧玉搔头^⑨。

君王^⑩掩面救不得，回看血泪相和流。

黄埃^⑪散漫风萧索，云栈萦纡登剑阁^⑫。

峨嵋山^⑬下少人行，旌旗无光日色薄^⑭。

蜀江水碧蜀山青，圣主^⑮朝朝暮暮情。

行宫^⑯见月伤心色，夜雨闻铃肠断声。

① 翠华：皇帝仪仗用翠鸟羽毛为饰的旗帜。
② 六军：此指皇帝的扈从部队。
③ 宛转：缠绵委屈貌。
④ 蛾眉：这里指杨贵妃。
⑤ 花钿：金玉制花形首饰。
⑥ 委地：落地。
⑦ 翠翘：形似翠鸟尾的首饰。
⑧ 金雀：钗名。
⑨ 玉搔头：玉簪。
⑩ 君王：指唐玄宗。
⑪ 黄埃：黄色尘土。
⑫ "云栈"句：高耸入云的栈道。萦纡，弯曲盘旋。剑阁，在今四川剑阁县东北大、
　　小剑山之间。
⑬ 峨嵋山：在今四川峨眉山市南，此泛指蜀山。
⑭ 日色薄：日光黯淡。
⑮ 圣主：指唐玄宗。
⑯ 行宫：皇帝出行时的住所。

Imperial flags moved slowly now and halted then.

And thirty miles from Western Gate they stopped again.

Six armies-what could be done-would not march with speed

Unless fair Lady Yang be killed before the steed.

None would pick up her hairpin fallen on the ground

Nor golden bird nor comb with which her head was crowned.

The monarch could not save her and hid his face in fear;

Turning his head, he saw her blood mix with his tear.

The yellow dust widespread, the wind blew desolate;

A serpentine plank path led to cloud-capped Sword Gate.

Below the Eyebrow Mountains wayfarers were few;

In fading sunlight royal standards lost their hue,

On Western water blue and Western mountains green

The monarch's heart was daily gnawed by sorrow keen.

The moon viewed from his tent shed a soul-searing light;

The bells heard in night rain made a heart-rending sound.

天旋地转①回龙驭②，到此踌躇不能去。

马嵬坡下泥土中，不见玉颜③空死处。

君臣相顾尽沾衣④，东望都门⑤信马⑥归。

归来池苑皆依旧，太液⑦芙蓉⑧未央⑨柳。

芙蓉如面柳如眉，对此如何不泪垂。

春风桃李花开日，秋雨梧桐叶落时。

西宫⑩南内⑪多秋草，落叶满阶红不扫。

梨园弟子⑫白发新，椒房阿监⑬青娥⑭老。

① 天旋地转：形容时局大变。
② 回龙驭：指唐玄宗还京。
③ 玉颜：美女，此指杨贵妃。
④ 沾衣：指落泪。
⑤ 都门：长安城门。
⑥ 信马：任马奔走，不加约束。
⑦ 太液：池名。
⑧ 芙蓉：荷花。
⑨ 未央：宫名，此泛指唐代宫苑。
⑩ 西宫：太极宫。
⑪ 南内：兴庆宫。太极宫和兴庆宫为唐玄宗返京后的两处住所。
⑫ 梨园弟子：由玄宗执教的宫内习艺者。
⑬ 椒房阿监：后妃宫中的女官。
⑭ 青娥：青春美貌。

许渊冲译唐诗三百首

Suddenly turned the tide. Returning from his flight,

The monarch could not tear himself away from the ground

Where' mid the clods beneath the Slope he couldn't forget

The fair-faced Lady Yang who was unfairly slain.

He looked at his courtiers, with tears his robe was wet;

They rode east to the capital but with loose rein.

Come back, he found her pond and garden in old place,

With lotus in the lake and willows by the hall,

Willow leaves like her brows and lotus like her face,

At the sight of all these, how could his tears not fall?

Or when in vernal breeze were peach and plum full-blown

Or when in autumn rain parasol leaves were shed?

In Western as in Southern Court was grass o'ergrown;

With fallen leaves unswept the marble steps turned red,

Actors, although still young, began to have hair grey.

Eunuchs and waiting maids looked old in palace deep.

夕殿萤①飞思悄然②，孤灯挑尽未成眠。

迟迟③钟鼓初长夜，耿耿④星河⑤欲曙天。

鸳鸯瓦⑥冷霜华⑦重，翡翠衾⑧寒谁与共。

悠悠生死别经年，魂魄不曾来入梦。

临邛道士鸿都客，能以精诚致⑨魂魄。

为感君王辗转⑩思，遂教方士殷勤觅。

排空驭气奔如电，升天入地求之遍。

上穷碧落⑪下黄泉，两处茫茫皆不见。

忽闻海上有仙山，山在虚无缥缈间。

楼阁玲珑五云起，其中绰约多仙子。

中有一人字太真，雪肤花貌参差是。

---

① 萤：萤火虫。
② 思悄然：情意萧瑟寂寞。
③ 迟迟：缓慢悠长。
④ 耿耿：明亮貌。
⑤ 河：指银河。
⑥ 鸳鸯瓦：指嵌合成对的瓦片。
⑦ 霜华：霜花。
⑧ 翡翠衾：指绣有成双翡翠鸟的被子。
⑨ 致：招来。
⑩ 辗转：翻来覆去。
⑪ 碧落：道家称天界为碧落。

Fireflies flitting the hall, mutely he pined away;
The lonely lampwick burned out, still he could not sleep.
Slowly beat drums and rang bells, night began to grow long;
Bright shone the Starry Stream, daybreak seemed to come late,
The lovebird tiles grew chilly with hoar frost so strong;
His kingfisher quilt was cold, not shared by a mate.
One long, long year the dead with the living was parted;
Her soul came not in dreams to see the broken-hearted.
A taoist sorcerer came to the palace door,
Skilled to summon the spirits from the other shore.
Moved by the monarch's yearning for the departed fair,
He was ordered to seek for her everywhere.
Borne on the air, like flash of lightning flew;
In heaven and on earth he searched through and through.
Up to the azure vault and down to deepest place,
Nor above nor below could he e'er find her trace.
He learned that on the sea were fairy mountains proud,
Which now appeared now disappeared amid the cloud
Of rainbow colors, where rose magnificent bowers
And dwelt so many fairies as graceful as flowers.
Among them was a queen whose name was Ever True;
Her snow-white skin and sweet face might afford a clue,

金阙西厢叩玉扃，转教小玉报双成。

闻道汉家①天子使，九华帐里梦魂惊。

揽衣②推枕起徘徊，珠箔银屏迤逦开。

云鬓半偏新睡觉③，花冠不整下堂来。

风吹仙袂④飘飖举，犹似霓裳羽衣舞。

玉容寂寞⑤泪阑干⑥，梨花一枝春带雨。

含情凝睇谢⑦君王，一别音容两渺茫。

昭阳殿里恩爱绝，蓬莱宫中日月长。

回头下望人寰⑧处，不见长安见尘雾。

① 汉家：唐朝。
② 揽衣：披衣。
③ 觉：睡醒。
④ 袂：衣袖。
⑤ 寂寞：黯淡失神貌。
⑥ 阑干：纵横流淌。
⑦ 谢：告诉。
⑧ 人寰：人世间。

Knocking at western gate of palace hall, he bade

The fair porter to inform the queen's waiting maid,

When she heard that there came the monarch's embassy,

The queen was startled out of dreams in her canopy.

Pushing aside the pillow, she rose and got dressed,

Passing through silver screen and pearl shade to meet the guest.

Her cloud-like hair awry, not full awake at all,

Her flowery cap slanted, she came into the hall.

The wind blew up her fairy sleeves and made them float

As if she danced still "Rainbow Skirt and Feathered Coat."

Her jade-white face crisscrossed with tears in lonely world

Like a spray of pear blossoms in spring rain impearled.

She bade him thank her lord, lovesick and broken-hearted;

They knew nothing of each other after they parted,

Love and happiness long ended within palace walls;

Days and nights appeared long in the Fairyland halls.

Turning her head and fixing on the earth her gaze,

She found no capital 'mid clouds of dust and haze.

惟将旧物表深情，钿合金钗寄将去。

钗留一股合一扇^①，钗擘黄金合分钿。

但教^②心似金钿坚，天上人间会相见。

临别殷勤^③重寄词，词中有誓两心知。

七月七日长生殿，夜半无人私语时。

在天愿作比翼鸟，在地愿为连理枝^④。

天长地久有时尽，此恨绵绵无绝期^⑤。

① 一扇：一片。
② 但教：只要让。
③ 殷勤：反复多次。
④ 连理枝：不同根的树木枝条连在一起。
⑤ 绝期：中断的时候。

To show her love was deep, she took out keepsakes old

For him to carry back, hairpin and case of gold.

Keeping one side of the case and one wing of the pin;

She sent to her lord the other half of the twin.

"If our two hearts as firm as the gold should remain,

In heaven or on earth some time we'll meet again,"

At parting, she confided to the messenger

A secret vow known only to her lord and her.

On seventh day of seventh moon when none was near,

At midnight in Long Life Hall he whispered in her ear:

"On high, we'd be two birds flying wing to wing;

On earth, two trees with branches twined from spring to spring."

The boundless sky and endless earth may pass away,

But this vow unfulfilled will be regretted for aye.

This long poem relates the life-and-death love story of Emperor Xuan Zong in the Tang Dynasty and his favorite Lady Yang Yuhuan.

遣悲怀三首（其二）

元　稹

昔日戏言身后意，
今朝都到眼前来。
衣裳已施行看尽①，
针线犹存未忍开。
尚想旧情怜婢仆，
也曾因梦送钱财。
诚知此恨②人人有，
贫贱夫妻百事哀。

① 行看尽：即将送完了。
② 此恨：指夫妻死别之情。

To My Deceased Wife (II)

Yuan Zhen

"What if one of us should die?" we said for fun one day;
But now it has come true and passed before my eyes.
I can't bear to see your clothes and give them away;
I seal your embroidery lest it should draw my sighs.
Remembering your kindness, I'm kind to our maids;
Dreaming of your bounty, I give bounties as before.
I know there is no mortal but returns to the shades,
But a poor couple like us have more to deplore.

遣悲怀三首（其三）

元　稹

闲坐悲君① 亦自悲，

百年② 都是几多时。

邓攸无子寻知命③，

潘岳悼亡④ 犹费词。

同穴窅冥何所望⑤，

他生缘会更难期⑥。

唯将终夜长开眼⑦，

报答平生⑧ 未展眉⑨。

---

① 君：指韦氏。

② 百年：指一生。

③ "邓攸"句：邓攸。字伯道，西晋时人，曾任河东太守，在战乱中舍弃自己的儿子而保全侄子，后来终生无子，当时人有"天道无知，使伯道无儿"之叹。知命，认识到是命中注定的。

④ 潘岳悼亡：西晋诗人潘岳在妻子死后写了三首悼亡诗悼念妻子。这也指诗人自己。

⑤ "同穴"句：同穴，指夫妻合葬。窅（yǎo）冥，深远幽暗的样子。何所望，意思是死后同穴合葬，也难以倾诉衷情。

⑥ "他生"句：他生，来生。缘会，姻缘遇合。期，期待。

⑦ "唯将"句：唯将，只将。长开眼，指彻夜不眠。

⑧ 平生：指韦氏生前。

⑨ 未展眉：指韦氏生前一直着过清苦的生活，很少欢悦。

To My Deceased Wife (III)

Yuan Zhen

Sitting idle, I grieve for myself as for you;

How many days are left of my declining years?

Another childless man fared better than I do;

Another widower lavished vain verse and tears.

Could I await a better fate than our same tomb?

Could you be born again and again be my wife?

With eyes unclosed all night long I'll lie in the gloom

To repay you for your unknit brows in your life.

许渊冲译唐诗三百首

The poet has written three poems for his deceased wife and two of them are selected here.

六年春遣怀八首（其二）

元　稹

检^①得旧书三四纸，
高低阔狭粗成行。
自言并食^②寻高事，
唯念山深驿路长。

---

① 检：翻检。
② 并食：两天只吃一天的粮食。

Elegy on My Deceased Wife (II)

Yuan Zhen

I find three or four sheets of your letters fine;

The words of your handwriting often go out of line.

You cared not for your hunger every other day,

If I was fed in deep mountains on my long way.

许渊冲译唐诗三百首

The poet remembers his wife who would suffer hunger every other day to provide for him on his way in the mountains.

离思五首（其四）

元　稹

曾经沧海^①难为水，
除却巫山不是云。
取次^②花丛懒回顾，
半缘修道半缘君。

① 沧海：大海。
② 取次：任意；随便。

Thinking of My Dear Departed (IV)

Yuan Zhen

No water's wide enough when you have crossed the sea;
No cloud is beautiful but that which crowns the peak.
I pass by flowers which fail to attract poor me
Half for your sake and half for Taoism I seek.

The poet no longer loves nature as before after the death of his dear wife but tries to seek consolation from Taoism.

赠别二首（其一）

杜 牧

娉娉袅袅^①十三余，
豆蔻^②梢头二月初。
春风十里扬州路，
卷上珠帘^③总不如。

---

① 娉娉袅袅：这里用来形容女子的姿态姣弱、美好。《乐府诗集·春歌》："娉婷扬袖舞，阿那曲身轻。"《玉台新咏》中沈约《十咏》："不声如动吹，无风自袅枝。"娉，貌美。袅，柔弱。
② 豆蔻：多年生草本植物，外形像芭蕉，叶子细长，开花淡黄，有香气。后来称女子十三四岁的年纪为豆蔻年华。
③ 珠帘：有珍珠缀饰的帘子。谢朓《谢宣城集·玉阶怨》："夕殿下珠帘，流萤飞复息。"

At Parting (I)

Du Mu

Not yet fourteen, she's fair and slender
Like early budding flower tender.
Though Yangzhou Road's beyond compare,
Pearly screen uprolled, none's so fair.

赠别二首（其二）

杜 牧

多情却似总无情，

唯觉樽^①前笑不成。

蜡烛有心还惜别，

替人垂泪到天明。

---

① 樽：又作"尊"。一种盛酒器。李白有诗《前有一樽酒行二首》："春风东来忽
相过，金樽绿酒生微波。"

At Parting (II)

Du Mu

Deep, deep our love, too deep to show;
Deep, deep we drink, silent we grow.
The candle grieves to see us part,
It melts in tears with burnt-out heart.

The poet describes his young love in Yangzhou as incomparable in the first quatrain and compares their heart to the burnt-out candle wick in the second.

忆扬州

徐　凝

萧娘[①]脸薄难胜泪，

桃叶[②]眉长易觉愁。

天下三分明月夜，

二分无赖[③]是扬州。

---

① 萧娘：女子的代称。
② 桃叶：女子的代称。
③ 无赖：蛮不讲理，或顽皮可爱之意。

To One in Yangzhou

Xu Ning

Your bashful face could hardly bear the weight of tears;
Your long, long brows would easily feel sorrow nears.
Of all the moonlit nights on earth when people part,
Two-thirds shed sad light on Yangzhou with broken heart.

The poet regrets his parting from his lover in Yangzhou so much that he feels the moon heart-broken to see them part, and thus the place is beautified by their parting.

悼伤后赴东蜀[①]辟至散关遇雪

李商隐

剑外[②]从军远，
无家与寄衣。
散关三尺雪，
回梦旧鸳机。

---

① 东蜀：东川（治所在梓州，今四川三台县）。
② 剑外：剑阁之南的蜀中。

Dreaming of My Deceased Wife at Her Loom

Li Shangyin

I join the army far away.

Who'd send me warm clothes for cold day?

The mountain pass is clad in snow;

My dream of her loom brings me woe.

许

渊

冲

译

唐

诗

三

百

首

The poet in the army dreams of his deceased wife on a cold day.

为有

李商隐

为有^①云屏^②无限娇，
凤城^③寒尽怕春宵。
无端嫁得金龟婿，
辜负香衾^④事早朝。

① 为有：以首句前两字为题，也属于无题诗一类。
② 云屏：用云母石做成的屏风。
③ 凤城：京城。
④ 衾：被子。

A Nobleman's Wife

Li Shangyin

Behind the screen his wife is charming without peer,

But she's afraid the vernal night should be too short.

Why should she be wed to her noble lord so dear?

At early dawn he'd leave her pillow for the court.

This quatrain describes the sorrow of a nobleman's wife whose lord should rise early to go to court.

无题

李商隐

相见时难别亦难，

东风无力百花残。

春蚕到死丝^①方尽，

蜡炬成灰泪^②始干。

晓镜但愁云鬓改，

夜吟应觉月光寒。

蓬山^③此去无多路，

青鸟^④殷勤为探看。

① 丝：与"思"谐音。
② 泪：烛泪，即蜡油。喻人的眼泪。
③ 蓬山：蓬莱山。传说中的三仙山之一。
④ 青鸟：《汉武故事》载，西王母下见汉武帝，有青鸟先到殿前报信，此句指托青
鸟代主人探望对方。

To One Unnamed

Li Shangyin

It's difficult for us to meet and hard to part;

The east wind is too weak to revive flowers dead.

Spring silkworm till its death spins silk from love-sick heart;

A candle but when burned out has no tears to shed.

At dawn I'm grieved to think your mirrored hair turns grey;

At night you would feel cold while I croon by moonlight.

To the three fairy hills it is not a long way.

Would the blue birds oft fly to see you on the height?

The poet writes this poem for his unnamed lover compared to a fairy living in the three mountains on the sea where only the mythical blue birds could bring messages.

嫦娥①

李商隐

云母②屏风烛影深，
长河③渐落晓星④沉。
嫦娥应悔偷灵药，
碧海⑤青天夜夜心⑥。

① 嫦娥：姮娥，又称羲娥。《搜神记》："羿请不死药于西王母，嫦娥窃之以奔月。"
② 云母：一种矿石，晶体透明有光泽，古代常用来装饰屏风等家具。
③ 长河：指天上的银河。
④ 晓星：启明星。
⑤ 碧海：形容蓝天一碧如海。
⑥ 夜夜心：指夜夜感到心情孤寂。

许渊冲译唐诗三百首

To the Moon Goddess

Li Shangyin

Upon the marble screen the candlelight is winking;

The Silver River slants and morning stars are sinking.

You'd regret to have stolen the miraculous potion;

Each night you brood over the lonely celestial ocean.

许渊冲译唐诗三百首

According to the myth, the archer who had shot down nine suns held miraculous potion, but his wife stole it, flew to the moon and became the lonely moon goddess.

无题四首（其一）

李商隐

来是空言去绝踪，

月斜楼上五更钟。

梦为远别啼难唤，

书被催成墨未浓。

蜡照① 半笼金翡翠②，

麝熏③ 微度绣芙蓉④。

刘郎⑤ 已恨蓬山⑥ 远，

更隔蓬山一万重。

① 蜡照：烛光。
② 金翡翠：指上面镶有翡翠鸟图案的金色屏风。
③ 麝熏：麝香的气味。
④ 绣芙蓉：指上面绣有芙蓉花图案的帷帐。
⑤ 刘郎：指刘晨。据说汉末（公元三世纪初）刘晨、阮肇上天台山采药，在山中迷路。
　遇二仙女，结成一段奇缘，返回家乡时人间已过了七世，后以"刘郎"指情郎。
⑥ 蓬山：海中三仙山之一，这里意中人的住处。

Untitled Poems (I)

Li Shangyin

You said you'd come but you have gone and left no trace;
I hear in the moonlit tower the fifth watch bell.
In dream my cry could not call you back from distant place;
In haste with ink unthickened I cannot write well.
The candlelight illuminates half our broidered bed;
The smell of musk still faintly sweetens lotus screen.
Beyond my reach the far-off fairy mountains spread;
But you're still farther off than fairy mountains green.

The poet writes for one unnamed lover who passed sweet nights together with him.

无题二首（其一）

李商隐

昨夜星辰昨夜风，
画楼西畔桂堂东①。
身无彩凤双飞翼，
心有灵犀②一点通。
隔座送钩③春酒暖，
分曹④射覆⑤蜡灯红。
嗟余听鼓⑥应官⑦去，
走马兰台⑧类转蓬。

---

① 画楼、桂堂：都是比喻富贵人家的屋舍。
② 灵犀：旧说犀牛有神异，角中有白纹如线，直通两头。
③ 送钩：也称藏钩。古代腊日的一种游戏，分二曹以较胜负。把钩互相传送后，藏于一人手中，令人猜。
④ 分曹：分组。
⑤ 射覆：在覆器下放着东西令人猜。分曹、射覆未必是实指，只是借喻宴会时的热闹。
⑥ 鼓：指更鼓。
⑦ 应官：犹上班。
⑧ 兰台：秘书省，掌管图书秘籍。李商隐曾任秘书省正字。

Untitled Poems (I)

Li Shangyin

As last night twinkle stars, as last night blows the breeze,
West of the painted bower, east of Cassia Hall.
Having no wings I can't fly to you as I please;
Our hearts at one, your ears can hear my inner call.
Maybe you're playing hook in palm and drinking wine
Or guessing what the cup hides under candle red,
Alas! I hear the drum call me to duties mine;
Like rootless weed to Orchid Hall I ride ahead.

The poet who works in Orchid Hall and lives in Cassia Hall recalls the night spent together with his unnamed lover and imagines what she is doing on his lonely night.

六、咏史怀古

. . . .

黄鹤楼①

崔　颢

昔人已乘黄鹤去，

此地空余黄鹤楼。

黄鹤一去不复返，

白云千载空悠悠。

晴川②历历汉阳树，

芳草萋萋鹦鹉洲③。

日暮乡关何处是？

烟波④江上使人愁。

① 黄鹤楼：因为处在汉水与长江交汇处的武昌黄鹤山（又名蛇山）而得名。黄鹤山，《齐谐志》中记载，仙人王子安乘黄鹤路过此地而得名。
② 晴川：晴天中的汉水。川，河道。
③ 鹦鹉洲：在汉水水滨，鄂州城南。李白《鹦鹉洲诗》中有"鹦鹉来过吴江水，江上洲传鹦鹉名"。
④ 烟波：朦胧得看不清的江波，像烟雾笼罩着一样。

Yellow Crane Tower

Cui Hao

The sage on yellow crane was gone amid clouds white.

To what avail is Yellow Crane Tower left here?

Once gone, the yellow crane will not on earth alight;

Only white clouds still float in vain from year to year.

By sunlit river trees can be counted one by one;

On Parrot Islet sweet green grass grows fast and thick.

Where is my native land beyond the setting sun?

The mist-veiled waves of River Han make me homesick.

The legend goes that the Yellow Crane Tower was built in memory of a sage who, riding on a yellow crane, flew to Heaven and became an immortal.

越中[①]览古

李 白

越王勾践[②]破吴归，

义士还家尽锦衣。

宫女如花满春殿，

只今惟有鹧鸪[③]飞。

① 越中：隋初将会稽郡改为越州，唐代沿用越州名，即现在的浙江绍兴。这里是春秋时越国领地。

② 勾践：春秋越国君王，曾被同时期的吴国打败。后来勾践卧薪尝胆，发愤图强，致力于国事、民事和军事，终于在二十年后又灭掉吴国。

③ 鹧鸪：产于我国南部，形似雌，体大如鸠。古人称它的鸣叫声为"钩辀格磔"，民间以为其叫声极像"行不得也哥哥"，所以古人常借其声以抒逐客流人之情，描绘荒芜凄凉之景。

The Ruined Capital of Yue

Li Bai

The King of Yue returned, having destroyed the foe;

His loyal men came home, with silken dress aglow.

His palace thronged with flower-like ladies fair;

Now we see but a flock of partridges flying there.

许渊冲译唐诗三百首

The poet sighs over the ruined palace of the King of Yue who revenged his defeat by over-throwing the Kingdom of Wu.

登金陵凤凰台 ①

李 白

凤凰台上凤凰游，

凤去台空江自流。

吴宫 ② 花草埋幽径，

晋代 ③ 衣冠成古丘。

三山 ④ 半落青天外，

二水中分白鹭洲 ⑤ 。

总为浮云能蔽日 ⑥ ，

长安不见使人愁。

---

① 凤凰台：位于金陵城（今江苏南京市）东南的凤凰山上。相传南朝刘宋永嘉年间，
有凤凰集于这座山上，于是朝廷筑造楼台，并将山和台都命名为凤凰。凤凰，在
古代是一种代表祥瑞的动物，如果凤凰出现就意味着国家昌盛、君主贤明。唐代
武则天时期有年号为"仪凤"，即"有凤来仪"的意思，就是因为当年有个地方
官上奏说凤凰出现，武则天认为是因为自己治理的国家昌盛凤凰才出现的，于是
改年号为"仪凤"以示纪念。
② 吴宫：这里指三国时期吴国的宫殿。
③ 晋代：这里专指东晋，因为东晋和三国时吴均定都金陵。
④ 三山：位于金陵城西南长江边。南宋陆游《入蜀记》载："三山，自石头及凤凰
山望之，杳杳有无中耳。及过其下，距金陵才五十余里。"
⑤ 白鹭洲：位于金陵城西长江中，将长江分为两道。
⑥ 浮云能蔽日：这里浮云蔽日是指皇帝受到奸臣的蒙蔽，不能明辨贤臣的状况。汉
陆贾《新语·慎微篇》："邪臣之蔽贤，犹浮云之障日月也。"

The Phoenix Terrace at Jinling

Li Bai

On Phoenix Terrace once phoenixes came to sing;

The birds are gone but still roll on the river's waves.

The ruined palace's buried under weeds in spring;

The ancient sages in caps and gowns all lie in graves.

The three-peaked mountain is half lost in azure sky;

The two-forked stream by Egret Isle is kept apart.

As floating clouds can veil the bright sun from the eye,

Imperial Court now out of view saddens my heart.

The disgraced poet visits Phoenix Terrace and compares himself to a phoenix and the emperor to the bright sun veiled by floating clouds.

谢公亭 [1]

李 白

许渊冲译唐诗三百首

谢公离别处，

风景每生愁。

客散青天月，

山空碧水流。

池花 [2] 春映日，

窗竹 [3] 夜鸣秋。

今古一相接 [4]，

长歌 [5] 怀旧游。

[1] 谢公亭：位于今安徽省宣城城北。因为南朝诗人谢朓曾任宣城太守，并曾在此亭送别他的好友范云，后就称此地为谢公亭，成为送别饯行的场所。《水经注》记载，在宣城有泀水流过，这首诗中的"碧水"可能就是指泀水。

[2] 池花：池塘中的鲜花。

[3] 窗竹：窗外的翠竹。

[4] 相接：精神相同、契合无间。

[5] 长歌：指作一首诗歌的意思。古时，诗歌是可以歌唱的，至唐代时仍有"歌诗"的说法，后随着诗歌的发展，才逐渐与歌唱分离，成为一种独立的文学形式。

Pavilion of Xie Tiao

Li Bai

Where the two poets parted,
The scene seems broken-hearted.
The moon's left in the sky;
The stream flows with deep sigh.
The pool reflects sunlight;
Bamboos shiver at night.
The present like the past;
Long, long will friendship last.

許
渊
冲
译
唐
诗
三
百
首

Xie Tiao (464—499) was a poet who parted with another poet at Xuancheng and built a pavilion there. Disfavored, he was put in jail and died in prison. Disgraced, Li Bai came to the pavilion and sighed for Xie's misfortune.

夜泊牛渚①怀古

李 白

牛渚西江②夜，

青天无片云。

登舟望秋月，

空忆谢将军③。

余亦能高咏，

斯人不可闻。

明朝挂帆席，

枫叶落纷纷。

---

① 牛渚（zhǔ）：山名，位于今安徽省当涂县西北，紧靠长江，其北端突入江中，形成了著名的采石矶。

② 西江：从南京以西到江西境内的一段长江，古代称为西江。《水经注》的"江水三"记载江水与湘水汇合，然后流入江西境内，冲刷出二夏浦，此处被称为西江口。

③ 谢将军：李白诗题下原来有个注释说："此地即谢尚闻袁宏咏史处。"谢将军即谢尚。

Mooring at Night Near Cattle Hill

Li Bai

I moor near Cattle Hill at night,

When there's no cloud to fleck the sky.

On deck I gaze at the moon bright,

Thinking of General Xie with a sigh.

I too can chant, to what avail?

None has like him a listening ear.

Tomorrow I shall hoist my sail,

Amid fallen leaves I'll leave here.

许渊冲译唐诗三百首

The poet thinks of General Xie who appreciated a poet chanting near Cattle Hill, but he can no longer find a connoisseur here now.

蜀相 ①

杜 甫

丞相祠堂 ② 何处寻？

锦官城 ③ 外柏森森。

映阶碧草自春色，

隔叶黄鹂空好音。

三顾频烦天下计 ④ ，

两朝 ⑤ 开济老臣心。

出师未捷身先死 ⑥ ，

长使英雄泪满襟。

① 蜀相：三国时期蜀国的丞相诸葛亮，字孔明，山东琅琊人，曾辅佐刘备建立蜀国，
使三国鼎立局面得以形成。
② 丞相祠堂：《三国志·蜀书》中记载，诸葛亮去世后被葬在汉中定军山上，因山
为坟，蜀后主赐谥爵为"忠武侯"，后来又为他立了祠堂，成为"武侯祠"，位
于今成都城南。
③ 锦官城：成都的别称。
④ "三顾"句：《三国志·蜀书》曾记载，刘备三顾茅庐向诸葛亮询问兴复汉室的
计谋，诸葛亮由此出山，这里就指这一典故。三顾，诸葛亮《出师表》中称刘备
"三顾臣于草庐之中"。天下计，指的是诸葛亮《隆中对》中所说东连孙权、北
抗曹操、西取刘璋的计划。
⑤ 两朝：指诸葛亮辅佐刘备建立蜀国，又辅佐刘禅坚守蜀国。
⑥ "出师"句：《三国志·蜀书》记载，诸葛亮在刘备去世后，曾出岐山攻魏，想
要成就"北定中原，兴复汉室"的大业，但是六出岐山，大业未竟，反因为身患
重病，在五丈原军中去世。

Temple of the Premier of Shu

Du Fu

The Premier's Temple's in the shade

Of cypress woven with brocade.

The steps are green with grass in spring;

In vain amid leaves orioles sing.

Consulted thrice on state affair,

He served two reigns beyond compare.

He died before he won success.

Could heroes' tears not wet their dress?

The premier of Shu was Zhuge Liang (181—234) and the Town of Brocade is Chengdu.

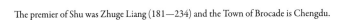

禹庙 ①

杜 甫

禹庙空山里，
秋风落日斜。
荒庭垂橘柚 ②，
古屋画龙蛇 ③。
云气嘘青壁，
江声走白沙。
早知乘四载 ④，
疏凿控三巴 ⑤。

① 禹庙：位于忠州临江的山崖上（今重庆忠县），是为了纪念古代君王大禹治水而建造的。

② 橘柚：《尚书·禹贡》记载，大禹治理洪水成功后，天下百姓能够安定生产生活，百姓们都对大禹十分感激，于是东南的一个部落就把丰收的橘柚包好，献给大禹以报答他的恩情。

③ 龙蛇：《孟子·滕文公》记载，大禹将兴风作浪的龙蛇赶入水草丰盛的大泽中，龙蛇有了归宿，也就不再祸害人民了。

④ 四载：传说大禹治水时一直奔波在外，水中乘舟，陆地乘车，泥路乘輴，山路乘檋，所以称为"四载"。

⑤ 三巴：指巴郡、巴东、巴西，也就是今天的重庆忠县、云阳及南充的阆中。传说这一带古时是沼泽之地，后来大禹凿通三峡，这里变成了陆地。

Temple of Emperor Yu

Du Fu

Your temple stands in empty hills,
The autumn breeze with sunset fills.
Oranges still hang in your courtyard;
Dragons on your old walls breathe hard.
Over green cliff float clouds in flight;
The river washes the sand white.
On water as on land you'd go
To dredge the streams and make them flow.

许
渊
冲
译
唐
诗
三
百
首

Emperor Yu was said to have stemmed the flood about 2000 BC.

八阵图 ①

杜 甫

功盖三分国，

名成八阵图。

江流石不转 ②，

遗恨失吞吴 ③。

---

① 八阵图：由天、地、风、云、龙、虎、鸟、蛇八种阵势组成的一种作战图，是诸葛亮的一项军事创造。八阵图遗址在夔州（今重庆奉节）永安宫前平沙上。

② 石不转：化用《诗经·邶风·柏舟》中的诗句"我心匪石，不可转也"，表现事物的不易变更。

③ 吞吴：吞并吴国的计划。《三国志·蜀书》记载，先主刘备称帝的第二年，也就是章武元年，刘备想以关羽被吴国杀害为借口讨伐吴国，实际上是想要借机吞并东吴，进而统一中原。但不幸的是，吴国大将陆逊等击退了刘备的进攻，并将刘备追到当时的鱼复县，也就是夔州永安县，刘备病重并逝于军中。诸葛亮从成都赶到永安，刘备将蜀国托付给诸葛亮。这时，黄元攻打蜀军，被诸葛亮生擒至成都。这就是刘备企图吞并吴国而以失败告终的历史事实。

The Stone Fortress

Du Fu

With his exploits history is crowned;
For the stone fortress he's renowned.
The river flows but stones still stand,
Though he'd not taken back lost land.

The stone fortress was the exploit of Zhuge Liang, premier of the Kingdom of Shu.

咏怀古迹五首（其二）

杜 甫

摇落深知宋玉悲^①，

风流儒雅^②亦吾师。

怅望千秋一洒泪，

萧条异代不同时。

江山故宅^③空文藻，

云雨荒台岂梦思^④？

最是楚宫俱泯灭，

舟人指点到今疑。

① "摇落"句：宋玉，战国时期楚辞作家，传说是屈原的学生。他的著名作品有《九辩》《高唐赋》和《神女赋》。《九辩》中的"悲哉，秋之为气也，萧瑟兮草木摇落而变衰"一语，被称为"千古悲秋之祖"。
② 风流儒雅：出自南北朝时期庾信的《枯树赋》，用来形容东晋名士殷仲文的人格高远。
③ 江山故宅：宋玉宅在归州和荆州各有一处，这里是指归州的宋玉宅。归州在三峡内，所以将宋玉宅说成江山故宅。
④ "云雨"句：宋玉《高唐赋》中有这样一个故事，楚怀王在高唐梦到巫山神女，并与之欢会，"旦为朝云，暮为行雨"，所以后人用"云雨"来代指楚怀王与巫山神女欢会一事。学者认为宋玉的这篇赋是为了劝诫楚帝王不要沉迷女色，唤醒他重新关心国事。

The Poet Song Yu's Abode (II)

Du Fu

When leaves shiver and fall, I see the poet drear;

Gallant and elegant, he is my master dear.

Looking back a thousand springs, can I not shed tears?

Desolate for long, we are not of the same years.

His autumn song's left in his old home by the stream.

Did clouds bring showers for flowers in the king's dream?

Even the royal palace falls now in decay,

The boatman points to the ruins in doubt today.

Song Yu (298BC—222BC) was famous for his Ode to Autumn (when leaves shiver and fall)
and his Goddess of Mount Witch (who brings showers for thirsting flowers).

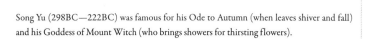

咏怀古迹五首（其五）

杜　甫

诸葛[①]大名垂宇宙，
宗臣遗像肃清高。
三分割据[②]纡筹策，
万古云霄一羽毛。
伯仲之间见伊吕[③]，
指挥若定失萧曹[④]。
运移汉祚终难复，
志决身歼军务劳。

① 诸葛：诸葛亮，蜀国开国丞相，辅佐刘备和刘禅二代，最终在五丈原病死于与司
　马懿对垒的军中。
② 三分割据：指三国时期三足鼎立的形势。据《三国志》记载，"三分天下而有蜀"
　的策略是诸葛亮提出和实施的。
③ 伊吕：指古代的贤相伊尹和吕尚。伊尹是商汤的辅佐之臣，帮助商汤建立商朝；
　吕尚是周武王的辅臣，帮助武王打败商代，建立西周。
④ 萧曹：指西汉的萧何和曹参，二人都是汉高祖刘邦的辅政之臣、西汉的开国元勋、
　著名的汉代丞相。

To the Prime Minister of Shu (V)

Du Fu

Your fame spreads far and wide, honored for long, long time:

Your noble image looks so solemn and sublime.

The world divided into three, Shu in the west;

You drove all clouds away with a plume on the crest.

You could rival all premiers of the olden day;

Beside you, all generals look pale and fade away.

But the kingdom at stake, you could not turn the tide;

Busy with your campaigns, with labor lost you died.

许
渊
冲
译
唐
诗
三
百
首

The Prime Minister refers to Zhuge Liang in the time of the Three Kingdoms (220—280).

汴河[①]曲

李　益

汴水东流无限春，
隋家宫阙[②]已成尘。
行人莫上长堤[③]望，
风起杨花愁杀人[④]。

① 汴河：唐人习惯上用汴河指隋炀帝所开的通济渠的东段，也就是运河从板渚（今河南荥阳北）到盱眙县进入淮河的一段。

② 隋家宫阙：指汴水边上的隋炀帝行宫。唐代刘禹锡《杨柳枝》中有"炀帝行宫汴水滨"。

③ 长堤：隋堤。隋炀帝为了游览江都（今江苏扬州），驱使百万民工开凿通济渠，沿岸堤上种植柳树，被称为"隋堤"。

④ 杨花愁杀人：唐代朱放《送魏校书》诗中有"杨花撩乱扑流水，愁杀人行知不知"，这里是李益化用朱放的诗句。

Song of River Bian

Li Yi

The River Bian flows eastward, overwhelmed with spring;

To dust have gone ruined palaces and their king.

Don't gaze afar from the long bank of willow trees!

The willow down will grieve your heart when blows the breeze.

The River Bian refers to the canal built by the pleasure-making Emperor Yong of the Sui Dynasty (581—618), which was soon overthrown by the up-rising armies.

蜀先主庙 ①

刘禹锡

许渊冲译唐诗三百首

天下英雄气，
千秋尚凛然。
势分三足鼎 ②，
业复五铢钱 ③。
得相 ④ 能开国，
生儿 ⑤ 不象贤 ⑥。
凄凉蜀故妓，
来舞魏宫前。

① 蜀先主庙：蜀先主，就是刘备。先主庙在夔州（今重庆奉节）。
② 三足鼎：三国时期魏、蜀、吴三国鼎立的局势。
③ 五铢钱：汉武帝元狩五年铸造的钱币，后来王莽新朝将五铢钱废掉。在原诗的题
注中，刘禹锡写道："汉末章谣：'黄牛白腹，五铢当复。'"这里五铢钱代指
刘备兴复汉室的希望。
④ 得相：指刘备三顾茅庐邀请诸葛亮出山，并任命其为蜀国丞相。
⑤ 生儿：指刘备的儿子刘禅，后来做了蜀国后主。
⑥ 象贤：学习先祖治国的贤才。《礼记·士冠礼》中说："继世以立诸侯，象贤也。"
象，即法，就是学习的意思。

Temple of the King of Shu

Liu Yuxi

Your heroism under the sky

From year to year spread far and nigh.

Like tripod did three kingdoms reign;

Old royal coins were used again.

Your premier struck your kingdom's root;

But your son did not follow suit.

Even Western dancers felt sad

To make Northern conquerors glad.

The Han Empire was divided into three kingdoms: Wei in the north, Wu in the east and Shu in the west where coins of the Han Dynasty were used. After the death of the King of Shu, his son surrendered to the King of Wei and enjoyed the Western dance as if he were not a captive of the Northern Kingdom, and even dancers of Shu were grieved.

金陵怀古

刘禹锡

潮满冶城渚①，

日斜征虏亭②。

蔡洲③新草绿，

幕府④旧烟青。

兴废由人事，

山川空地形。

后庭花⑤一曲，

幽怨不堪听。

① 冶城渚：位于今江苏南京朝天宫一带，据说是东吴时期冶炼吴钩、吴刀的场所。
② 征虏亭：位于南京市玄武湖北，东晋时征虏将军谢石的哥哥谢万曾在这里送客。
③ 蔡洲：长江过南京江段中心的小岛。
④ 幕府：指金陵门户幕府山，因东晋王导曾在这里建立幕府屯兵而得名。
⑤ 后庭花：指《玉树后庭花》这首曲子，由南朝陈后主陈叔宝创作，后人一般用"后庭花"来象征导致陈灭亡的陈叔宝的骄奢淫逸。

Memories at Jinling

Liu Yuxi

The tide overwhelms the forge's site,

The tower drowned in slanting sunlight.

The islet covered with grass green,

And hills are veiled by a smoke screen.

Man decides a state's rise and fall,

Hills and streams can do nothing at all.

O hear the captive ruler's song!

How can you bear his grief for long?

Jinling was the capital of six dynasties. The last ruler fond of pleasure-making became a captive and the place where weapons were forged was overwhelmed by the tide.

西塞山^①怀古

刘禹锡

王濬^②楼船^③下益州,

金陵王气黯然收。

千寻铁锁沉江底,

一片降幡出石头^④。

人世几回伤往事,

山形依旧枕寒流。

今逢四海为家日,

故垒萧萧芦荻^⑤秋。

---

① 西塞山:位于今湖北省大冶县东,长江中流的要塞之一。
② 王濬:西晋大将,曾被晋武帝任命为益州(今四川成都)刺史,后受诏讨伐东吴。
③ 楼船:有楼的大船。古代多用于作战。
④ 石头:石头城,位于南京清凉山,孙权时建城。
⑤ 芦荻:荻,长得像芦苇,这里是指芦苇等杂草。

Mount Western Fort

Liu Yuxi

The Northern galleys went along the stream;
The Eastern kingdom vanished like a dream.
The iron chains could not bar the barges light;
The Eastern king surrendered with flags white.
How many times have we grieved over the past!
Mountains commanding the river still last.
We're glad the world is unified today,
But the fort shivers to see the reed sway.

The King of Wu in the East tried to bar the river with iron chains, but the galleys of Jin in the North broke through and captured the King of Wu in 280. The fort shivers for it has witnessed the rise and fall of kingdoms.

石头城 ①

刘禹锡

山围故国②周遭在，
潮打空城寂寞回。
淮水东边旧时月，
夜深还过女墙③来。

The Town of Stone

Liu Yuxi

The changeless hills round ancient capital still stand;
Waves beating on ruined walls, unheeded, roll away.
The moon which shone by riverside on flourished land
Still shines at dead of night over ruined town today.

The town of stone refers to Jinling capital of six dynasties.

乌衣巷 [1]

刘禹锡

朱雀桥 [2] 边野草花，
乌衣巷口夕阳斜。
旧时王谢 [3] 堂前燕，
飞入寻常百姓家。

[1] 乌衣巷：位于今南京市东南，因三国时为东吴乌衣营的驻地而得名，东晋时为高门大族聚居的地方。

[2] 朱雀桥：原是秦淮河上的浮桥，今已不存在。从建康城去乌衣巷要经过朱雀桥，东晋时桥上曾经建有装饰两只铜雀的重楼，据说是东晋大臣谢安建的。朱雀桥位于建康城南，也与古代的"东苍龙，北玄武，西白虎，南朱雀"的说法相符。

[3] 王谢：指东晋的高门大族王家和谢家。当时，有种说法："王与马，共天下"，王就是指开国元勋大将军王导所在的琅玡王氏；而陈郡谢氏也是代代都出高官，取得淝水之战胜利的就是谢氏家族的谢安。

The Street of Mansions

Liu Yuxi

Beside the Bridge of Birds rank grasses overgrow;

Over the Street of Mansions the setting sun hangs low.

Swallows that skimmed by painted eaves in days gone by,

Are dipping now in homes where humble people occupy.

许渊冲译唐诗三百首

The Street of Mansions were inhabited by the noble and the rich during the Jin Dynasty (266—420).

途经秦始皇墓 ①

许　浑

龙盘虎踞树层层，

势入浮云亦是崩 ②。

一种青山秋草里，

路人唯拜汉文陵 ③。

---

① 秦始皇墓：位于陕西省临潼下河村附近，南倚骊山，北临渭水，建于公元前210年。原高五十丈，因为是土筑，经过两千年的风吹日晒，现在的秦始皇墓有四十三米，周长两千米。秦始皇，是中国第一个统一国家的皇帝，尽管功劳卓著，但是异常残暴，不但大征徭役，而且焚书坑儒，破坏了大量的中国传统文化遗产。

② 崩：古代把皇帝去世称为"驾崩"，以避讳"死"这个字。

③ 汉文陵：汉文帝的陵墓霸陵，位于陕西西安东十余里，与秦始皇陵靠近。汉文帝，即汉高祖刘邦的儿子刘恒，他在位期间，励精图治，勤俭持国，奠定了汉代富强的基业，成就了"文景之治"的盛况。

Passing by the Tomb of the First Emperor of the Qin Dynasty

Xu Hun

The dragon coils and tiger crouches amid the trees;

The sky-scraping imperial tomb can't but fall down.

The hill's still green with grass when blows the autumn breeze,

But the passers-by worship only the new crown.

The imperial tomb was built in 210 BC.

金铜仙人①辞汉歌并序

李　贺

魏明帝青龙元年②八月，诏宫官牵车西取汉孝武捧露盘仙人，欲立置前殿。宫官既拆盘，仙人临载乃潸然泪下③。唐诸王孙李长吉遂作《金铜仙人辞汉歌》。

茂陵④刘郎秋风客⑤，夜闻马嘶晓无迹。

画栏桂树悬秋香，三十六宫土花⑥碧。

魏官牵车指千里，东关⑦酸风射眸子。

空将汉月⑧出宫门，忆君清泪如铅水。

衰兰送客咸阳道，天若有情天亦老。

携盘独出月荒凉，渭城⑨已远波声小。

① 金铜仙人：后文所说的捧露盘仙人。《三辅黄图》中曾记载汉武帝时建造了神明台，上面有承露盘，有铜仙人"舒掌捧铜盘玉杯"来接"云表之露"，然后用露水调匀玉屑，汉武帝认为吃下这露水所和的玉屑就可以成仙。

② 青龙元年：青龙元年与历史不符，据《三国志·魏书·明帝纪》记载，在青龙五年三月改元为景初元年，迁徙长安铜人承露盘即在这一年。

③ 潸然泪下：《汉晋春秋》记载魏明帝迁徙铜人时，拆承露盘的声音响彻数十里，金铜仙人也落下了眼泪，所以被留在了霸城。其实是因为铜人太重，难以运到洛阳。

④ 茂陵：汉武帝刘彻的陵墓，在今陕西省兴平市东北。

⑤ 秋风客：这里是指悲秋的人。汉武帝曾写有《秋风辞》，其中有名句"欢乐极兮哀情多，少壮几时兮奈老何"。

⑥ 土花：这里是指青苔。

⑦ 东关：从长安到魏的国都洛阳要经过长安东门，所以称为东关。

⑧ 汉月：这里指承露盘。李白曾有一首诗《古朗月行》中说"小时不识月，呼作白玉盘"，是将月亮比作白玉盘，这里则用月比喻玉盘。

⑨ 渭城：秦国国都咸阳，汉代改为渭城县，此代指长安。

The Bronze Statue Leaving Han Palace

Li He

The emperor was gone just like his autumn breeze;

At night his steed would neigh, at dawn no trace was seen.

By painted rails fragrance still wafts over laurel trees,

His thirty palaces overgrown with mosses green.

Wei eunuch drove a dray to go a long, long way;

In Eastern Pass the sour wind stung the bronze's eyes.

Only the moon of yore saw him leave palace door;

Thinking of his dear lord, he shed tears and heaved sighs.

Withered orchid would say, "Farewell and go your way."

Heaven would have grown old if it could feel as man.

He went with moon-shaped plate beneath the moon desolate;

The waves unheard, far from the town the horses ran.

The Martial Emperor of the Han Dynasty, author of Ode to the Autumn Breeze. built a bronze statue with a moon-shaped plate, but the Bright Emperor of the Wei Dynasty ordered his eunuch to move it out of the palace, and the bronze was said to have shed tears. This poem shows the poet, like the bronze, is unwilling to leave the capital after his failure in the civil service examinations.

金陵怀古

许 浑

玉树^①歌残王气终，

景阳^②兵合戍楼空。

松楸^③远近千官冢，

禾黍^④高低六代宫。

石燕^⑤拂云晴亦雨，

江豚^⑥吹浪夜还风。

英雄一去豪华尽，

唯有青山似洛中。

① 玉树：指《玉树后庭花》曲，据说是南朝陈后主创作的。
② 景阳：指景阳宫，陈后主所居住的宫殿。
③ 松楸（qiū）：指坟墓上栽的树。李白《拟恨赋》称"一望蒿里，松楸骨寒"。
④ 禾黍：《诗经》有《黍离》篇，后人用"黍离之悲"来写亡国之痛。
⑤ 石燕：据《湘中记》记载，零陵有石燕，遇见风雨就能飞翔，风雨停止又会回归石形。
⑥ 江豚：据《南越志》记载，江豚像猪，生活在水中，如果江豚在水中跳跃，就会起风。

Memories of Jinling

Xu Hun

The kingdom collapsed after the Song of Jade Tree;

The garrison deserted when came the enemy.

Planted with pines, a thousand tombs spread far and nigh;

Buried amid the weed, palaces stand low and high.

The swallow of stone scrapes the white cloud, rain or shine;

The night breeze blows with waves raised by the river swine.

The splendor fades when heroes are gone one and all;

Only green hills look like the ancient capital.

Jinling was the capital of the six dynasties. The last king of Chen, author of the Song of Jade Tree, surrendered and the kingdom collapsed in 604. The swallow of stone was a statue in the palace and the river swine was said to be capable of raising waves.

题宣州开元寺①水阁，阁下宛溪②，夹溪居人

杜 牧

六朝③文物草连空，

天淡云闲④今古同。

鸟去鸟来山色里，

人歌人哭水声中。

深秋帘幕千家雨，

落日楼台一笛风。

惆怅无因见范蠡⑤，

参差烟树五湖⑥东。

① 宣州开元寺：宣州，今安徽省宣城。开元寺，始建于东晋，初名永安寺，后改为景德寺，唐开元二十六年（738年）又改名开元寺。
② 宛溪：源于安徽省宣城东南峄山，东北流也叫九曲河，向西流过城东，称为宛溪，又名东溪，与青弋江汇合后注入长江。
③ 六朝：历史上把三国时的吴、东晋和南朝的宋、齐、梁、陈合称为六朝。
④ 天淡云闲：这里用以形容六朝遗迹的祥和宁静。淡，宁静。闲，闲适。
⑤ 范蠡：春秋时期越国的大夫，曾帮助勾践报仇雪耻，灭吴之后，泛舟而去。《国语·越语下》记载范蠡在灭吴之后："遂乘轻舟，以浮于五湖，莫知其所终极。"
⑥ 五湖：太湖及周围的四个湖泊，合称为五湖。这里泛指太湖一带。

Ruined Splendor

Du Mu

Rank grasses grow, six dynasties' splendors no more;

The sky is lightly blue and clouds free as of yore.

Birds come and go into the gloom of wooded hills,

And songs and wails alike merge in murmuring rills.

Like countless window curtains falls late autumn rain:

High towers steeped in sunset, wind and flute's refrain.

O how I miss the lakeside sage of bygone days!

I see but ancient trees loom rugged in the haze.

许渊冲译唐诗三百首

The poet describes the ruins to show his regret for the past splendor. The lakeside sage refers to General Fan who was said to have retired by the lakeside with the beautiful Lady of the West after his victory over the King of Wu in 473 BC.

赤壁 ①

杜 牧

折戟 ② 沉沙铁未销 ③，

自将磨洗认前朝 ④。

东风不与周郎便，

铜雀 ⑤ 春深锁二乔 ⑥。

① 赤壁：赤壁山，在今湖北蒲圻市西北，在长江南岸。《元和郡县图志》记载："鄂州蒲圻县赤壁山，在县西一百二十里，北临大江，其北岸即乌林，与赤壁相对，即周瑜用黄盖策，焚曹公舟船败走处。"三国时的孙权、周瑜在这里用火攻大败曹操，取得赤壁之战的胜利，之后形成魏、蜀、吴三国鼎立的局面。

② 戟：古代的一种武器，在长杆的一端装有青铜或铁制成的枪尖，旁边附有月牙形锋刃。

③ 未销：一作"半销"。销，腐蚀。

④ 前朝：历史上的朝代，这里指三国时期。

⑤ 铜雀：指铜雀台，汉末建安十五年由曹操建造，故址在今河北省临漳县西南。铜雀台高十丈，周围殿屋一百二十间。于楼顶置大铜雀，舒翼若飞，故名铜雀台。

⑥ 二乔：三国时东吴乔公的两个女儿：其长者名大乔，嫁给了孙权之兄孙策；幼者名小乔，嫁给了东吴大将周瑜。

The Red Cliff

Du Mu

We dig out broken halberds buried in the sand
And wash and rub these relics of an ancient war.
Had the east wind refused General Zhou a helping hand,
His foe'd have locked his fair wife on Northern shore.

许渊冲译唐诗三百首

The Red Cliff was a scene of battle in 208 when General Zhou defeated the Northern enemy by setting their warships on fire with the help of the east wind.

题乌江亭 ①

杜 牧

胜败兵家事不期 ②，
包羞忍耻是男儿。
江东 ③ 子弟多才俊，
卷土重来未可知。

① 乌江亭：在今安徽省和县东北的乌江镇，唐时属乌江县。楚汉相争时，项羽兵败于此，自刎于乌江岸边。
② 不期：难以预料。期，预料。
③ 江东：长江南岸苏州一带。项羽跟从叔父项梁从这里起兵。

On the Black River Pavilion

Du Mu

A hero can't foretell victory or defeat.

Why should a loser not stand again on his feet?

There are so many talents on the Southern shore.

Who dare say, once defeated, he can't win the war?

许渊冲译唐诗三百首

The Herculean King of Chu, when defeated by the king of Han, killed himself on the Black River in 202 BC.

题木兰庙①

杜　牧

弯弓征战作男儿，
梦里曾经与画眉②。
几度思归还把酒，
拂云堆③上祝明妃④。

---

① 木兰庙：在今湖北省黄冈县木兰山，上有木兰庙，供奉替父从征的女英雄木兰。据《演繁露》记载："乐府有木兰，乃女子，代父征戍，十年而归，不受爵赏，人为作诗，然不著何代人。或者疑为寓言。"
② 画眉：古代妇女以黛色描画眉毛，以为装饰。《玉台新咏》："新妆莫点黛，余还自画眉。"
③ 拂云堆：在黄河北崖岸，今内蒙古自治区的乌喇特西北。旧有神祠，是当时祭祀求福的地方。这里是说木兰在黄河以北的边疆与胡人作战。
④ 明妃：王昭君，本名王嫱，南郡秭归人。

Temple of the Heroine

Du Mu

She played the role of a man bending his bow,
But she dreamed of penciling her eyebrow.
How many times, homesick, wine cup in hand,
Would she bless the princess of her homeland?

The heroine refers to Hua Mulan who served in the army instead of her father, and the princess to Wang Zhaojun who was married to the Chief of the Tartars in 33 BC.

咏史

李商隐

北湖①南埭②水漫漫，

一片降旗百尺竿。

三百年间同晓梦，

钟山③何处有龙盘④？

---

① 北湖：玄武湖，相传南朝刘宋时湖中有黑龙出现而得名。湖的东面为钟山，湖的
南面为鸡笼山。

② 南埭（dài）：鸡鸣埭，位于鸡笼山东麓的山阜上，此处在南朝梁时建有同泰寺，
为南京佛教首刹，后因侯景之乱而荒废。直到明代重建同泰寺，并更名为鸡鸣寺。

③ 钟山：紫金山，位于南京东北十里左右，历史上曾用金山、蒋山等名字。

④ 龙盘：张勃《吴录》中记载，刘备派诸葛亮出使吴国，诸葛亮看到金陵的景观后
称赞说"钟山龙盘，石头（石头城）虎踞，帝王之宅也"。这里借用"龙盘"来
指帝王之气。

On History

Li Shangyin

Water shimmers in Northern Lake and by Southern Tower,
All kings surrendered with white flags to a new power.
Three hundred years have passed like a dream one and all;
No Coiling Dragon could keep kingdoms from downfall.

The Northern Lake, Southern Tower, Mount Coiling Dragon are all in the vicinity of the capital of the six dynasties, but neither mountains nor rivers could defend the kingdom against the invading power.

马嵬^①二首（其二）

李商隐

海外^②徒闻更九州^③，

他生未卜此生休。

空闻虎旅^④传宵柝^⑤，

无复鸡人^⑥报晓筹。

此日六军同驻马，

当时七夕笑牵牛。

如何四纪^⑦为天子，

不及卢家有莫愁^⑧。

① 马嵬（wéi）：指马嵬驿，位于陕西西安兴平市西。安史之乱中这里发生兵变，兵变中陈玄礼迫使唐玄宗诛杀杨国忠和杨贵妃。

② 海外：相传，唐玄宗思念杨贵妃，道士在海外仙山寻找到贵妃，在唐诗人白居易的《长恨歌》和陈鸿《长恨歌传》中有详细记载。

③ 九州：战国邹衍曾经说，中国只是赤县神州，海外还有像中国这样大小的九个州。

④ 虎旅：古人称勇士为"虎贲"，这里虎旅指跟随玄宗逃难的禁军。

⑤ 宵柝（tuò）：指夜晚报更所敲的木梆。

⑥ 鸡人：皇宫中一般不养鸡，而是设有报时的卫士，每当到了鸡叫的时候，就到宫中报晓，所以被称为"鸡人"。

⑦ 四纪：一纪为十二年，四纪就是四十八年。唐玄宗在位四十五年，这里取成数。

⑧ 卢家有莫愁：南朝梁萧衍的《河中之水歌》中记载，有个洛阳女子叫莫愁，后来嫁给了卢家。

On Lady Yang's Death (II)

Li Shangyin

Tis said there is a fairyland over the sea.

When this life is no more, can there another be?

In vain the watchman beat at night the warning gong;

No cock would wake her from dream with morning song.

The six armies demanded her death left and right.

Could she still laugh at severed lover-stars at night?

Though the emperor reigned as long as forty years,

She's not so happy as a griefless maid appears.

Lady Yang was the favorite mistress of the Bright Emperor of the Tang Dynasty. When the six armies in revolt demanded her death, the emperor could not protect her.

苏武庙 ①

温庭筠

苏武 ② 魂销汉使前，

古祠高树两茫然。

云边雁断胡天月，

陇上羊归塞草烟。

回日楼台非甲帐 ③，

去时冠剑是丁年 ④。

茂陵 ⑤ 不见封侯印，

空向秋波 ⑥ 哭逝川 ⑦。

① 苏武庙：苏武庙位置尚不确定，但是诗中的景色与河北丰宁的苏武庙有相吻合之处。丰宁苏武庙，又叫宏济寺，它的始建年代说法有二：一说建于西汉宣帝年间，二说建于宋代，现在尚难确定。但是丰宁现存苏武庙就是康熙时重修、雍正时扩建的苏公祠。

② 苏武：汉武帝时名臣，在武帝天汉元年出使匈奴，被扣留。匈奴多次逼降，但是他坚贞不屈。后被匈奴流放到北海牧羝羊（公羊），称只有当羝羊哺乳时才可以被放还，直至昭帝始元六年，才返回汉朝，前后长达十九年。

③ 甲帐：据《汉武故事》记载，武帝用琉璃、珠玉、明月、夜光错杂天下珍宝做成甲帐，又做乙帐。甲帐给神居住，乙帐给自己住。

④ 丁年：壮年。

⑤ 茂陵：汉武帝的陵寝。

⑥ 秋波：秋水。

⑦ 逝川：《论语·子罕》中说："子在川上，曰：'逝者如斯夫！不舍昼夜。'"这里指像流水一样倏然而逝的武帝。

Temple of Su Wu

Wen Tingyun

How could Su Wu, before the envoi, not shed tears?

The ancient temple and tree bespeak bygone years.

Wild geese flew into clouds in moonlit Northern sky;

The sheep returned to west of frontier when grass grew high.

The palace looked unlike that of olden day;

Su was no longer strong as when he went away.

Ennobled when the emperor was in the grave,

He wept in vain over him gone with the autumn wave.

Su Wu (?—60BC) was an envoy retained by the Tartars for eighteen years. He was ennobled on his return when the emperor who sent him to the Tartars was dead. A temple was built in honor of Su's loyalty.

黄陵庙 ①

李群玉

小姑 ② 洲北浦云边，

二女容华自俨然。

野庙向江春寂寂，

古碑无字草芊芊。

风回日暮吹芳芷，

月落山深哭杜鹃。

犹似含颦望巡狩，

九疑 ③ 如黛隔湘川 ④。

① 黄陵庙：又名湘妃祠，位于湖南省湘阴县北洞庭湖畔，是为了纪念舜帝的二妃娥皇、女英而建造的，据说建于春秋年间，具体年代不可考。
② 小姑：蒋子文第三妹，即青溪神女，因为汉乐府《青溪小姑曲》而得名。杨炯《少姨庙碑》："虞帝二妃，湘水之波澜未歇；蒋侯三妹，青溪之轨迹可寻。"将小姑与二妃并举，所以这里"小姑"应该代指娥皇、女英，因为她们溺湘水后成为湘水之神。一说小姑是山名，即小孤山的俗称，位于安徽宿松县城东南六十公里的长江中，与江西彭泽临界，因为一峰独立，故名孤山，圆形如锥髻，又称髻山。又因为鄱阳湖中有大孤山，所以又称为小孤山。半山有启秀寺，称为"小姑庙"，始建于唐代，庙内有小姑像。但是小姑山距离黄陵庙很远，与诗歌不大相符。
③ 九疑：指九疑山，传说舜帝向南巡狩，死于苍梧，葬在江南九疑山。
④ 湘川：湘水。传说娥皇、女英听说舜帝的死讯，溺于湘水，后来成了湘水的女神，又被称为湘夫人。

476

The Temple of Emperor Shun's Wives

Li Qunyu

North of the Maiden's Islet, by the riverside,

The two princesses shed tears in attire dignified.

The temple faces the river in lonely spring.

What could the wordless monument amid grass sing?

At sunset blows the breeze among the clovers white;

The cuckoos cry in hills from moon-down till deep night.

The princesses seem to gaze on Nine Peaks in dream.

Where was buried their emperor beyond the stream.

Emperor Shun was buried at the foot of the Nine Mysterious Peaks and his two wives came to weep over him by the riverside, where a temple was built in his memory.

馆娃宫 [①] 怀古五绝（其一）

皮日休

绮阁 [②] 飘香下太湖 [③]，

乱兵侵晓上姑苏 [④]。

越王 [⑤] 大有堪羞处，

只把西施赚得吴。

[①] 馆娃宫：春秋时期吴王夫差为西施建造的宫殿，故址在今苏州市西南灵岩山上。吴国打败越国后，越王采纳大夫文种的建议，把西施献给了吴王夫差，以换得越国的生存，并慢慢强大起来，后来越国终于打败吴国。

[②] 绮阁：织有素色花纹的衣料。用它做成的衣服是一种上层身份的象征。

[③] 太湖：古代又有震泽、笠泽等几个名称，春秋时为吴国和越国的分界。

[④] 姑苏：常用来指苏州。苏州西南有姑苏山，姑苏山上有姑苏台，是春秋时吴王阖闾建造的。这里应该指姑苏山和姑苏台。

[⑤] 越王：指当时越国国君勾践。

The Palace of the Beauty (I)

Pi Rixiu

Her dress shed fragrance on the lake;

The Southern soldiers took the capital at daybreak.

It would be a shame for the Southern king to win

The Eastern Kingdom by a lady fair and thin.

许渊冲译唐诗三百首

The King of the Southern Yue, defeated by the Eastern King of Wu, offered beautiful lady of the west, the Beauty to him, who loved her so much as to lose his kingdom in 473 BC.

汴河①怀古（其二）

皮日休

尽道隋亡为此河，

至今千里赖通波。

若无水殿龙舟事②，

共禹论功③不较多。

① 汴河：唐人习惯上用汴河指隋炀帝所开的通济渠的东段，也就是运河从板渚（今河南荥阳北）到盱眙县进入淮河的一段。当时，炀帝从洛阳西苑引谷、洛二水入黄河，又经黄河入汴水，再沿着春秋时吴王夫差所开的运河故道引汴水入泗水，最后到达淮水。
② 水殿龙舟事：大运河竣工后，隋炀帝率众二十万出游江都，造了一艘高达四层的"龙舟"，还有九艘高三层被称为"浮景"的"水殿"。据说当时要百姓捐出全部香油，使龙舟水殿能从陆地进入水中，劳民伤财，极尽奢侈，最终民怨载道，这成为隋末之乱的直接导火索。
③ 共禹论功：指大禹治水的功绩。

The Great Canal (II)

Pi Rixiu

The Great Canal was blamed for the Sui Empire's fall,
But on its waves the goods and food are brought to all.
Could the flood-fighting emperor do anything more
Than the Sui dragon-boats of three stories or four?

Emperor Yang of the Sui Dynasty (581—618) built the Great Canal and dragon-boats for
pleasure-makiag, but it would facilitate the transportation and communication between
North and South, and the poet praises him as high as the flood-fighting Emperor Yu of the
Xia Dynasty (ca.2000 BC)

焚书坑 ①

章 碣

竹帛 ② 烟销帝业虚，
关河 ③ 空锁祖龙 ④ 居。
坑灰未冷山东 ⑤ 乱，
刘项 ⑥ 原来不读书。

① 焚书坑：旧址在今陕西省西安市临潼区东南的骊山上，据传是秦始皇时焚书的一个洞穴。秦始皇三十四年（公元前213年），秦始皇采纳丞相李斯的奏议，下令在全国范围内搜集焚毁儒家《诗经》《书经》和百家之书，诏令下发之后三十日不烧者，罚做筑城的苦役。这是一场文化的浩劫，使得汉代承担了传统文化复兴的艰巨任务。
② 竹帛：西汉蔡伦发明纸以前，中国的书籍大多刻写在竹简上，还有一些写在帛上。因为帛质料好价格高，所以所写书籍较少。
③ 关河：指函谷关和黄河，是秦国可以凭借的天险。
④ 祖龙：秦始皇自称。祖，"始"的意思；"龙"，皇帝的象征。
⑤ 山东：战国时指秦国函谷关以东的六国，此处是指秦末山东农民起义。
⑥ 刘项：指刘邦、项羽，他们是秦末农民起义最大的两支力量，后来经过楚汉之争，刘邦胜利，建立汉朝。

The Pit Where Emperor Qin Burned the Classics

Zhang Jie

Smoke of burnt classics gone up with the empire's fall;

Fortresses and rivers could not guard the capital.

Before the pit turned cold, eastern rebellions spread,

The leaders of revolts were not scholars well-read.

许

渊

冲

译

唐

诗

三

百

首

The poet satirizes the first emperor of the Qin Dynasty who burned up all classics for fear his empire be overthrown without knowing the rebel leaders were not well-read.

七、边塞军旅
·
·
·

从军行^①

杨　炯

烽火^②照西京，
心中自不平^③。
牙璋辞凤阙^④，
铁骑绕龙城^⑤。
雪暗凋旗画^⑥，
风多杂鼓声。
宁为百夫长^⑦，
胜作一书生。

---

① 从军行：乐府旧题，属《相和歌辞·平调曲》，题材大多为边塞军旅战争。
② 烽火：古代边防报警的信号。
③ 不平：难以平静。
④ "牙璋"句：牙璋，调兵的符牒。两块合成，朝廷和主帅各执其半，嵌合处呈齿状，故名。这里指代奉命出征的将帅。凤阙，汉武帝所建的建章宫上有铜凤，故称凤阙。后来常用作帝王宫阙的泛称。
⑤ "铁骑"句：铁骑，精锐的骑兵，指唐军。绕，围。龙城，汉时匈奴大会祭天之处，故址在今蒙古国鄂尔浑河东侧。这里泛指敌方要塞、据点。
⑥ "雪暗"句：大雪弥漫，落满军旗，使旗帜上的图案黯淡失色。凋，原意是草木枯败凋零，此指失去了鲜艳的色彩。
⑦ 百夫长：周朝兵制以百人为一队，队长称"百夫长"。后世泛指下级武官。

I Would Rather Fight

Yang Jiong

The beacon fires spread to the capital;

My agitated mind can't be calmed down.

By royal order to leave palace hall;

Our armored steeds besiege the Dragon Town.

Darkening snow damages our banners red;

With the howling wind mingle our drumbeats.

I'd rather fight at a hundred men's head

Than pore over books without performing feats.

The poet would rather fight than write.

凉州词 ①

王之涣

黄河远上白云间，

一片孤城万仞 ② 山。

羌笛 ③ 何须怨杨柳 ④，

春风不度玉门关 ⑤。

---

① 凉州词：凉州歌的唱词，不是诗题，是盛唐时流行的一种曲调名。开元年间，陇右节度使郭知运搜集了一批西域的曲谱，进献给唐玄宗。玄宗交给教坊翻成中国曲谱，并配上新的歌词演唱，以这些曲谱产生地的名称为曲调名。后来许多诗人都喜欢这个曲调，为它填写新词，因此唐代许多诗人都写有《凉州词》。"凉州词"又作"出塞"。

② 万仞：一仞八尺。万仞是形容山很高的意思。

③ 羌笛：古代羌人所制的一种管乐器。有二孔。

④ 杨柳：指《折杨柳》曲，是一种哀怨的曲调。

⑤ 玉门关：关名，在今甘肃省敦煌市西北，是古代通往西域的要道。

Out of the Great Wall

Wang Zhihuan

The Yellow River rises to the white cloud;

The lonely town is lost amid the mountains proud.

Why should the Mongol flute complain no willow grow?

Beyond the Gate of Jade no vernal wind will blow.

This quatrain describes a desolate scene out of the Gate of Jade, a part of the Great Wall.

古从军行 [1]

李 颀

白日登山望烽火，
黄昏饮马傍交河 [2]。
行人刁斗风沙暗 [3]，
公主琵琶 [4] 幽怨多。
野营 [5] 万里无城郭，
雨雪纷纷连大漠。
胡雁哀鸣夜夜飞，
胡儿 [6] 眼泪双双落。
闻道玉门犹被遮 [7]，
应将性命逐轻车 [8]。
年年战骨埋荒外 [9]，
空见蒲桃入汉家。

① 古从军行：从军行乃乐府旧题，这首诗是拟古，所以称"古从军行"。
② 交河：在今新疆维吾尔自治区西北部的吐鲁番市。
③ "行人"句：行人，行军之人。刁斗，古代军队用的铜器，白天作锅，夜晚用来打更。
④ 公主琵琶：相传汉武帝时以江都王刘建女细君嫁乌孙国王昆莫，恐其途中烦闷，
　　故弹琵琶以娱之。这句用此典故，写征途中听到的幽怨的琵琶声。
⑤ 野营：一作"野云"。
⑥ 胡儿：少数民族人民。
⑦ "闻道"句：遮，阻拦。据《汉书·李广利传》，汉武帝曾命李广利攻大宛，欲
　　至贰师城取良马，战不利，广利上书请撤兵回国，武帝大怒，发使遮玉门关。曰：
　　"军有敢入，斩之！"
⑧ "应将"句：逐，跟随。轻车，轻车将军的简称，这里指将帅。
⑨ 荒外：极边远的地方。

Army Life

Li Qi

We climb up mountains to watch for beacon fires,
And water horses by riverside when day expires.
We beat the gong in sand-darkened land where wind blows,
And hear the pipa tell the princess' secret woe.
There is no town for miles and miles but tents in rows;
Beyond the desert there's nothing but rain and snow.
The wild geese honk from night to night, that's all we hear;
We see but Tartar soldiers shedding tear on tear.
'Tis said we cannot go back through the Jade Gate Pass;
We'd risk our lives to follow war-chariots, alas!
The dead are buried in the desert year by year,
Only to bring back grapes from over the frontier.

许渊冲译唐诗三百首

The poet draws a desolate picture of the army life on the frontier.

从军行七首（其四）

王昌龄

青海^①长云暗雪山^②，
孤城^③遥望玉门关^④。
黄沙百战穿^⑤金甲，
不破楼兰^⑥终不还。

① 青海：青海湖，在今青海省西宁市西。
② 雪山：此当指祁连山脉。
③ 孤城：一说为青海地区的一座城池；一说孤城即玉门关。两说都可通。今取后者，乃考虑到格律诗经常有为了格律谐整而把正常语序调整成非正常语序的情况。"孤城遥望"，即即为"遥望孤城"之调整。
④ 玉门关：汉武帝置，因西域输入玉石取道于此而得名。故址在今甘肃敦煌市西北小方盘城。六朝时关址东移至今安西双塔堡附近。
⑤ 穿：磨穿；磨破。
⑥ 楼兰：汉时西域的鄯善国，在今新疆维吾尔自治区鄯善县东南一带。西汉时，楼兰国与匈奴联合，屡次截杀汉朝派往西域的使臣。傅介子奉命前往，用计刺杀楼兰王，"遂持王首还诣阙，公卿将军议者咸嘉其功"（《汉书·傅介子传》）。此以楼兰泛指西北地区的敌人。

Poems on Army Life (IV)

Wang Changling

Clouds on frontier overshadow mountains clad in snow;
A lonely town afar faces Pass of Jade Gate.
Our golden armor pierced by sand, we fight the foe;
We won't come back till we destroy the hostile State.

This quatrain shows the fighting spirit of the army.

从军行七首（其五）

王昌龄

大漠①风尘日色昏，

红旗半卷出辕门②。

前军夜战洮河③北，

已报生擒吐谷浑④。

① 大漠：此泛指西北沙漠，非确指某处之沙漠。
② 辕门：军营的大门。古代行军扎营时，一般用车环卫，出口处把两车的车辕相对竖起，对立如门。
③ 洮河：黄河上游支流，在甘肃省甘南藏族自治州境内，源出甘青两省边界西倾山东麓，东流到岷县折向北，经临洮县到永靖县城附近入黄河。长五百余公里。
④ 吐谷浑：晋代鲜卑族慕容氏的后裔，唐前期据有青海洮水西南等处，地势险要，唐朝三次征讨均无功而返。后李靖挂帅，一改先前正面进攻的策略，几十万唐军从青海甘肃交界的狭窄小路穿越，从吐谷浑身后发起攻击，一举歼灭吐谷浑。一说王昌龄此诗即记此次大捷。一说此诗非实写，此处吐谷浑乃只借指边境之敌而已。考察此次战役发生在唐太宗时期，而王昌龄生活在武后、玄宗时期，所以后说为当。

Poems on Army Life (V)

Wang Changling

The wind and sand in the desert have dimmed sunlight;
With red flags half unfurled we go through the camp gate.
North of River Tao, after nocturnal fight,
Our vanguards have captured the chief of hostile State.

The poet describes the victory won by the army after one battle at night.

出塞 ①

王昌龄

秦时明月汉时关，
万里长征人未还。
但使龙城 ② 飞将 ③ 在，
不教胡 ④ 马度阴山 ⑤。

---

① 出塞：乐府《横吹曲》旧题。唐人乐府中的《出塞》《前出塞》《后出塞》《塞上曲》《塞下曲》等均由此演变而出。

② 龙城：汉时匈奴大会祭天之地，在今蒙古国境内，汉车骑将军卫青曾率兵到此。有的版本作"卢城"或"陇城"。

③ 飞将：《史记·李将军传》："（李）广居右北平，匈奴闻之，号曰'汉之飞将军'"，因此不敢犯汉境。此处可理解为两典合用，指古代卫青、李广这样的守边名将，也可泛指一切良将。

④ 胡：指匈奴等北方部族。

⑤ 阴山：西起河套，绵亘于今内蒙古自治区境内，东与内兴安岭相接。汉时匈奴常据此犯边。

On the Frontier

Wang Changling

The moon still shines on mountain passes as of yore.

How many guardsmen of the Great Wall are no more!

If the flying general were still there in command,

No hostile steeds would have dared to invade our land.

The poet sympathizes with the guardsmen and glorifies General Li who defeated the foe.

出塞作

王　维

居延^①城外猎天骄^②，

白草^③连天野火烧。

暮云空碛^④时驱马，

秋日平原好射雕^⑤。

护羌校尉^⑥朝乘障，

破虏将军^⑦夜渡辽。

玉靶角弓珠勒马，

汉家将赐霍嫖姚^⑧。

① 居延：中国汉唐以来西北地区的军事重镇，位于今内蒙古额济纳旗东南。
② 天骄：匈奴自称。此指吐蕃。
③ 白草：西域所产牧草。《汉书·西域传》颜师古注："白草似莠而细，无芒，其干熟时正白色，牛马所嗜也。"
④ 碛：沙漠。
⑤ 射雕：雕剽疾难射，匈奴人因以之称善射者。
⑥ 护羌校尉："护羌校尉，武帝置，秩比二千石，持节以护西羌。"（《后汉书·光武帝纪》）此指唐将领。
⑦ 破虏将军："表术表孙坚行破虏将军。"（《三国志·魏志》）此指唐将领。
⑧ 霍嫖姚：汉霍去病曾任嫖姚校尉，此代指战功显赫的崔希逸。

Out of the Frontier

Wang Wei

The proud Tartar sons are hunting out of the town;

White grass spreads to the sky, wild fire burns up and down.

They ride on the desert when evening clouds hang low;

In autumn days on the vast plain they bend their bow.

Our officers strengthen the defense by daylight;

Our victorious generals cross the river at night.

The swords, bows and bridles mounted with gems and jade

Are awarded generals and their brave cavalcade.

This poem describes the Tartar forces and glorifies the Han generals defeating them.

关山月①

李 白

明月出天山②,
苍茫云海间。
长风几万里,
吹度玉门关③。
汉下白登道④,
胡窥青海湾⑤。
由来征战地,
不见有人还。
戍客⑥望边色,
思归多苦颜。
高楼⑦当此夜,
叹息未应闲。

① 关山月:乐府《鼓角横吹曲》十五曲之一。《乐府古题要解》:"《关山月》,
　　伤离别也。"唐玄宗开元后期和天宝年间,唐王朝不断发动与周边少数民族的战
　　争。李白借此乐府旧题,写远离家乡的戍边将士与家中妻子的相互思念之情。
② 天山:祁连山,位于甘肃省西北部。匈奴语呼天为"祁连",故祁连山亦称"天山"。
③ 玉门关:为古时通往西域的要道,故址在今甘肃省敦煌市西北。此处泛指西北边地。
④ "汉下"句:下,出兵。白登,山名,在今山西省大同市东北。据《史记·匈奴
　　列传》记载,汉高祖刘邦曾在白登山附近与匈奴作战,并被围困七日。
⑤ "胡窥"句:窥,窥伺、侵扰。青海湾,即青海湖,在今青海省东北部,唐玄宗
　　开元年间,唐军曾多次在此与吐蕃交战。
⑥ 戍客:指戍边将士。
⑦ 高楼:戍边将士妻子的居所,代指戍边将士的妻子。

The Moon over the Mountain Pass

Li Bai

From Heaven's Peak the moon rises bright
Over a boundless sea of cloud.
Winds blow for miles with main and might
Past the Jade Gate which stands so proud.
Our warriors march down the frontier,
While Tartars peer across Blue Bays.
From the battlefield outstretched here,
None have come back since olden days.
Guards watch the scene of borderland,
Thinking of home with wistful eyes.
Tonight upstairs their wives would stand,
Looking afar with longing sighs.

Seeing the moon, warriors on the frontier and their wives at home long for each other.

塞下曲

李 白

五月天山[1]雪，

无花只有寒。

笛中闻折柳[2]，

春色未曾看。

晓战随金鼓[3]，

宵眠抱玉鞍。

愿将[4]腰下剑，

直为斩楼兰[5]。

---

① 天山：今祁连山。

② 折柳：指《折杨柳》曲，为汉乐府《横吹曲》之一。

③ 金鼓：金，军中乐器，用金属制成，战时敲击用以号令将士停止进攻，即所谓鸣金收兵。鼓是战鼓，敲响战鼓就是向敌人发起进攻的号令，所谓一鼓作气。

④ 将：拿。

⑤ 楼兰：汉代时西域国名，在今新疆维吾尔自治区鄯善县东南。此代指楼兰国王。汉武帝派遣使者通大宛，途经楼兰。楼兰国王阻挡通道，并攻杀汉使臣。昭帝元凤四年，大将军霍光派遣平乐监傅介子前往楼兰，用计杀死其国王。见《汉书·傅介子传》。

Frontier Song

Li Bai

In summer sky-high mountains white with snow,
In bitter cold no fragrant flowers blow.
Songs on the flute are heard of Willows Green,
But nowhere is the vernal color seen.
From dawn till dusk to beats of drums they fight;
With saddle in their arms they rest at night.
From scabbard at my waist I'd draw my sword
To kill the chieftain of the Turki horde.

The poet sympathizes with the warriors fighting in the bitter cold on the frontier.

许渊冲译唐诗三百首

从军行

李 白

百战沙场碎铁衣，
城南已合数重围。
突营①射杀呼延②将，
独领残兵千骑归。

---

① 突营：突围。
② 呼延：匈奴中地位仅次于左右贤王的四大贵族之一。诗中代指敌人的中军主将。

Song of a General after the Break-through

Li Bai

After a hundred battles, his armor is worn,
The southern town surrounded ring on ring in the morn.
When he breaks through and kills the chief of Tartar peers,
He comes back with a thousand beaten cavaliers.

许
渊
冲
译
唐
诗
三
百
首

This quatrain describes a general with his armor outworn and his cavaliers beaten after a breakthrough.

燕歌行

高 适

开元二十六年，客有从御史大夫张公①出塞而还者，作燕歌行②以示适，感征戍之事，因而和焉。

汉家烟尘在东北③，

汉将辞家破残贼。

男儿本自重横行④，

天子非常赐颜色⑤。

摐金伐鼓下榆关⑥，

旌旆逶迤⑦碣石间。

校尉羽书飞瀚海⑧，

单于猎火照狼山⑨。

① 张公：指张守珪。开元二十三年（735 年），张因为与契丹作战立功拜为辅国大将军兼御史大夫。二十六年，其部将假借张之命，与叛军余党战，先胜后败。张不据实上报，反而贿赂去调查情况的牛仙童。事败，张被贬。
② 燕歌行：属乐府《相和歌·平调曲》。
③ "汉家"句：汉家，汉朝，代指唐朝。烟尘，烽烟战尘，代指敌人入侵。
④ 横行：纵横驰骋，横行无阻。
⑤ 赐颜色：给面子，赐予荣耀。
⑥ "摐金"句：摐（chuāng），撞击。金，军中乐器。伐鼓，击鼓。下，往，直奔。榆关，即山海关。
⑦ 逶迤：穿行。
⑧ "校尉"句：校尉，武官名，仅次于将军。羽书，插有鸟羽毛的紧急军函。瀚海，大漠。
⑨ 狼山：在今内蒙古境内。

Song of the Northern Frontier

Gao Shi

A cloud of smoke and dust spreads over northeast frontier;
To fight the remnant foe our generals leave the rear.
Brave men should go no manes where beneath the sky;
The emperor bestows on them his favor high.
To the beat of drums and gongs through Elm Pass they go;
Round Mount Stone Tablet flags serpentine row on row,
But urgent orders speed over the Sea of Sand:
Mount Wolf aflame with fires set by the Tartar band.

许渊冲译唐诗三百首

山川萧条极边土^①,

胡骑凭陵^②杂风雨。

战士军前半死生^③,

美人帐下^④犹歌舞。

大漠穷秋塞草腓^⑤,

孤城落日斗兵稀。

身当恩遇恒轻敌,

力尽关山未解围。

铁衣^⑥远戍辛勤久,

玉箸^⑦应啼别离后。

少妇城南欲断肠,

征人蓟北^⑧空回首。

① 极边土:临边境的尽头。
② 凭陵:侵犯。
③ 半死生:形容伤亡惨重。
④ 帐下:指将帅的营帐。
⑤ 腓(féi):衰败;枯萎。
⑥ 铁衣:指远征战士。
⑦ 玉箸(zhù):少妇的眼泪。
⑧ 蓟北:唐蓟州治所在渔阳,今天津市蓟州区,这里泛指东北边地。

Both hills and streams are desolate on border plain;

The Tartar horsemen flurry like the wind and rain.

Half of our warriors lie killed on the battleground;

While pretty girls in camp still sing and dance their round.

Grass withers in the desert as autumn is late;

At sunset few men guard the lonely city gate.

Imperial favor makes them hold the foemen light;

Their town is under siege, though they've fought with their might.

In coats of mail they've served so long on the frontiers;

Since they left home their wives have shed streams of impearled

tears.

In southern towns the women weep with broken heart;

In vain their men look southward, still they're far apart.

边庭飘飖那可度①，

绝域②苍茫更何有。

杀气三时作阵云③，

寒声一夜传刁斗④。

相看白刃血纷纷，

死节从来岂顾勋⑤。

君不见沙场征战苦，

至今犹忆李将军⑥。

① "边庭"句：边庭，边疆。飘飖（yáo），此形容边地局势紧张。度，越过。
② 绝域：极僻远的地方。
③ "杀气"句：三时，指晨、午、晚，即一整天。阵云，战云。
④ 刁斗：军中的一种报更工具，铜器。
⑤ "死节"句：死节，此指为保卫国家而死。顾勋，顾及个人功勋。
⑥ 李将军：汉代李广，他作战勇敢，身先士卒，爱惜士兵。

The northern front at stake, how can they go away?

On border vast and desolate, how can they stay?

All day a cloud of slaughter mounts now and again;

All night the boom of gongs is heard to chill the plain.

Each sees the other's sword bloodstained in the hard strife.

Will they care for reward when they give up their life?

Do you not know the bitterness of fighting with the foe?

Can they forget General Li sharing their weal and woe?

The poet criticizes the proud generals defeated for they made light of the enemy, and glorifies General Li (1st century BC) who shared weal and woe with his soldiers.

前出塞九首（其六）

杜　甫

挽弓当挽强，

用箭当用长。

射人先射马，

擒贼先擒王。

杀人亦有限[1]，

列国自有疆[2]。

苟[3] 能制[4] 侵陵[5]，

岂在多杀伤?

① 亦有限：也应该有个限度。
② 自有疆：本来应该有个疆界。
③ 苟：如果。
④ 制：制止。
⑤ 侵陵：侵犯；侵略。

Song of the Frontier (VI)

Du Fu

The bow you carry should be strong;

The arrows you use should be long.

Shoot before a horseman his horse;

Capture the chief to beat his force,

Slaughter shan't go beyond its sphere;

Each State should guard its own frontier.

If an invasion is repelled,

Why shed more blood unless compelled?

The poet speaks of the art of war and his love of peace.

夜上受降城①闻笛

李　益

回乐峰②前沙似雪，
受降城外月如霜。
不知何处吹芦管③，
一夜征人尽望乡。

---

① 受降城：在灵州（今宁夏回族自治区灵武县西南）州治所在地回乐县。在唐代，这里是防御突厥、吐蕃的前线。贞观二十年（646年），唐太宗曾经亲临灵州接受突厥一部的投降，故称灵州为"受降城"。
② 回乐峰：烽火台名，当在回乐县境内，位于今宁夏灵武市西南。
③ 芦管：题中之"笛"。

On Hearing a Flute at Night atop the Victor's Wall

Li Yi

Before the beacon tower sand looks white as snow;
Beyond the Victor's Wall like frost cold moonbeams flow.
None knows from where a flute blows a nostalgic song,
All warriors lie awake homesick the whole night long.

Hearing a flute song, the warriors on the frontier are drowned in homesickness.

白雪歌送武判官归京

岑 参

北风卷地白草折^①，胡天八月即飞雪。

忽如一夜春风来，千树万树梨花开。

散入珠帘湿罗幕^②，狐裘不暖锦衾薄^③。

将军角弓不得控^④，都护铁衣冷难著^⑤。

瀚海阑干百丈冰^⑥，愁云惨淡万里凝^⑦。

中军置酒饮归客^⑧，胡琴琵琶与羌笛。

纷纷暮雪下辕门^⑨，风掣红旗冻不翻^⑩。

轮台^⑪东门送君去，去时雪满天山路。

山回路转不见君，雪上空留马行处^⑫。

① 白草折：白草，西北之地所长，牛马所嗜，干枯时，呈白色。折，断。
② "散入"句：珠帘，缀有珠子的门帘。罗幕，用绫罗制作的帷幕。
③ "狐裘"句：狐裘，用狐狸皮做的皮袄。锦衾（qīn），用锦缎做的被子。
④ "将军"句：角弓，用兽角装饰的弓。控，引、拉。
⑤ "都护"句：都护，镇守边疆的长官。唐代设六都护府，各设大都护一人。著，穿。
⑥ "瀚海"句：瀚海，沙漠。阑干，纵横的样子。
⑦ "愁云"句：惨淡，昏暗的样子。凝，凝结。
⑧ "中军"句：中军，古代分兵为左、中、右三军。中军为主帅亲自统帅的军队，这里指主帅的营帐。饮归客，招待归客饮酒。归客这里指将京都的武判官。
⑨ 辕门：军营门。古代军营前将两车车辕交叉作为门。
⑩ "风掣"句：掣，拉、牵拽。翻，这里是飘扬的意思。
⑪ 轮台：在今新疆乌鲁木齐市西南。
⑫ 马行处：指雪地上马蹄的痕迹。

Song of White Snow in Farewell to Secretary Wu Going Back to the Capital

Cen Shen

Snapping the pallid grass, the northern wind whirls low;
In the eighth moon the Tartar sky is filled with snow.
As if the vernal breeze had come back overnight,
Adorning thousands of pear trees with blossoms white.
Flakes enter pearled blinds and wet the silken screen;
No furs of fox can warm us nor brocade quilts green.
The general cannot draw his rigid bow with ease;
E'en the commissioner in coat of mail would freeze.
A thousand feet o'er cracked wilderness ice piles,
And gloomy clouds hang sad and drear for miles and miles.
We drink in headquarters to our guest homeward bound;
With Tartar lutes, pipas and pipes the camps resound.
Snow in huge flakes at dusk falls heavy on camp gate;
The frozen red flag in the wind won't undulate.
At eastern gate of Wheel Tower we bid goodbye
On the snow-covered road to Heaven's Mountain high.
I watch his horse go past a bend and, lost to sight,
His track will soon be buried up by snow in flight.

The poet describes the biting cold on the frontier.

走马川[1] 行奉送封大夫[2] 出师西征[3]

岑 参

君不见走马川，雪海[4]边，平沙莽莽黄入天[5]。

轮台[6]九月风夜吼，一川碎石大如斗，随风满地石乱走。

匈奴草黄马正肥，金山[7]西见烟尘飞，汉家大将[8]西出师。

将军金甲夜不脱，半夜军行戈相拨[9]，风头如刀面如割。

马毛带雪汗气蒸[10]，五花连钱旋作冰[11]，幕中草檄[12]砚水凝。

虏骑[13]闻之应胆慑，料知短兵不敢接[14]，车师[15]西门伫献捷。

---

① 走马川：又名左末河，即今新疆车尔臣河。
② 封大夫：封常清。天宝十三年受命为北庭都护、伊西节度、瀚海军使，奏请岑参为节度判官。这年冬，封常清西征播仙部族，岑参写此诗送行。
③ 西征：一作"西行"。
④ 雪海：《新唐书·西域传下》："行度雪海，春夏常雨雪。"泛指西北苦寒之地。
⑤ "平沙"句：莽莽，无边无际。黄入天，形容黄沙弥漫，与天相接。
⑥ 轮台：在今新疆米泉县境。
⑦ 金山：今新疆阿尔泰山。
⑧ 汉家大将：指封常清。
⑨ 拨：撞击。
⑩ 蒸：蒸发。
⑪ "五花"句：五花，开元天宝年间，社会上最考究马的装饰，常把马的鬃毛剪成花瓣形，剪三瓣的叫三花马，剪五瓣的叫五花马。连钱，一种宝马名，《尔雅·释畜》："色有深浅，斑驳隐粼，今之连钱骢。"旋，马上。
⑫ 草檄（xí）：起草声讨敌人的檄文。
⑬ 虏骑：指播仙部族的骑兵。
⑭ "料知"句：短兵，指刀、剑类的短武器。接，接战、交战。
⑮ 车师：一作"军师"。车师为唐安西都护府所在地，在今新疆吐鲁番市。

Song of the Running Horse River in Farewell to General Feng on His Western Expedition

Cen Shen

Do you not see the Running Horse River flow
Along the sea of snow
And the sand that's yellowed sky and earth high and low?
In the ninth moon at Wheel Tower winds howl at night;
The river fills with boulders fallen from the height;
With howling winds they run riot as if in flight.
When grass turns yellow and plump Hunnish horses neigh,
West of Mount Gold dusts rise, the foe in proud array.
Our general leads his army on his westward way.
He keeps his iron armor on the whole night long,
Spears clang at midnight when his army march along,
Their faces cut by winds that blow so sharp and strong.
Their sweat and snow turn into steam on horse's mane,
Which soon on horse's back turns into ice again;
Ink freezes when challenge's written before campaign.
On hearing this, the foe with fear should palpitate.
Dare they cross swords with our brave men in iron plate?
We'll wait for news of victory at the western gate.

This song glorifies General Feng in praise of his heroism against wind and snow.

凉州① 馆② 中与诸判官③ 夜集

岑 参

弯弯月出挂城头，
城头月出照凉州。
凉州七里④ 十万家，
胡人半解⑤ 弹琵琶。
琵琶一曲肠堪断，
风萧萧兮夜漫漫。
河西幕⑥ 中多故人，
故人别来三五春。
花门楼⑦ 前见秋草，
岂能贫贱相看老。
一生大笑能几回，
斗酒相逢须醉倒。

① 凉州：此指河西节度府治所武威（今甘肃武威）。
② 馆：客舍。
③ 判官：官名，唐代特派担任临时职务的大臣皆得自选中级官员奏请充任判官，以
　资佐理。中期以后，节度使、观察使均有判官，非正官。此诗作于天宝十三年赴
　北庭途经武威时。
④ 七里：《元和郡县图志》卷四十："（凉州）南北七里，东西三里。"一作"七
　城"。《资治通鉴》卷二一九："武威大城之中，小城有七。"
⑤ 半解：多半（人）懂得。
⑥ 幕：幕府。
⑦ 花门楼：指凉州馆舍的楼房。

Drinking with Friends at Night in Liangzhou

Cen Shen

The crescent moon rises and hangs on city wall;

The rising moon on city wall shines over all.

There're a thousand homes in seven districts on frontier;

Half of the Tartars play pipa for us to hear.

The heart would be broken to hear the pipa song,

When the wind sheds leaves in showers and night is long.

West of the River I have so many compeers;

Many friends are separated from me for many years.

Before the flowery gate we see autumn grass.

Could we bear to see friends grow old like it? Alas!

How many times can we laugh in a life so fleet?

So let us drink our fill till drunken, now we meet!

This poem sings of friendship and wine-drinking.

许渊冲译唐诗三百首

塞下曲六首（其二）

卢　纶

林暗草惊风^①，

将军夜引弓^②。

平明^③寻白羽^④，

没^⑤在石棱^⑥中。

① 惊风：突然被风吹动。
② 引弓：拉弓、开弓，这里包含下一步的射箭。
③ 平明：天刚亮的时候。
④ 白羽：箭杆后部的白色羽毛，这里指箭。
⑤ 没：陷入，这里是钻进的意思。
⑥ 石棱：石头的边角。

Border Songs (II)

Lu Lun

In gloomy woods grass shivers at wind's howl;
The general takes it for a tiger's growl.
He shoots and looks for his arrow next morn
Only to find a rock pierced amid the thorn.

塞下曲六首（其三）

卢 纶

月黑雁飞高，
单于夜遁逃。
欲将轻骑逐，
大雪满弓刀。

Border Songs (III)

Lu Lun

Wild geese fly high in moonless night;
The Tartars through the dark take flight.
Our horsemen chase them, armed with bow
And sword covered with heavy snow.

The poet glorifies the cavaliers in pursuit of the foe on a snowy night.

塞下曲

许 浑

夜战桑乾北^①，
秦兵半不归。
朝来有乡信，
犹自寄寒衣^②。

① 桑乾北：桑乾河北岸。桑乾河，永定河的上游，发源于山西，流经华北平原。
② 寒衣：御寒的衣服。

Frontier Song

Xu Hun

In snow our men did fight,
Half of them died at night.
But letters came next day:
Winter clothes on the way.

The poet is grieved over the soldiers' death for lack of winter clothes.

马诗二十三首（其五）

李 贺

大漠沙如雪，
燕山^① 月似钩。
何当^② 金络脑^③，
快走踏清秋。

② 何当：何时承受。
③ 金络脑：嵌金的马络头。《陌上桑》："黄金络马头。"这里指贵重的辔头、鞍具等。

Horse Poems (V)

Li He

The desert sand looks white as snow;
The crescent moon hangs like a bow.
When would the steed in golden gear
Gallop all night through autumn clear?

The poet who cannot serve his country compares himself to a battle horse which cannot gallop at full speed.

八、政治讽喻

古风（其二十四）

李　白

大车扬飞尘，

亭午暗阡陌①。

中贵②多黄金，

连云开甲宅③。

路逢斗鸡者，

冠盖④何辉赫⑤。

鼻息干虹蜺，

行人皆怵惕⑥。

世无洗耳翁⑦，

谁知尧与跖⑧！

① 阡陌：泛指大路。
② 中贵："中贵人"的简称。即宦官。
③ 甲宅：豪华的宅院。
④ 冠盖：衣冠和车盖。
⑤ 辉赫：光彩照人。
⑥ 怵惕（chù tì）：恐惧。
⑦ 洗耳翁：古代隐士许由。
⑧ 跖（zhí）：古代大盗，代指不肖之人。

Eunuchs and Cock-fighters (XXIV)

Li Bai

The dust which eunuchs' carriages raise

Darkens at noon the public ways.

Of their gold the eunuchs are proud;

Their mansions rise to scrape the cloud

I meet those who can make cocks fight,

With caps and cabs, so fair and bright.

Into rainbows they blow their breath,

Passers-by are frightened to death.

There is no connoisseur in this age.

Who can tell a thief from a sage?

The poet criticizes the rich and influential eunuchs and cock-fighters.

乌栖曲 ①

李 白

姑苏台②上乌栖时③，

吴王宫里醉西施④。

吴歌楚舞欢未毕，

青山欲衔半边日。

银箭金壶⑤漏水多，

起看秋月坠江波。

东方渐高⑥奈乐何！

① 乌栖曲：乐府《清商曲辞·西曲歌》旧题，西曲本是江汉一带民歌，与吴声歌曲相近。
② 姑苏台：故址在今江苏省苏州市，春秋时吴王夫差所建。
③ 乌栖时：黄昏时。
④ 西施：吴王夫差的宠妃。她本是越国的著名美女，越王勾践将她献给吴王，以销
　 蚀吴王的意志。
⑤ 银箭金壶：古代用壶和箭作计时的器具，用金属制成。
⑥ 高：同"皓"。白色。

Crows Flying Back to Their Nest

Li Bai

Over Royal Terrace when crows flew back to their nest,

The king in Royal Palace feasted his mistress drunk.

The Southern maidens sang and danced without a rest

Till beak-like mountain peaks would peck the sun half sunk.

The golden clepsydra could not stop water's flow,

Over the waves the autumn moon was hanging low.

Would not the king enjoy his fill in Eastern glow?

许
渊
冲
译
唐
诗
三
百
首

This is a satire on the King of Wu who held perpetual revelries with his favorite mistress in his Royal Palace in the 5th century BC.

咏史

戎　昱

汉家①青史②上，
计③拙④是和亲。
社稷⑤依明主，
安危托妇人。
岂能将玉貌⑥，
便拟⑦静胡⑧尘⑨。
地下千年骨，
谁为辅佐臣。

① 汉家：汉朝。
② 青史：史册。古人在青竹简上纪事，后世就称史册为青史。
③ 计：计策，计谋。
④ 拙：愚笨。
⑤ 社稷：本指古代天子诸侯祭祀土神、谷神的庙宇，后来用作国家政权的象征。
⑥ 玉貌：美好的容貌，这里代指和亲的女子。
⑦ 拟：意欲，打算。
⑧ 胡：汉唐时期，汉族称西、北方的少数民族为"胡人"。
⑨ 尘：指烟尘，代指战争。

On Appeasement by Marriage

Rong Yu

The kings in history sank so low

As to appease by marriage the foe.

To rule is a sovereign's duty.

Can safety depend on a beauty?

Could a face beautiful as jade

Repel the Tartars who invade?

Why were no loyal generals found

Among bones buried underground?

This is a satire against the kings who sought appeasement by marriage.

丽人行

杜　甫

三月三日天气新，长安水边多丽人。

态浓意远淑且真^①，肌理细腻骨肉匀。

绣罗衣裳照暮春，蹙^②金孔雀银麒麟。

头上何所有，翠微盍叶垂鬓唇^③。

背后何所见，珠压腰衱稳称身^④。

就中云幕椒房亲^⑤，赐名大国虢与秦^⑥。

紫驼之峰^⑦出翠釜，水精之盘行素鳞。

① "态浓"句：态浓意远，姿态浓艳，神情高远而显得超凡脱俗。淑且真，贤淑而又纯真。
② 蹙（cù）：古代刺绣的一种手法。在其下接有"金孔雀"和"银麒麟"两个宾语。
③ "翠微"句：翠微盍叶，用翠玉制成的妇女发髻上的雕花饰物。鬓唇，鬓角边。
④ "珠压"句：衱（jié），衣服后面的大襟。稳称身，珠玉压住后襟，使它下垂，显得衣服非常妥帖合身。
⑤ "就中"句：就中，宫内。云幕椒房，都指后妃居住的内宫。
⑥ 虢（guó）与秦：杨贵妃有三个姊妹，大姐嫁给崔家封为韩国夫人，三姐嫁给裴家封为虢国夫人，八姐嫁给柳家封为秦国夫人，这里用"虢与秦"指代杨氏姊妹。
⑦ 紫驼之峰：紫驼背上高突的肉峰。

Satire on Fair Ladies

Du Fu

The weather's fine in the third moon on the third day,

By riverside so many beauties in array.

Each of the ladies has a fascinating face,

Their skin is delicate, their manner full of grace.

Embroidered with peacocks and unicorns in gold,

Their dress in rich silks shines so bright when spring is old.

What do they wear on the head?

Emerald pendant leaves hang down in silver thread.

What do you see from behind?

How nice-fitting are their waistbands with pearls combined.

Among them there're the emperor's favorite kin,

Ennobled Duchess of Guo comes with Duchess of Qin.

What do they eat?

The purple meat of camels hump cooked in green cauldron as a

dish;

On crystal plate is served snow-white slices of raw fish.

犀箸厌饫久未下^①，鸾刀缕切空纷纶^②。

黄门飞鞚不动尘^③，御厨络绎送八珍。

箫鼓哀吟感鬼神，宾从杂遝实要津^④。

后来鞍马何逡巡^⑤，当轩下马入锦茵^⑥。

杨花雪落覆白苹，青鸟飞去衔红巾。

炙手可热势绝伦^⑦，慎莫近前丞相嗔。

① "犀箸"句：犀箸，用犀牛角制作的筷子。厌饫（yù），饱足。
② "鸾刀"句：鸾刀，环上有鸾铃的刀。缕切，切脍如丝缕般精细。纷纶，忙乱。
③ "黄门"句：黄门，太监。飞鞚（kòng），鞚指马笼头，这里指马飞驰。
④ "宾从"句：宾从，讨好杨氏一家的趋炎附势之人。杂遝（tà），杂乱而众多。
   实要津，津原指渡口，这里指担任各方面的重要职位。
⑤ 逡（qūn）巡：神气飞扬，旁若无人的样子。
⑥ 锦茵：地上铺有锦毯。
⑦ "炙手"句：炙手可热，气焰嚣张，触之熏灼。绝伦，无人可比。

See rhino chopsticks the satiated eaters stay,

And untouched morsels carved by belled knives on the tray.

When eunuchs' horses come running, no dust is raised;

They bring still more rare dishes delicious to the taste.

Listen to soul-stirring music of flutes and drums!

On the main road an official retinue comes.

A rider ambles on saddled horse, the last of all,

He alights, treads on satin carpet, enters the hall.

The willow down like snow falls on the duckweed white;

The blue bird picking red handkerchief goes in flight.

The prime minister's powerful without a peer.

His angry touch would burn your hand. Do not come near!

許
淵
冲
译
唐
诗
三
百
首

This is a satire against the emperor's favorite Lady Yang and her sisters and their brother who became the Prime Minister. The poet describes their beauty, their dress, their food. He hints at the incest by the frivolous willow-down and the blue bird which carries secret amorous message for them.

兵车行

杜　甫

车辚辚，马萧萧，行人弓箭各在腰。

耶娘妻子^①走相送，尘埃不见咸阳桥。

牵衣顿足拦道哭，哭声直上干^②云霄。

道傍过者问行人，行人但云点行频^③。

或从十五北防河，便至四十西营田^④。

去时里正^⑤与裹头^⑥，归来头白还戍边。

边庭流血成海水，武皇^⑦开边意未已。

君不闻汉家山东二百州^⑧，千村万落生荆杞。

① 妻子：妻子和儿女。
② 干：犯；冲。
③ 点行频：多次点兵出征。
④ 营田：戍边的士卒，兼从事垦荒工作。
⑤ 里正：里长。唐制，百户为一里，里有里正，管户口、赋役等事。
⑥ 与裹头：古以皂罗三尺裹头作头巾。因应征者年龄还小，故由里正替他裹头。
⑦ 武皇：汉武帝，他在历史上以开疆拓土著称。这里暗喻唐玄宗。
⑧ 山东二百州：指华山以东的广大土地。

Song of the Conscripts

Du Fu

Chariots rumble

And horses grumble.

The conscripts march with bow and arrows at the waist.

Their fathers, mothers, wives and children come in haste

To see them off; the bridge is shrouded in dust they've raised.

They clutch at their coats, stamp the feet and bar the way;

Their grief cries loud and strikes the cloud straight, straight away.

An onlooker by roadside asks an enrollee.

"The conscription is frequent," only answers he.

Some went north at fifteen to guard the river shore,

And were sent west to till the land at forty or more.

The elder bound their young heads when they went away;

Just home, they're sent to the frontier though their hair's gray.

The field on borderland becomes a sea of blood;

The emperor's greed for land is still at high flood.

Have you not heard

Two hundred districts east of the Hua Mountains lie,

Where briers and brambles grow in villages far and nigh?

纵有健妇把锄犁，禾生陇亩无东西。

况复秦兵耐苦战，被驱不异犬与鸡。

长者虽有问，役夫敢申恨。

且如今年冬，未休关西卒①。

县官②急索租，租税从何出。

信知生男恶，反是生女好。

生女犹得嫁比邻③，生男埋没随百草。

君不见，青海头，古来白骨无人收。

新鬼烦冤旧鬼哭，天阴雨湿声啾啾。

---

① 关西卒：指此次应征出发的秦地士卒。
② 县官：指官府。
③ 比邻：近邻。

Although stout women can wield the plough and the hoe,

Thorns and weeds in the east as in the west o'ergrow.

The enemy are used to hard and stubborn fight;

Our men are driven just like dogs or fowls in flight.

"You are kind to ask me

To complain I'm not free.

In winter of this year

Conscription goes on here.

The magistrates for taxes press.

How can we pay them in distress?

If we had known sons bring no joy,

We would have preferred girl to boy.

A daughter can be wed to a neighbor, alas!

A son can only be buried under the grass?"

Have you not seen

On borders green

Bleached bones since olden days unburied on the plain?

The old ghosts weep and cry, while the new ghosts complain;

The air is loud with screech and scream in gloomy rain.

许

渊

冲

译

唐

诗

三

百

首

诸将五首（其二）

杜 甫

韩公^①本意筑三城，
拟绝天骄^②拔汉旌。
岂谓尽烦回纥马，
翻然远救朔方兵^③。
胡^④来不觉潼关隘，
龙起犹闻晋水清。
独使至尊忧社稷，
诸君何以答升平？

---

① 韩公：指张仁愿，景龙二年（708 年）封韩国公。
② 天骄：指回纥。
③ 朔方兵：朔方镇的唐军。
④ 胡：指安禄山叛军。

Five Generals (II)

Du Fu

The Duke of Han planned to build three victorious walls

To stop the foe from coming near our capitals.

Could he anticipate the Western cavaliers,

After their victory, would not leave Northern frontiers?

The Pass could not prevent the foe from coming near;

After the dragon's rise, we can see our land clear.

Should the sovereign worry about the country's fate,

Generals could not have done their duty for the State.

The poet praises the Duke of Hart who has built three victor's walls, and criticizes other generals who cannot stop the enemy's invasion on Northern frontiers. The dragon refers to the new sovereign who has recaptured the Western capital.

哀江头

杜 甫

少陵野老^①吞声哭，春日潜行曲江^②曲。

江头宫殿锁千门，细柳新蒲为谁绿？

忆昔霓旌^③下南苑，苑中万物生颜色^④。

昭阳殿里第一人^⑤，同辇随君侍君侧。

辇前才人带弓箭，白马嚼啮^⑥黄金勒^⑦。

翻身向天仰射云，一笑正坠双飞翼。

明眸皓齿今何在？血污游魂归不得^⑧。

清渭^⑨东流剑阁^⑩深，去住彼此无消息。

人生有情泪沾臆，江水江花岂终极！

黄昏胡骑尘满城，欲往城南望城北。

① 少陵野老：杜甫自称。
② 曲江：长安城南著名的风景区。
③ 霓旌：皇帝的旌旗。
④ 生颜色：焕发生机。
⑤ 昭阳殿里第一人：指杨贵妃。
⑥ 啮（niè）：咬。
⑦ 勒：马衔的嚼口。
⑧ 归不得：指马嵬坡兵变，杨贵妃被缢死。
⑨ 清渭：渭水。
⑩ 剑阁：大剑山。

Lament along the Winding River

Du Fu

Old and deprived, I swallow tears on a spring day;
Along Winding River in stealth I go my way.
All palace gates and doors are locked on river shore;
Willows and reeds are green for no one to adore.
I remember rainbow banners streamed at high tide
To Southern Park where everything was beautified.
The first lady of the Sunny Palace would ride
In the imperial chariot by the emperor's side.
The horsewomen before her bore arrows and bow;
Their white steeds champed at golden bits on the front row.
One archer, leaning back, shot at cloud in the sky;
One arrow brought down two winged birds from on high.
Where are the first lady's pearly teeth and eyes bright?
Her spirit, blood-stained, could not come back from the height.
Far from Sword Cliff, with River Wei her soul flew east;
The emperor got no news from her in the least.
A man who has a heart will wet his breast with tears.
Would riverside grass and flowers not weep for years?
At dusk the rebels' horses overrun the town;
I want to go upward, but instead I go down.

The poet laments over the Winding River where the Bright Emperor made pleasure with his favorite Lady Yang who is dead, and where the rebels are running riot.

元和十年 ① 自朗州召至京师戏赠看花诸君子 ②

刘禹锡

紫陌 ③ 红尘 ④ 拂面来，

无人不道看花回。

玄都观 ⑤ 里桃千树，

尽是刘郎 ⑥ 去后栽。

① 元和十年：公元815年。
② 看花诸君子：指一起承召回京的柳宗元、韩愈等志同道合者。
③ 紫陌：京城长安繁华的街道。
④ 红尘：街道上行人车马扬起的尘土。
⑤ 玄都观：长安城南崇业坊（今西安市南门外）的一座道教庙宇。
⑥ 刘郎：诗人自指。

The Flower-admirers

Liu Yuxi

Dust raised by cabs on grassy lane caresses my face;
No flower-admirers but follow the cabs' trace.
Thousands of peach trees in the Taoist temple's place
Are all planted after I fell into disgrace.

In 815 the poet lamented over his banishment from the capital in 805 with the result that he could not admire the peach flowers in the Taoist temple.

再游玄都观

刘禹锡

百亩庭中半是苔^①，
桃花净尽菜花开。
种桃道士^②归何处，
前度^③刘郎今又来。

① 苔：青苔。
② 种桃道士：比喻昔日竭力打击革新派的执政者。
③ 前度：前次。

The Taoist Temple Revisited

Liu Yuxi

In half of the wide courtyard only mosses grow;
Peach blossoms all fallen, only rape-flowers blow.
Where is the Taoist planting peach trees in this place?
I come after I fell again into disgrace.

许渊冲译唐诗三百首

In 829 the poet came again to the Taoist temple after his second banishment in 815.

上阳[①] 白发人

白居易

上阳人，上阳人，红颜暗老[②] 白发新。

绿衣监使[③] 守宫门，一闭上阳多少春。

玄宗末岁初选入，入时十六今六十。

同时采择[④] 百余人，零落年深残此身[⑤]。

忆昔吞悲别亲族，扶入车中不教哭。

皆云入内便承恩，脸似芙蓉胸似玉。

未容君王得见面，已被杨妃遥侧目[⑥]。

妒令潜配上阳宫，一生遂向空房宿。

宿空房，秋夜长，夜长无寐天不明。

耿耿残灯背壁影，萧萧暗雨打窗声。

---

① 上阳：唐代别宫名，在东都洛阳西南。
② 红颜暗老：人的青春容颜在不知不觉中衰老。
③ 绿衣监使：唐代管理宫闱事务的宦官，唐时京都诸苑各设监一人，从六品下；副
  监一人，从七品下。六、七品官服为深、浅绿色。
④ 采择：选入宫女。
⑤ "零落"句：零落，凋谢，这里指宫女死亡。残，剩余、留下。
⑥ "已被"句：杨妃，杨贵妃。遥侧目，斜着眼睛看，形容忌恨的样子。

The White-haired Palace Maid

Bai Juyi

The Shangyang Palace maid,
Her hair grows white, her rosy cheeks grow dark and fade.
The palace gate is guarded by eunuchs in green.
How many springs have passed, immured as she has been!
She was first chosen for the imperial household
At the age of sixteen; now she's sixty years old.
The hundred beauties brought in with her have all gone,
Flickering out through long years, leaving her alone.
She swallowed grief when she left home in days gone by,
Helped into the cab, she was forbidden to cry.
Once in the palace, she'd be favored, it was said;
Her face was fair as lotus, her bosom like jade.
But to the emperor she could never come nigh,
For Lady Yang had cast on her a jealous eye.
She was consigned to Shangyang Palace full of gloom,
To pass her lonely days and nights in a bare room.
In empty chamber long seemed each autumnal night;
Sleepless in bed, it seemed she'd never see daylight.
Dim, dim the lamplight throws her shadow on the walls;
Shower by shower on her windows chill rain falls.

春日迟，日迟独坐天难暮；

宫莺百啭^①愁厌闻，梁燕双栖老休妒。

莺归燕去长悄然，春往秋来不记年。

唯向深宫望明月，东西四五百回圆。

今日宫中年最老，大家遥赐尚书号^②。

小头鞋履窄衣裳，青黛点眉眉细长。

外人不见见应笑，天宝末年时世妆。

上阳人，苦最多。

少亦苦，老亦苦，少苦老苦两如何！

君不见昔时吕向《美人赋》^③，

又不见今日上阳白发歌！

---

① 百啭：鸟婉转地叫。
② "大家"句：大家，古代宫中侍从对皇帝的称谓。尚书，女尚书，宫中女官的名称。
③ 吕向《美人赋》：作者自注云："天宝末，有密采艳色者，当时号花鸟使，吕向献《美人赋》以讽之。"吕向，字子回，事迹见《新唐书·文艺传》。《美人赋》载《全唐文》卷三零一。

Spring days drag slow;

She sits alone to see light won't be dim and low.

She's tired to hear the palace orioles sing and sing,

Too old to envy pairs of swallows on the wing.

Silent, she sees the birds appear and disappear,

And counts nor springs nor autumns coming year by year.

Watching the moon o'er palace again and again,

Four hundred times and more she's seen it wax and wane.

Today the oldest honorable maid of all,

She is entitled Secretary of Palace Hall.

Her gown is tightly fitted, her shoes like pointed prows;

With dark green pencil she draws long, long slender brows.

Seeing her, outsiders would even laugh with tears;

Her old-fashioned dress has been out of date for years.

The Shangyang maid, to suffer is her fate, all told;

She suffered while still young; she suffers now she's old.

Do you not know a satire spread in days gone by?

Today for white-haired Shangyang Palace maid we'll sigh.

The poet pities the palace maid who lived the palace from sixteen to sixty without even seeing the emperor's face.

轻肥 ①

白居易

意气②骄满路，鞍马光照尘。

借问何为者？人称是内臣③。

朱绂④皆大夫，紫绶⑤或将军。

夸赴军中宴，走马去如云。

樽罍⑥溢九酝⑦，水陆罗八珍⑧。

果擘⑨洞庭橘⑩，脍⑪切天池⑫鳞。

食饱心自若，酒酣气益振。

是岁江南旱，衢州⑬人食人！

① 轻肥：轻裘肥马，指达官显贵，兼喻其生活的豪奢。《论语·雍也》云："乘肥马，衣轻裘。"
② 意气：意态与神气。
③ 内臣：宦官。
④ 朱绂（fú）：朱红色朝服。唐制，官分九品，四五品衣朱，二三品佩紫绶。
⑤ 紫绶（shòu）：紫色的系印绶带。
⑥ 樽罍（léi）：古代盛酒的器具。
⑦ 九酝：泛指最醇美的酒。
⑧ 八珍：八样贵重食物。
⑨ 擘（bò）：剖开。
⑩ 洞庭橘：江苏太湖洞庭山产的名橘。
⑪ 脍（kuài）：细切的鱼肉。
⑫ 天池：这里指大海。
⑬ 衢州：今浙江省衢州市。

许渊冲译唐诗三百首

Sleek Horse and Light Furs

Bai Juyi

The road is overwhelmed with their pride,

Saddled steeds brighten the roadside.

How proud these officers appear

For they are eunuchs without fear!

They wear official tassels red

And violet ribbon round the head.

To feast in the army they're proud,

Their horses run as light as cloud.

They drink and eat, wine cup in hand,

Delicious food from sea and land.

The oranges come from the lakeside;

The fish from Heaven's Pool well fried.

Full fed, they set their heart at ease;

Drunken, they would do as they please.

This year in the south the drought rages;

Men eat human flesh like savages.

The poet criticizes the luxurious eunuchs and reminds them of the drought in the south.

买花

白居易

帝城①春欲暮，喧喧车马度。

共道牡丹时，相随买花去。

贵贱无常价，酬直②看花数。

灼灼③百朵红，戋戋五束素④。

上张幄幕⑤庇⑥，旁织笆篱护。

水洒复泥封⑦，移来色如故。

家家习为俗，人人迷不悟。

有一田舍翁⑧，偶来买花处。

低头独长叹，此叹无人喻。

一丛深色花，十户中人赋⑨！

---

① 帝城：指京城长安。

② 酬直：酬值。

③ 灼灼：形容花鲜艳有光彩的样子。

④ "戋戋"句：戋戋，众多的样子。束，量词，古时帛五匹为一束。素，白绸子。

⑤ 幄幕：帐篷。

⑥ 庇：庇护。

⑦ 泥封：用土培植。

⑧ 田舍翁：老农。

⑨ 中人赋：中等人家一年缴的赋税。唐时赋税，按户口征收，分为上户、中户、下户。（《旧唐书·食货志》）

Buying Flowers

Bai Juyi

The capital's in parting spring,
Steeds run and neigh and cab bells ring.
Peonies are at their best hours
And people rush to buy the flowers.
They do not care about the price,
Just count and buy those which seem nice.
For hundred blossoms dazzling red,
Twenty-five rolls of silk they spread.
Sheltered above by curtains wide,
Protected with fences by the side,
Roots sealed with mud, with water sprayed,
Removed, their beauty does not fade.
Accustomed to this way for long,
No family e'er thinks it wrong.
What's the old peasant doing there?
Why should he come to Flower Fair?
Head bowed, he utters sigh on sigh
And nobody understands why.
A bunch of deep-red peonies
Costs taxes of ten families.

The poet compares the rich who buy flowers and the poor who pay taxes.

卖炭翁

白居易

卖炭翁，伐薪烧炭南山^①中。

满面尘灰烟火色，两鬓苍苍^②十指黑。

卖炭得钱何所营？身上衣裳口中食。

可怜身上衣正单，心忧炭贱愿天寒。

夜来城外一尺雪，晓驾炭车辗冰辙^③。

牛困人饥日已高，市南门^④外泥中歇。

翩翩两骑来是谁？黄衣使者白衫儿^⑤。

手把文书口称敕^⑥，回车叱牛牵向北^⑦。

一车炭，千余斤，宫使驱将惜不得^⑧。

半匹^⑨红纱一丈绫，系^⑩向牛头充炭直^⑪！

① 南山：终南山。
② 苍苍：形容鬓发斑白。
③ 辗冰辙：轧着结冰的车道行走。
④ 市南门：唐代长安有东、西两个市场，每个市场都有东、南、西、北门。
⑤ "黄衣"句：黄衣使者，指太监，唐代级别较高的太监穿黄衣。白衫儿，太监手下的爪牙。
⑥ "手把"句：口称敕，嘴里说着皇帝的命令。敕，君主的诏命。
⑦ "牵向北"：唐代长安市场在城南，宫廷在城北，所以叱牛向北行。
⑧ "宫使"句：宫使，即上面所说的黄衣使者。驱将，把牛车赶走。将，语气助词。
⑨ 半匹：唐代四丈为一匹，半匹为二丈。
⑩ 系：绑扎。
⑪ 直：同"值"。

The Old Charcoal Seller

Bai Juyi

What does the old man fare?
He cuts the wood in southern hill and fires his ware.
His face is grimed with smoke and streaked with ash and dust,
His temples grizzled and his fingers all turned black.
The money earned by selling charcoal is not just
Enough for food for his mouth and clothing for his back.
Though his coat is thin, he hopes winter will set in,
For cold weather will keep up the charcoals good price.
At night a foot of snow falls outside city walls;
At dawn his charcoal cart crushes ruts in the ice.
The sun is high, the ox tired out and hungry he;
Outside the southern gate in snow and slush they rest.
Two riders canter up. Alas! Who can they be?
Two palace heralds in the yellow jackets dressed.
Decree in hand, which is imperial order, one says;
They turn the cart about and at the ox they shout.
A cartload of charcoal a thousand catties weighs;
They drive the cart away. What dare the old man say?
Ten feet of silk and twenty feet of gauze deep red,
That is the payment they fasten to the ox's head.

The poet sympathizes with the old charcoal seller in poverty and in misery.

悯农二首（其一）

李 绅

春种一粒粟，
秋收万颗子。
四海无闲田，
农夫犹饿死。

The Peasants (I)

Li Shen

Each seed that's sown in spring,
Will make autumn yields high.
What will fertile fields bring?
Of hunger peasants die.

悯农二首（其二）

李　绅

锄禾[①]日当午[②]，

汗滴禾下土。

谁知盘中餐[③]，

粒粒皆辛苦。

① 禾：禾苗。
② 日当午：指中午。
③ 餐：饭菜。

The Peasants (II)

Li Shen

At noon they weed with hoes;

Their sweat drips on the soil.

Each bowl of rice, who knows?

Is the fruit of hard toil.

许
渊
冲
译
唐
诗
三
百
首

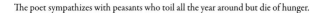

The poet sympathizes with peasants who toil all the year around but die of hunger.

秦王①饮酒

李 贺

秦王骑虎游八极②，剑光照空天自碧。

羲和敲日玻璃声③，劫灰飞尽古今平④。

龙头泻酒邀酒星⑤，金槽琵琶夜枨枨⑥。

洞庭雨脚来吹笙，酒酣喝月使倒行。

银云栉栉瑶殿明⑦，宫门掌事⑧报一更。

花楼玉凤声娇狞⑨，海绡红文⑩香浅清，

黄鹅跌舞千年觥⑪。仙人烛树⑫蜡烟轻，

清琴⑬醉眼泪泓泓⑭。

① 秦王：秦始皇。
② 八极：四面八方，这里指天下各地。
③ "羲和"句：羲和，传说为太阳驾车的神。敲日，鞭打着太阳。玻璃声，发出敲打玻璃的声音。
④ "劫灰"句：劫灰，劫火的余灰。飞尽，灾难结束。
⑤ 酒星：传说中主管饮宴的星君。
⑥ "金槽"句：金槽，用金装饰琵琶上端架弦的地方。枨枨（chéng），琵琶声。
⑦ "银云"句：银云，映着月光的云彩。栉栉（zhì），排列整齐的样子。瑶殿，华美的宫殿。
⑧ 宫门掌事：掌管宫里杂事的人。
⑨ "花楼"句：玉凤，歌女。娇狞，歌声婉转。
⑩ 海绡（xiāo）红文：用海绡纱做的红色花纹的舞衣。
⑪ "黄鹅"句：黄鹅，即黄娥，歌姬舞女。跌舞，献酒时的舞蹈动作。觥（gōng），酒器。
⑫ 仙人烛树：指高大的烛台。
⑬ 清琴：借指宫女。
⑭ 泪泓泓：眼泪汪汪。

The Drinking Song of the King of Qin

Li He

The King of Qin rode the tiger to eight Poles high:

His sword shone in the air and brightened the blue sky.

His driver struck the sun with a glass-breaking sound;

All were reduced to ashes on the battleground.

Stars were invited to drink wine poured from dragon's head;

The golden pipa played at night would grieve the dead.

The rain treading on Dongting Lake would blow the lute;

The King ordered the moon to go back to its root.

Silver cloud on cloud made the crystal palace bright;

The gate-keeper announced it was still early night.

The phoenix in the tower sang her bewitching song;

Clear fragrance of ladies' silken dress wafted long.

The dancers drank to his health of a thousand years.

From the candles on the fairy trees rose smoke light.

From the lutist's drunken eyes streamed down copious tears.

The poet imagines how the King of Qin drank like an immortal.

老夫采玉歌

李 贺

采玉采玉须水碧[①]，
琢作步摇徒好色[②]。
老夫饥寒龙为愁，
蓝溪水气无清白[③]。
夜雨冈头食蓁子[④]，
杜鹃口血[⑤]老夫泪。
蓝溪之水厌生人[⑥]，
身死千年恨溪水。
斜山柏风雨如啸[⑦]，
泉脚挂绳青袅袅[⑧]。
村寒白屋念娇婴[⑨]，
古台石磴悬肠草[⑩]。

① 水碧：碧玉名。
② "琢作"句：琢作，雕琢成。步摇，贵族妇女的首饰，用银丝穿宝玉作花枝形，插在头上，走路时随步摇动，增加美感。徒好色，仅仅使贵妇容貌美丽。
③ "蓝溪"句：蓝溪，今陕西省蓝田县西蓝田山下，出产美玉。无清白，清白不分，指溪水浑浊。
④ 蓁子：榛树的果实。
⑤ 杜鹃口血：杜鹃的喙是红色，啼叫声悲切，所以人们称杜鹃啼血。
⑥ 厌生人：溺死了许多人。
⑦ "斜山"句：斜山，陡峭的山崖。柏风，柏林中的风雨。
⑧ "泉脚"句：泉脚，从山崖上流下的瀑布。挂绳，采玉工人身系绳索，从山崖垂到溪水之中。青袅袅（niǎo），形容人攀着绳索飘摇不定的样子。
⑨ "村寒"句：白屋，简陋的房屋。娇婴，言娇儿。
⑩ "古台"句：石磴（dèng），山路的石级。悬肠草，蔓生植物，又名思子蔓。

Song of an Old Jade-digger

Li He

He digs up jade, he digs up jade in water green
To make a headdress for a lady or a queen.
When he's hungry and cold, the dragon would be sad;
Nor clear nor pure, the water of Blue Creek turns bad.
He eats hazelnuts when it rains in mountains deep;
With tears like the blood shed by the cuckoo, he'd weep.
The Blue Creek dislikes a digger when he appears;
He too dislikes it though dead for a thousand years.
By the mountainside the wind soughs and the rain falls;
A rope hangs around his waist over waterfalls.
How can he not think of his children in his hut cold,
When he sees the forget-me-not on the cliff old?

The poet sympathizes with the poor old man who digs up jade from the Blue Creek.

汴河亭^①

许 浑

广陵^②花盛帝^③东游，

先劈昆仑一派流。

百二禁兵^④辞象阙^⑤，

三千宫女下龙舟。

凝云鼓震星辰动，

拂浪旗开日月浮。

四海义师^⑥归有道，

迷楼^⑦还似景阳楼^⑧。

---

① 汴河亭：隋炀帝在汴河之滨建造的行宫。汴河，又称汴水、汴渠、通济渠，自今河南荥阳市北引黄河水东南流，经开封、商丘、夏邑与今安徽宿州市、泗县及江苏泗洪，至盱眙县境入淮河及洪泽湖。
② 广陵：今扬州。
③ 帝：指隋炀帝杨广。
④ 禁兵：中国古代皇帝的亲兵，即侍卫宫中及护从的军队。
⑤ 象阙：这里代指隋宫。
⑥ 义师：隋末农民起义军。
⑦ 迷楼：隋炀帝建在今扬州纵欲玩乐的宫殿。
⑧ 景阳楼：南朝陈后主在今南京所建的宫殿。

Royal Pavilion on the Great Canal

Xu Hun

The emperor went east to see the flowering town;

Mount Kunlun was cleft to let its water flow down.

Royal escorts leaving the palace went afloat;

Three thousand maids of honor mounted the dragon boat.

Drums were beaten to make clouds tremble and stars shiver;

Flags caressed waves, sun and moon floated on the river.

But by revolting armies the empire overthrown,

The emperor in the pavilion lost his crown.

This is a satire against the last emperor of the Sui Dynasty who lost his crown in 618.

过华清宫^①绝句三首（其一）

杜 牧

长安回望绣成堆^②，

山顶千门次第开。

一骑红尘^③妃子笑，

无人知是荔枝来。

---

① 华清宫：故址在陕西临潼骊山之上，原称温泉宫，天宝六年（747 年）改名为
华清宫。
② 绣成堆：骊山左侧有西绣岭，右侧有东绣岭。唐玄宗时，岭上广植树木花卉，远
远望去，犹如锦绣。唐玄宗李隆基和妃子杨玉环常来游乐。
③ 红尘：飞扬的尘土。

The Spring Palace (I)

Du Mu

Viewed from afar, the hill's paved with brocade in piles;

The palace doors on hilltops opened one by one.

A steed which raised red dust won the fair mistress' smiles.

How many steeds which brought her fruit died on the run!

许渊冲译唐诗三百首

过华清宫绝句三首（其二）

杜　牧

新丰^①绿树起黄埃，
数骑渔阳^②探使回。
霓裳^③一曲千峰上，
舞破中原始下来。

① 新丰：唐县名，在陕西临潼东北，与华清宫相距不远。
② 渔阳：唐郡名，在天津市蓟州区附近，当时是安禄山的根据地。
③ 霓裳：《霓裳羽衣曲》。

The Spring Palace (II)

Du Mu

Yellow dust raised by the steeds veiled trees like a screen;
The messenger deceived came to deceive the crown.
The Song of Rainbow Cloak over a thousand peaks green
Would not stop till the Central Plain was broken down.

許
渊
冲
译
唐
诗
三
百
首

The report said that General An Lushan would rise in revolt and the Bright Emperor sent messengers to An's headquarters, who, bribed by An, reported An's loyalty. The emperor deceived continued to enjoy the dance and music of Rainbow Cloak in the Spring Palace until the Central Plain was lost to An's revolting army.

九、人格境界……

送陈章甫

李 颀

四月南风大麦黄，枣花未落桐叶长。

青山朝别暮还见，嘶马出门思旧乡。

陈侯①立身何坦荡，虬须②虎眉仍③大颡④。

腹中贮书一万卷，不肯低头在草莽。

东门⑤酤酒饮我曹⑥，心轻万事如鸿毛。

醉卧不知白日暮，有时空望孤云高。

长河浪头连天黑，津吏⑦停舟渡不得。

郑国游人⑧未及家，洛阳行子⑨空叹息。

闻道故林⑩相识多，罢官昨日今如何。

① 陈侯：对陈章甫的敬称。
② 虬须：胡须拳曲。
③ 仍：再加上。
④ 大颡（sǎng）：宽大的前额。
⑤ 东门：指洛阳东门。
⑥ 我曹：我辈。
⑦ 津吏：管理渡口的小吏。
⑧ 郑国游人：指陈章甫。时居河南洛阳的嵩山，故称。
⑨ 洛阳行子：作者自称。
⑩ 故林：故乡；故园。

许渊冲译唐诗三百首

Farewell to Chen Zhangfu

Li Qi

To yellow barley the summer wind sings its song,
Date flowers not yet fallen, the plain leaves grow long.
Green hills left at dawn can be seen at dusk again;
The horse neighing outdoors thinks of its familiar plain.
My friend, you are so dignified and frank and true.
With dragon beard, tiger brows and large forehead too,
In your bosom there must be ten thousand books you've read;
To the officialdom you would not bow your head.
By the east gate you drink wine with us in delight;
At heart you take everything as a feather light.
Without knowing the sun has set, so drunk you lie;
Sometimes you gaze in vain at lonely cloud on high.
Waves in the long river surge to join the dark sky;
No boat at the ferry would take the passers-by.
Roamer, you cannot go back to your native land,
Sighing in vain by the riverside where you stand.
You have many friends in your country, people say,
Dismissed yesterday, how will they greet you today?

The poet bids farewell at the ferry to a friend dismissed from his office.

将进酒 [1]

李 白

君不见 [2] 黄河之水天上来，奔流到海不复回。

君不见高堂 [3] 明镜悲白发，朝如青丝暮成雪。

人生得意须尽欢，莫使金樽空对月。

天生我材必有用，千金散尽还复来。

烹羊宰牛且为乐，会须 [4] 一饮三百杯。

岑夫子，丹丘生 [5]，将进酒，杯莫停。

---

[1] 将（qiāng）进酒：乐府旧题，属《鼓吹曲·铙歌》，内容多写饮酒放歌的情感。将，请。

[2] 君不见：你没有看见。这是乐府诗中常用的套语，"君不闻"，也是这样的。君，多为泛指。

[3] 高堂：高大的厅堂。

[4] 会须：应该。

[5] 岑夫子，丹丘生：岑勋、元丹丘。两人均为李白好友。

Invitation to Wine

Li Bai

Do you not see the Yellow River come from the sky,

Rushing into the sea and ne'er come back?

Do you not see the mirrors bright in chambers high

Grieve o'er your snow-white hair though once it was silk-black?

When hopes are won, oh! Drink your fill in high delight,

And never leave your wine-cup empty in moonlight!

Heaven has made us talents, we're not made in vain.

A thousand gold coins spent, more will turn up again.

Kill a cow, cook a sheep and let us merry be,

And drink three hundred cupfuls of wine in high glee!

Dear friends of mine,

Cheer up, cheer up!

I invite you to wine.

Do not put down your cup!

许渊冲译唐诗三百首

与君歌一曲，请君为我倾耳听。

钟鼓馔玉^①不足贵，但愿长醉不愿醒。

古来圣贤皆寂寞，唯有饮者留其名。

陈王^②昔时宴平乐^③，斗酒十千恣欢谑。

主人^④何为言少钱，径须沽取对君酌。

五花马^⑤，千金裘^⑥，

呼儿将出换美酒，与尔同销万古愁。

① 钟鼓馔（zhuàn）玉：代指豪门富贵。古时富贵人家宴会上常鸣钟击鼓作乐。馔玉，"玉馔"的倒文，喻精美的饮食。
② 陈王：三国魏曹植，他是曹操的第三个儿子，曾被封为陈王。
③ 宴平乐：曹植《名都篇》："归来宴平乐，美酒斗十千。"平乐，即平乐观（guàn），汉宫阙名，旧址在今河南省洛阳市附近。
④ 主人：作者自称。
⑤ 五花马：五色花纹的好马。
⑥ 千金裘：价值千金的皮衣。《史记·孟尝君列传》："孟尝君有一狐白裘，直千金。"裘，皮衣。

I will sing you a song, please hear,

O hear! Lend me a willing ear!

What difference will rare and costly dishes make?

I only want to get drunk and never to wake.

How many great men were forgotten through the ages?

But great drinkers are more famous than sober sages.

The Prince of Poets feast'd in his palace at will,

Drank wine at ten thousand a cask and laughed his fill.

A host should not complain of money he is short,

To drink with you I will sell things of any sort.

My fur coat worth a thousand coins of gold

And my flower-dappled horse may be sold

To buy good wine that we may drown the woes age-old.

˙ The poet invites his friends to wine so as to drown the age-old sorrow.

行路难 ①

李 白

金樽 ② 清酒斗十千 ③，玉盘 ④ 珍羞 ⑤ 直万钱。

停杯投箸 ⑥ 不能食，拔剑四顾心茫然。

欲渡黄河冰塞川，将登太行 ⑦ 雪满山。

闲来垂钓碧溪上 ⑧，忽复乘舟梦日边 ⑨。

行路难！行路难！多歧路 ⑩，今安在？

长风破浪 ⑪ 会有时，直挂云帆 ⑫ 济 ⑬ 沧海 ⑭！

① 行路难：古乐府"杂曲歌辞"调名，内容多写世路艰难和离别悲伤，多以"君不见"开头。原诗有三首，这是第一首。
② 樽：古代盛酒的器具。
③ 斗十千：形容酒价昂贵。
④ 玉盘：玉制的盘子。
⑤ 珍羞：精美的食品。羞，同"馐"。直，同"值"。
⑥ 箸（zhù）：筷子。
⑦ 太行（háng）：山名，位于山西河北交界处。
⑧ 垂钓碧溪上：据《史记·齐太公世家》记载，吕尚（姜太公）曾在渭水边垂钓，后来遇到周文王，被重用。
⑨ 乘舟梦日边：传说伊尹在受成汤重用前，曾梦见自己乘船经过日月旁边。
⑩ 歧路：岔路。
⑪ 长风破浪：比喻远大抱负得以实现。据《宋书·宗悫传》载：宗悫（què）少年时，叔父宗炳问他的志向，他说："愿乘长风破万里浪。"
⑫ 云帆：像白云一样的船帆。
⑬ 济：渡过。
⑭ 沧海：大海。

许渊冲译唐诗三百首

Hard Is the Way of the World

Li Bai

Pure wine in golden cup costs ten thousand coins, good!

Choice dish in a jade plate is worth as much, nice food!

Pushing aside my cup and chopsticks. I can't eat;

Drawing my sword and looking round, I hear my heart beat.

I can't cross Yellow River: ice has stopped its flow;

I can't climb Mount Taihang: the sky is blind with snow.

I poise a fishing pole with ease on the green stream

Or set sail for the sun like the sage in a dream.

Hard is the way. Hard is the way.

Don't go astray! Whither today?

A time will come to ride the wind and cleave the waves;

I'll set my cloud-like sail to cross the sea which raves.

The poet sighs for the hard way of the world, but he will brave the wind and waves to cross the sea of perils.

答王十二寒夜独酌有怀

李 白

昨夜吴中雪，子猷①佳兴发。

万里浮云卷碧山，青天中道流孤月。

孤月沧浪②河汉③清，北斗错落长庚④明。

怀余对酒夜霜白，玉床金井冰峥嵘⑤。

人生飘忽百年内，且须酣畅万古情。

君不能狸膏金距⑥学斗鸡，坐令鼻息吹虹霓⑦。

君不能学哥舒⑧，横行青海夜带刀，西屠石堡取紫袍。

① 子猷（yóu）：王徽之，王羲之之子。《世说新语·任诞》记载：王子猷居山阴，夜大雪，眠觉，开室，命酌酒，四望皎然。因起彷徨，咏左思《招隐》诗，忽忆戴安道。时戴在剡，即便夜乘小船就之。经宿方至，造门不前而返。人问其故，王曰："吾本乘兴而行，兴尽而返，何必见戴？"

② 沧浪：沧凉，寒冷之意。

③ 河汉：这里指银河。

④ 长庚：黄昏时出现在西方的金星的名称。

⑤ "玉床"句：晨见东方为启明，昏见西方为长庚。床，井栏。玉床金井，言其美丽之饰，如玉如金。峥嵘，高峻突出的样子。

⑥ 狸膏金距：狸膏，即狸猫的膏脂。斗鸡时，取狸膏涂于鸡头，则斗无敌。因为狸善捕鸡，鸡闻到狸味就会恐惧逃走。金距，施金芒于距，即给鸡爪套上锐利的金属爪套。距，鸡附足膏。

⑦ "坐令"句：出自李白《古风其二十四》，原诗为讽刺斗鸡之徒不可一世的嚣张气焰："路逢斗鸡者，冠盖何辉赫。鼻息干虹霓，行人皆怵惕。"斗鸡者趾高气扬，吹出的气息都能冲上天，使路边的行人胆战心惊，表现其小人得志之态。

⑧ 哥舒：哥舒翰，唐朝赫赫有名的战将，曾为安西节度使。天宝七年（748年）大破吐蕃军于青海，又筑城于青海中龙驹岛，吐蕃屏迹不敢近青海。天宝八年（749年）攻下吐蕃要塞石堡城，功勋卓著。

许渊冲译唐诗三百首

For Wang the Twelfth Who Drank Alone on a Cold Night

Li Bai

It snowed on southern shore last night;

You drank alone with keen delight.

Clouds float for miles and miles like rolled-up mountains high;

The lonely moon drifts in the midst of the sky.

The same lonely moon swims in Silver River dear;

The evening star is bright when Dipper stars appear.

You think of me drinking on a night white with frost;

The golden well with rails of jade in ice is lost.

Men live like floating clouds within a hundred years,

So we should drink our fill like our ancient compeers.

You cannot do as the eunuchs fond of cock fight,

Who blow their breath like rainbow bright.

You cannot do as the general with sword in hand,

Who won his violet robe by slaughter on the land.

吟诗作赋北窗里，万言不直一杯水。

世人闻此皆掉头，有如东风射马耳。

鱼目亦笑我，谓与明月①同。

骅骝拳跼②不能食，蹇驴得志鸣春风。

折杨黄华③合流俗，晋君听琴枉清角④。

巴人谁肯和阳春，楚地犹来贱奇璞⑤。

黄金散尽交不成，白首为儒身被轻。

---

① 明月：明月珠，夜明珠。此句源自成语"鱼目混珠"。
② 骅骝（huá liú）拳跼：骅骝，骏马名。拳跼，不伸也，约束窘促，喻不能发挥才能。
③ 折杨、黄华：与"巴人"皆古流行通俗乐曲。
④ "晋君"句：典出《韩非子·十过》。清角是古代悲壮乐调，据说只能给有才德者听。晋平公德薄，却强迫师旷奏，结果风雨大作，裂帷破幕，屋瓦飞散。平公大惊而病，晋大旱三年。
⑤ "楚地"句：用卞和献玉事。出自《韩非子·和氏第十三》：楚人和氏得玉璞楚山中，奉而献之厉王，厉王使玉人相之，玉人曰："石也。"王以和为诳，而刖（yuè）其左足。及厉王薨（hōng），武王即位，和又奉其璞而献之武王，武王使玉人相之，又曰："石也。"王又以和为诳，而刖其右足。武王薨，文王即位，和乃抱其璞而哭于楚山之下，三日三夜，泣尽而继之以血。王闻之，使人问其故，曰："天下之刖者多矣，子奚哭之悲也？"和曰："吾非悲刖也，悲夫宝玉而题之以石，贞士而名之以诳，此吾所以悲也。"王乃使玉人理其璞而得宝焉，遂命曰："和氏之璧。"

Writing verse or prose, by north window you remain;

Ten thousand words not worth a cup of water plain.

Hearing of this, people would turn their heads away,

Just as a horse with ears hurt by east wind would neigh.

The fish's eye mistaken for a pearl laughs at me,

Saying I cannot shine as the moon or as he.

A horse can't gallop when it has nothing to eat;

A donkey brays in spring breeze though crippled in fret.

The common people like to sing the vulgar thing.

How could the sacred lute please a secular king?

By popular musicians no fine music's played;

The Southerners usually look down on rare jade.

No friendship will be made when I've spent all my gold,

Though my hair turns white, I receive but glances cold.

一谈一笑失颜色，苍蝇贝锦①喧谤声。

曾参岂是杀人者？谗言三及慈母惊②。

与君论心握君手，荣辱于余亦何有？

孔圣犹闻伤凤麟③，董龙④更是何鸡狗！

一生傲岸苦不谐，恩疏媒劳志多乖。

严陵⑤高揖⑥汉天子，何必长剑拄颐⑦事玉阶。

达亦不足贵，穷亦不足悲。

① 苍蝇贝锦：苍蝇，即青蝇。出自《诗经·小雅·青蝇》："营营青蝇，止于樊。岂弟君子，无信谗言。营营青蝇，止于棘。谗人罔极，交乱四国。营营青蝇，止于榛。谗人罔极，构我二人。"贝锦，锦上贝状图案，比喻花言巧语。出自《诗经·小雅·巷伯》："萋兮斐兮，成是贝锦。彼谮（zèn）人者，亦已大甚！"苍蝇、贝锦均是讽刺妄进谗言的小人的。
② "谗言"句：曾参，春秋时孔丘学生。在郑时，有同姓名者杀人，别人误以为他，告诉其母。其母正织布，不信安坐。又两人来告，其母疑，投杼下机，越墙逃走。
③ "孔圣"句：孔圣，丘曾为凤鸟不至而哀叹，又为麒麟被获而伤悲。以为生逢乱世。
④ 董龙：北朝秦主符坚宠臣。宰相王堕刚直，上朝每不交言董，人劝他敷衍，曰："董龙是何鸡狗，而令国士与之言乎？"后为董龙所杀。
⑤ 严陵：东汉隐士严光，字子陵，曾与光武帝刘秀同学。秀为皇帝，请严去。严到宾馆高卧不起，不行君臣之礼，仍愿回富春江钓鱼。
⑥ 高揖：长揖而不下拜，是平交之礼。
⑦ 长剑拄颐：佩剑长及面颊。

My face has lost color when I speak in low voice;

For slanderers like flies make a deafening noise.

The sage's a murderer, how could that be believed?

The rumor thrice heard, the sage's mother was deceived.

We speak our bosom hand in hand and face to face.

What do I care about vain glory or disgrace?

Confucius only grieved no phoenix would appear.

Why should we hold these lower animals in fear?

Proud all my life long, with them I'm not in accord;

In disfavor, I'm alienated from the lord.

The hermit said to the emperor goodbye.

Why should he serve with his long sword in palace high?

The successful are not those we adore,

Nor the unsuccessful those we deplore.

韩信羞将绛灌比^①，祢衡耻逐屠沽儿^②。

君不见李北海^③，英风豪气今何在！

君不见裴尚书^④，土坟三尺蒿棘居！

少年早欲五湖去^⑤，见此弥将钟鼎疏。

① "韩信"句：汉淮阴侯韩信一向自视颇高，《史记·淮阴侯列传》："信知汉王
畏恶其能，尝称病不朝从。……居常鞅鞅，羞与绛、灌等列"。绛、灌是指绛侯
周勃和灌婴这两个汉初功臣。

② 屠沽儿：指屠户与酒家。《后汉书·祢衡传》记载，建安初年，祢（mí）衡从荆
州游历至许昌。"是时许都新建，贤士大夫四方来集。"有人建议他去拜见当时
的名士陈长文和司马伯达，谁知祢衡根本看不起他们，回答说："吾焉能从屠沽
儿耶！"意思是我怎么能跟杀猪卖酒的人混在一起呢？

③ 李北海：李邕，字泰和，广陵江都人。拜左拾遗。开元初，历殿中侍御史，执政
忌其才，频被贬斥。后为北海太守，李林甫傅以罪，杖杀之。

④ 裴尚书：指刑部尚书裴敦复。奸相李林甫利用户部尚书裴宽和刑部尚书裴敦复之
间的矛盾，趁势挑拨，怂恿裴敦复买通杨玉环的姐姐在皇上面前说裴宽坏话，致
使裴宽被贬为睢阳太守。李林甫另以明迁暗降的手法，任命裴敦复为岭南五府经
略等使。裴敦复稍有迟疑，便被李林甫反奏一本，以逗留不到任为由，贬为淄州
太守。

⑤ 五湖去：春秋越大夫范蠡助勾践败吴，功成身退，泛舟五湖。

594

General Han was ashamed of his compeers;

A loyal man despises one at whom he jeers.

Have you not seen Li of North Sea?

Brave as he was, where now is he?

Have you not seen Secretary Pei

Buried among thorns? What to say?

While young, I wished to wander on the lake;

Now older, born the dreams of glory I'm awake.

许
渊
冲
译
唐
诗
三
百
首

The poet talks about his friendship, his despise of slanderers, his love for the hermit and the loyal general, his sympathy with Li and Pei unjustly punished by the prime minister, and his wish to wander on the lake like General Fan with the Beauty in 473 BC.

山中问答

李　白

问余何意栖^①碧山^②，
笑而不答心自闲^③。
桃花流水窅然^④去，
别有天地非人间。

① 栖：休息。
② 碧山：一座青翠苍绿的小山。一说在湖北安陆，山下有桃花岩，李白读书处。
③ 闲：自由自在。
④ 窅然：远去的样子。窅，深邃、深远。

A Reply

Li Bai

I dwell among green hills and someone asks me why;

My mind carefree, I smile and give him no reply.

Peach petals fallen on running water pass by,

This is an earthly paradise beneath the sky.

The poet prefers to live carefree in the hills or by the riverside.

望蓟门 [①]

祖　咏

燕台 [②] 一望客心惊，

笳鼓喧喧汉将营。

万里寒光生积雪，

三边 [③] 曙色动危旌。

沙场烽火连胡月，

海畔云山拥蓟城。

少小虽非投笔吏，

论功还欲请长缨。

---

① 蓟门：今北京德胜门外西北，相传当年其地树木葱茏，晴烟拂空，故名之"蓟门
烟树"，为燕京八景之一。
② 燕台：幽州台。
③ 三边：古称幽、并、凉三州为三边。天宝末年，安禄山兼领三镇（平卢、范阳、
云中），皆重镇。

Gazing on Northern Gate

Zu Yong

My mind is startled when I've left the Northern town,

To hear horns and drums in General's camp up and down.

For miles and miles cold light grows out of piled-up snow;

In twilight on frontier flags flutter high and low.

The beacon fire brightens the moon on battleground

And clouds over the seaside town, mountains surround.

While young, I did not give up the pen for the sword;

To do a feat, I would capture the Tartar lord.

Gazing on the Norther frontier, the poet wishes to do a feat.

饮中八仙歌

杜 甫

知章骑马似乘船，

眼花落井水底眠。

汝阳三斗始朝天，

道逢麹车①口流涎，

恨不移封向酒泉②。

左相日兴费万钱，

饮如长鲸吸百川，

衔杯乐圣称避贤。

宗之潇洒美少年，

举觞③白眼望青天，

皎如玉树临风前。

苏晋长斋绣佛前，

醉中往往爱逃禅。

---

① 麹车：酒车。
② 酒泉：今属甘肃，相传那里"城下有金泉，泉味如酒，故名酒泉"（见《三秦记》）。
③ 觞（shāng）：古代酒器。

Songs of Eight Immortal Drinkers

Du Fu

Zhizhang feels dizzy on his horse as in a boat.

Should he fall into the well, asleep there he should float.

Prince Lian would go to court after drinking three jars;

His mouth would water, seeing wine-transporting cars.

He would have as his fief the Spring of Wine in dreams.

Left Minister buys wine with thousand coins by day,

He would drink like a whale a hundred streams,

Dismissed now, he would drink impure wine as he may.

Without restraint, Zongzhi is a gallant young guy.

Like one of the jade trees standing in vernal breeze.

The Buddhist Su Jin should neither drink nor eat the meat,

But drunk, to run away from Buddha he is fleet.

李白斗酒诗百篇,

长安市上酒家眠。

天子呼来不上船,

自称臣是酒中仙。

张旭三杯草圣传,

脱帽露顶王公前,

挥毫落纸如云烟。

焦遂五斗方卓然[①],

高谈雄辩惊四筵。

① 卓然:超然;卓越。

Li Bai would turn sweet nectar into verses fine.

Drunk in the capital, he'd lie in shops of wine.

Even imperial summons proudly he'd decline,

Saying immortals could leave the drink divine.

In cursive writing Zhang Xu's worthy of his fame.

After three drinks he bares his head before lord and dame,

And splashes cloud and mist on paper as with flame.

Jiao Sui is sober after drinking jar on jar;

His eloquence astonishes guests near and far.

许
渊
冲
译
唐
诗
三
百
首

The poet describes eight drinkers: He Zhizhang who writes Home-Coming. Prince Lian, the
Left Minister, Zuo Zongzhi for whom Li Bai writes Farewell to a Friend, a Buddhist who wor-
ships wine more than Buddha, Li Bai who could turn wine into verse, Zhang Xu who paints
better when drinks, and Jiao Sui more eloquent after drinking.

房兵曹①胡马

杜 甫

胡马大宛名②，

锋棱③瘦骨成。

竹批双耳峻④，

风入四蹄轻。

所向无空阔，

真堪托死生⑤。

骁腾⑥有如此，

万里可横行。

① 兵曹：兵曹参军的省称，是唐代州府中掌管军防、驿传等事的小官。房兵曹不详
为何人。
② "胡马"句：胡，此指西域。大宛，汉西域国名，其地在今乌兹别克斯坦境内，
盛产良马。大宛名，著名的大宛马。
③ 锋棱：锋利的棱角。形容马的神俊健悍之状。
④ "竹批"句：竹批，形容马耳尖如竹尖。峻，尖锐。这是良马的特征之一。
⑤ "真堪"句：堪，可以、能够。托死生，马值得信赖，对人的生命有保障。
⑥ 骁腾：健步奔驰。

General Fang's Steed

Du Fu

The steed from the barbaric west
Has angular frame and strong chest.
Likc pointed bamboo its sharp ear,
As swift wind its fleet hoofs, O hear!
The way it runs will never end;
Life or death on it may depend.
When you have such a fiery steed,
You can ride where you will indeed.

许渊冲译唐诗三百首

The poet writes this poem in praise of the fiery steed of General Feng.

望岳

杜 甫

岱宗①夫如何?

齐鲁②青未了③。

造化钟④神秀,

阴阳⑤割昏晓。

荡胸生曾云,

决眦⑥入归鸟。

会当凌绝顶,

一览众山小。

---

① 岱宗:指泰山。泰山别名岱,为五岳之首,故又名岱宗。
② 齐鲁:泰山之北为古齐地,之南为古鲁地。
③ 了:尽。
④ 钟:集中;赋予。
⑤ 阴阳:山北为阴,山南为阳。
⑥ 决眦:眼角裂开。眦,眼角。

Gazing on Mount Tai

Du Fu

O peak of peaks, how high it stands!

One boundless green overspreads two States.

A marvel done by Nature's hands,

Over light and shade it dominates.

Clouds rise therefrom and lave my breast;

I stretch my eyes to see birds fleet.

I will ascend the mountain's crest;

It dwarfs all peaks under my feet.

许渊冲译唐诗三百首

Gazing on Mount Tai, the poet seems to ascend in and dwarf all peaks under his feet.

奉赠韦左丞丈二十二韵

杜 甫

纨绔不饿死，儒冠多误身①。

丈人试静听，贱子请具陈②：

甫昔少年日，早充观国宾③。

读书破万卷，下笔如有神。

赋料扬雄敌，诗看子建亲④。

李邕求识面，王翰愿卜邻⑤。

自谓颇挺出，立登要路津⑥。

致君尧舜上，再使风俗淳⑦。

① "纨绔"二句：纨绔，指富贵子弟。不饿死，不学无术却无饥饿之忧。儒冠多误身，满腹经纶的儒生却穷困潦倒。
② "丈人"二句：丈人，对长辈的尊称，这里指韦济。贱子，年少位卑者自谓，这里是杜甫自称。
③ "甫昔"二句：这两句是指开元二十三年（735年），杜甫以乡贡（由州县选出）的资格在洛阳参加进士考试的事。杜甫当时才二十四岁，就已是"观国之光"（参观王都）的国宾了，故曰"早充"。"观国宾"语出《周易·观卦·象辞》："观国之光尚宾也。"
④ "赋料"二句：扬雄，字子云，西汉辞赋家。料，差不多。敌，匹敌。子建，曹植的字，曹操之子，建安时期著名文学家。看，比拟。亲，接近。
⑤ "李邕（yōng）"二句：李邕，唐代文豪、书法家，曾任北海郡太守。杜甫年少在洛阳时，李邕奇其才，曾主动去结识他。王翰，当时著名诗人，《凉州词》的作者。
⑥ "自谓"二句：挺出，杰出。立登要路津，很快就要得到重要的职位。
⑦ "致君"二句：这两句说，如果自己得到重用的话，可以辅佐皇帝实现超过尧舜的业绩，使已败坏的社会风俗再恢复到上古那样淳朴敦厚。这是当时一般儒者的最高政治理想。尧舜，传说中上古的圣君。

For Minister Wei

Du Fu

The rich of hunger never die;
The poor of their misfortune sigh.
Minister Wei, would you please hear
What I would confide to your ear?
While young, I was a candidate
In Civil Exams of the State.
Having ten thousand volumes read,
I wrote as if by God I was led.
In prose I was second to none;
In verse I vied with the best one.
Ministers would like to know me,
And poets my neighbors would be.
I thought, outstanding as was I,
A job was not hard to come by.
I would help the crown in my strife
To purify the ways of life.

许渊冲译唐诗三百首

此意竟萧条，行歌非隐沦。

骑驴十三载，旅食京华春。

朝扣富儿门，暮随肥马尘。

残杯与冷炙，到处潜悲辛。

主上顷见征，欻然欲求伸[1]。

青冥却垂翅，蹭蹬无纵鳞[2]。

甚愧丈人厚，甚知丈人真。

每于百僚上，猥诵佳句新。

窃效贡公喜，难甘原宪贫[3]。

① "主上"二句：主上，指唐玄宗。顷，不久前。见征，被征召。欻（xū）然，忽然。欲求伸，希望表现自己的才能，实现致君尧舜的志愿。
② "青冥"二句：青冥却垂翅，飞鸟折翅从天空坠落。蹭蹬，行进困难的样子。无纵鳞，本指鱼不能纵身远游，这里是说理想得不到实现。
③ "窃效"二句：贡公，西汉人贡禹。他与王吉为友，闻吉显贵，高兴得弹冠相庆，因为知道自己也将出头。杜甫说自己也曾自比贡禹，并期待韦济能荐拔自己。难甘，难以甘心忍受。原宪，孔子的学生，以贫穷出名。

I could not do what I desired;

Singing, I would not be retired.

Riding a donkey thirteen years,

I suffered the capital's sneers.

I knock at the mansions by day;

At dusk I hear dusty steeds neigh.

I eat leftovers of a meal;

In vain I suffer a great deal.

The Crown showed his favor and love;

I saw a chance to rise above.

In the sky the roe folds its wings;

On the sea swim no scaly kings.

I thank you for your kindness true,

Knowing you're kind in what you do.

Whenever you meet a good friend,

It's my new verse you recommend.

Though glad of your prosperity,

How could I bear my poverty?

许
渊
冲
译
唐
诗
三
百
首

焉能心快快，只是走踆踆①。

今欲东入海，即将西去秦②。

尚怜终南山，回首清渭滨。

常拟报一饭，况怀辞大臣③。

白鸥没浩荡，万里谁能驯④！

① 走踆踆（qūn）：且进且退的样子。
② "今欲"二句：东入海，指避世隐居。孔子曾言："道不行，乘桴浮于海"（《论语》）。去秦，离开长安。
③ "常拟"二句：报一饭，报答一饭之恩。春秋时灵辄报答赵宣子（见《左传》宣公二年），汉代韩信报答漂母（见《史记·淮阴侯列传》），都是历史上有名的报恩故事。辞大臣，指辞别韦济。
④ "白鸥"二句：没浩荡，投身于浩荡的烟波之间。谁能驯，谁还能拘束我呢？

I'm not unhappy in my place;

But it's a dilemma I face.

Should I go seaward for my rest,

Or to the capital in the west?

I love the Southern Mountains high

And the clear River flowing by.

I can't forget what I owe you,

Nor what to ministers is due.

Like a white gull on the vast sea,

I'd fly for miles and miles, carefree.

许渊冲译唐诗三百首

The poet thanks Minister Wei for his kind help but he would be free like a gull.

江汉

杜 甫

江汉^①思归客^②，

乾坤^③一腐儒^④。

片云天共远，

永夜^⑤月同孤。

落日^⑥心犹壮，

秋风病欲苏^⑦。

古来存老马，

不必取长途。

① 江汉：长江、汉水之间。当时杜甫在湖北公安，地处江汉。
② 思归客：杜甫自谓，因为身在江汉，却时刻思归故乡。
③ 乾坤：天地间。
④ 腐儒：迂腐的儒者，这里实际是指不会迎合世俗的、正直的读书人。
⑤ 永夜：长夜。
⑥ 落日：借指暮年。这时杜甫五十六岁。
⑦ 病欲苏：病快要好了。苏，复苏。

On River Han

Du Fu

On River Han my home thoughts fly,
Bookworm with worldly ways in fright.
The cloud and I share the vast sky;
I'm lonely as the moon all night.
My heart won't sink with sinking sun;
West wind blows my illness away.
A jaded horse may not have done,
Though it cannot go a long way.

The poet compares himself to a jaded horse which can still run but not a long way.

致酒行

李　贺

零落栖迟^①一杯酒，
主人奉觞客长寿。
主父^②西游困不归，
家人折断门前柳。
吾闻马周^③昔作新丰客，
天荒地老无人识。
空将笺上两行书，
直犯龙颜请恩泽。
我有迷魂^④招不得，
雄鸡一声天下白。
少年心事当拏云^⑤，
谁念幽寒坐呜呃^⑥。

---

① 零落栖迟：零落，指身世飘零。栖迟，指困顿失意。此言自己潦倒闲居，漂泊落魄，寄人篱下。
② 主父：《汉书》：汉武帝时主父偃西入关见卫将军，卫将军数言上，上不省。资用乏，留久，诸侯宾客多厌之。后来主父偃上书终于被采纳，当上了郎中。
③ 马周：《旧唐书》：马周西游长安，宿于新丰，逆旅主人唯供诸商贩而不顾待。周遂命酒一斗八升，悠然独酌。主人深异之。至京师，舍于中郎将常何家。贞观五年（631 年），太宗令百僚上书言得失，常何以武吏不涉经学。周乃为陈便宜二十余事，令奏之，皆合旨。太宗怪其能，问何，对曰："此非臣所能，家客马周具草也。"太宗即日招之，未至间，遣使催促者数四。及谒见，与语甚悦，令值门下省。贞观六年（632 年）授监察御史。
④ 迷魂：此指执迷不悟。宋玉曾作《招魂》，以招屈原之魂。
⑤ 拏云：凌云，高举入云。
⑥ 呜呃：悲叹之声。

616

Drinking Song

Li He

Unsuccessful I stay but with a cup of wine;
The kind host wishes me to live to ninety-nine.
An ancient could not but stay in the west for long;
In vain his household waited with their willow song.
"A young talent often met with contemptuous eye,
Unknown on the old earth under the dreary sky.
You may write letters of two lines now and again,
And you may not court imperial favor in vain."
I would not call back my soul lost in a sad plight,
But when the cock crows, all the world will see daylight.
"While young, you should aim high and soar into the cloud.
Who pities a lonely man sobbing in the crowd?"

安定^①城楼

李商隐

迢递^②高城百尺楼，
绿杨枝外尽汀洲^③。
贾生^④年少虚垂涕，
王粲^⑤春来更远游。
永忆江湖归白发，
欲回天地入扁舟。
不知腐鼠成滋味，
猜意鹓雏^⑥竟未休。

① 安定：唐代泾原节度使府所在地，故址在今甘肃省泾川县北。唐文宗大和九年（835 年），李商隐的岳父王茂元任泾原节度使，李商隐于唐文宗开成三年（838 年）在其幕府中任掌书记，诗当写于此时。

② 迢递：遥远连绵。此形容楼高而且连续绵延。

③ 汀洲：汀指水边之地，洲是水中之泥沙淤积的陆地。

④ 贾生：指西汉人贾谊。贾谊年少即颇通诸子百家之书，文帝召以为博士，一岁中官至太中大夫。贾谊认为"时事可为痛哭者一，可为流涕者二，可为太息者六"，因此"教上书陈政事，多所欲匡建"，但文帝并未采纳他的建议。后来他呕血而亡，年仅三十三岁。李商隐此时二十七岁，以贾生自比。

⑤ 王粲：东汉末年人，建安七子之一。《三国志·魏书·王粲传》载：王粲年轻时曾流寓荆州，依附刘表，但并不得志。他曾于春日作《登楼赋》，其中有句云："虽信美而非吾土兮，曾何足以少留？"李商隐此以寄人篱下的王粲自比。

⑥ 鹓（yuān）雏：古代传说中一种像凤凰的鸟。《庄子·秋水》："惠子相梁，庄子往见之。或谓惠子曰：'庄子来，欲代子相。'于是惠子恐，搜于国中三日三夜。庄子往见之，曰：'南方有鸟，其名为鹓雏……发于南海而飞于北海，非梧桐不止，非练实不食，非醴泉不饮。于是鸱得腐鼠，鹓雏过之。仰而视之曰：吓！今子欲以子之梁国而吓我邪？'"李商隐以庄子和鹓雏自比，表明自己有高远的心志，并非汲汲于官位利禄之辈，但谗佞之徒却以小人之心度之。

On the Tower of the City Wall

Li Shangyin

From hundred-foot-high city wall I look afar;
Beyond green willow trees the sandy islets are.
I remember a scholar while young shed vain tears,
And a famed scholar roamed in the spring of his years.
I can't forget white-haired General on the lake floating,
After changing the face of the world he went boating.
An owl might feed on dead rats with good appetite,
But a phoenix would perch on trees of lofty height.

許
渊
冲
译
唐
诗
三
百
首

谒山

李商隐

从来系日乏长绳，
水去云回恨不胜。
欲就麻姑买沧海，
一杯春露冷如冰。

Homage to the Mountain

Li Shangyin

Since olden days there is no rope to bind the sun.

How could we stop the cloud and water on the run?

I'd like to buy the vast sea from the goddess nice,

But a cup of spring dew soon turns as cold as ice.

許淵沖譯唐詩三百首

韩冬郎①即席为诗相送，一座尽惊。他日余方追吟"连宵侍坐徘徊久"之句，有老成之风②，因成二绝寄酬，兼呈畏之员外（其一）

李商隐

十岁裁诗走马成③，

冷灰残烛④动离情。

桐花万里丹山路⑤，

雏凤清于老凤声⑥。

① 冬郎：晚唐诗人韩偓的乳名，其父韩瞻（字畏之）与李商隐同年进士登第，同是王茂元的女婿。"连宵侍坐徘徊久"是残句，原诗已佚。大中五年（851年）李商隐离开长安赴东川幕府时，韩氏父子为之饯行，偓曾作诗相送，其诗有"连宵侍坐徘徊久"句。至大中十年（856年），李回长安，因作二首绝句追答。
② 老成之风：指冬郎虽年少，但诗风老练成熟。
③ "十岁"句：十岁，大中五年，韩偓十岁。裁诗，作诗。走马成，言其作诗文思敏捷，走马之间即可成章。
④ 冷灰残烛：当时饯别时宴席上的情景。
⑤ "桐花"句：凤凰非梧桐不栖。
⑥ "雏凤"句：此戏谑韩瞻，并赞其子韩偓的诗才。

For Han Wo, Poet Prodigy (I)

Li Shangyin

You wrote a verse with highest speed at ten years old;
We would not part though candle ashes turned cold.
The flowery mountain path extends for miles long;
The young surpass the old in singing phoenix's song.

许
渊
冲
译
唐
诗
三
百
首

长安秋望

杜 牧

楼倚霜树①外，
镜天无一毫②。
南山③与秋色，
气势④两相高。

① 霜树：秋天经霜之后树叶变红的树木，泛指秋天的树木。
② 毫：毫毛，细而尖的毛，这里指云彩。
③ 南山：终南山，又名中南山、太一山，位于西安城南二十五公里处。它东接骊山、
  华山，西连太白山，是秦岭的主峰。
④ 气势：气魄；气概。

Autumn in the Capital

Du Mu

The tower overlooks frosty trees;
Speckless is the mirror-like sky.
The South Mountain and autumn bre
Vie to be more sublime and high.

杨柳枝词九首（其一）

刘禹锡

塞北梅花 ① 羌笛吹，
淮南桂树 ② 小山词。
请君莫奏前朝曲，
听唱新翻杨柳枝。

① 梅花：指汉乐府《横吹曲》中的《梅花落》曲，用笛子吹奏。
② 桂树：指代《楚辞》中的《招隐士》篇。相传西汉淮南王刘安门客小山之徒作《招
　隐士》篇来哀悼屈原。

Willow Branch Song (I)

Liu Yuxi

The flute played on "Mume Blossoms" on Northern Frontier,

"The Laurel Branch" to Southern River shore was dear.

They were sung in the former dynasties for long.

Now listen to my newly composed "Willow Song".

剑客

贾　岛

十年磨一剑，
霜刃未曾试。
今日把示君，
谁有不平事？

A Swordsman

Jia Dao

I've sharpened my sword for ten years;
I do not know if it will pierce.
I show its blade to you today.
O who has any grievance? Say!

许渊冲译唐诗三百首

登鹳雀楼

王之涣

白日依山尽，
黄河入海流。
欲穷千里目，
更上一层楼。

On the Stork Tower

Wang Zhihuan

The sun along the mountain bows;

The Yellow River seawards flows.

You will enjoy a grander sight

By climbing to a greater height.

许渊冲译唐诗三百首

金缕衣

无名氏

劝君莫惜金缕衣 [①] ，
劝君须惜少年时。
花开堪 [②] 折直须 [③] 折，
莫待无花空折枝。

---

① 金缕衣：以金线制成的华丽衣裳。
② 堪：可以。
③ 直须：不必犹豫。

The Golden Dress

Anonymous

Love not your golden dress, I pray,

More than your youthful golden hours.

Gather sweet blossoms while you may,

And not the twig devoid of flowers!

十、人生感悟····

代悲白头翁

刘希夷

洛阳城东桃李花，

飞来飞去落谁家？

洛阳女儿惜颜色，

坐见落花长叹息。

今年花落颜色改，

明年花开复谁在？

已见松柏摧为薪[1]，

更闻桑田变成海[2]。

古人无复洛城东，

今人还对落花风。

年年岁岁花相似，

岁岁年年人不同。

寄言全盛红颜子，

应怜半死白头翁。

① 松柏摧为薪：松柏被砍伐作柴薪。《古诗十九首》："古墓犁为田，松柏摧为薪。"
② 桑田变成海：《神仙传》："麻姑谓王方平曰：'接待以来，已见东海三为桑田。'"

Admonition on the Part of a White-haired Old Man

Liu Xiyi

The peach and plum flowers east of the capital
Fly up and down and here and there. Where will they fall?
The maiden in the capital loves rosy hue;
She would sigh for the flowers falling out of view.
Her rosy color fades when flowers fall this year.
When flowers blow again, will she pretty appear?
I've seen cypress cut down as fuel with pine trees;
I've heard the mulberry fields turn into the seas.
We see no ancients now east of capital town,
But we still see today the wind blow flowers down.
The flowers of this year look like those of last year;
But next year the same people will not reappear.
I'd like to tell the rosy faces in their prime
Not to forget the old before their dying time.

此翁白头真可怜，

伊昔红颜美少年。

公子王孙芳树下①，

清歌妙舞落花前。

光禄②池台文锦绣③，

将军④楼阁画神仙。

一朝卧病无相识，

三春行乐在谁边？

宛转蛾眉⑤能几时？

须臾鹤发乱如丝。

但看古来歌舞地，

唯有黄昏鸟雀悲！

① "公子"二句：这两句说，白头翁年轻时曾和公子王孙在树下花前共赏清歌妙舞。
② 光禄：光禄勋。用东汉马援之子马防的典故。《后汉书·马援传》（附马防传）载：马防在汉章帝时拜光禄勋，生活很奢侈。
③ 池台文锦绣：指以锦绣装饰池台中物。
④ 将军：指东汉贵戚梁冀，他曾为大将军。《后汉书·梁冀传》载：梁冀大兴土木，建造府宅。
⑤ 宛转蛾眉：本为年轻女子的面部化妆，此处代指青春年华。

Pitiable is the old man whose hair turns white,

But in his prime he was rosy-cheeked, fair and bright.

Noble sons and daughters under the leafy trees

Sing and dance before the flowers blown down by the breeze.

By lakeside stand ministers' richly brocaded bowers;

Pictures of immortals hang in generals' towers.

When you're ill and cast down, with you none would abide.

Who would then make merry in spring days by your side?

How long can your finely arched eyebrows remain fair?

Your head will soon be covered with disheveled hair.

See where the noble sang and danced in merriment,

Now you can only hear at dusk the birds' lament.

许渊冲译唐诗三百首

The poet admonishes young men and maidens not to waste their golden hours of youth.

登幽州台歌

陈子昂

前不见古人，
后不见来者。
念天地之悠悠，
独怆然①而涕下。

① 怆然：凄伤的样子。

On the Tower at Youzhou

Chen Zi'ang

Where are the great men of the past
And where are those of future years?
The sky and earth forever last;
Here and now I alone shed tears.

The poet sighs for he has not done great deeds as the great men of yore.

許渊冲译唐诗三百首

秋夜独坐

王　维

独坐悲双鬓，

空堂欲二更。

雨中山果落，

灯下草虫鸣。

白发①终难变，

黄金不可成②。

欲知除老病③，

唯有学无生④。

---

① 白发：《列仙传》载，稷丘君朱璜入山八十余年，"白发尽黑"。此处反用典故。
② "黄金"句：古道士、方士谓烧炼丹药化为金银之事，又叫黄白之术。《史记·孝武本纪》："致物而丹砂可化为黄金，黄金成，以为饮食器则益寿。"
③ 老病：佛教称生老病死为四苦。《释迦谱》："以畏生老病死之苦，故于五欲不敢爱者。"
④ 无生：无生即无灭。佛家把世界看成绝对静止，认为一切皆虚幻。《仁王经》："一切法性真实空，不来不去，无生无灭。"

Sitting Alone on an Autumn Night

Wang Wei

Sitting alone, I grieve over my hair white;

In empty room it approaches midnight.

With the rain I hear in the mountain fruit fall;

By lamplight the insects chirp in my hall.

I cannot blacken my white hair while old,

Nor can I turn a metal into gold.

If you want to get rid of ills of old age,

You can only learn from the Buddhist sage.

許
渊
冲
译
唐
诗
三
百
首

The poet thinks it best to learn from the Buddhist sage.

行路难

李　白

大道如青天，

我独不得出。

羞逐长安社中儿，

赤鸡白雉^①赌梨栗。

弹剑作歌^②奏苦声，

曳裾王门^③不称情。

淮阴市井笑韩信^④，

汉朝公卿忌贾生^⑤。

① 赤鸡白雉：指当时斗鸡走狗的博戏。
② 弹剑作歌：战国时齐公子孟尝君门下食客冯谖曾屡次弹剑作歌怨己不如意。《史记》："冯谖闻孟尝君好客，蹑蹻而见之，孟尝君置传舍十日，孟尝君问传舍长曰：客何所为，答曰：冯先生甚贫，犹有一剑耳。又蒯缑，弹其剑而歌曰：长铗归来乎，食无鱼。孟尝君迁之幸舍，食有鱼矣。五日又问传舍长，答曰：客复弹剑而歌曰：长铗归来乎，出无舆。孟尝君迁之代舍，出入乘舆车矣。五日孟尝君复问传舍长，答曰：先生又尝弹剑而歌曰：长铗归来乎，无以为家。孟尝君不悦。"
③ 曳裾王门：寄食公卿王侯门下。裾，长裙。《汉书》："邹阳曰：饰固陋之心，则何王之门不可曳长裾乎？"
④ "淮阴"句：淮阴，地名。即今江苏淮阴区。汉封韩信为淮阴侯，即此。韩信，汉初淮阴人，少时受辱胯下，全市皆笑韩信怯懦，后为大将。《史记》："韩信淮阴人，淮阴屠中少年有侮信者，曰：若虽长大，好带刀剑，中情怯耳。众辱之曰：信能死，刺我，不能死，出我胯下。于是，信孰视之，俯出胯下，蒲伏。一市人皆笑信，以为怯。"
⑤ 贾生：洛阳贾谊，曾上书汉文帝，劝其改制兴礼，受大臣反对。《史记》："天子议以为贾生任公卿之位，绛、灌、东阳侯、冯敬之属尽害之，乃短贾生曰：洛阳之人，年少初学，专欲擅权，纷乱诸事。于是天子后亦疏之，不用其议。"

Hard Is the Way of the World

Li Bai

The way is broad like the blue sky,

But no way out before my eye.

I am ashamed to follow those who have no guts,

Gambling on fighting cocks and dogs for pears and nuts.

Feng would go homeward way, having no fish to eat;

Zhou did not think to bow to noblemen was to meet.

General Han was mocked in the market place;

The brilliant scholar, Jia was banished in disgrace.

君不见昔时燕家重郭隗[①]，

拥篲折节[②]无嫌猜。

剧辛乐毅[③]感恩分，

输肝剖胆效英才。

昭王白骨萦蔓草，

谁人更扫黄金台[④]。

行路难，归去来。

许渊冲译唐诗三百首

[①] 郭隗：战国时燕人，昭王筑台师事之，乐毅、剧辛等闻风而至，燕以大治。
[②] 拥篲折节：比喻谦恭下士。篲，扫帚。拥篲，长者未来之前，持帚扫尘，以示恭敬。折节，弯腰，降低身份，礼待臣下。燕昭王曾亲自扫路，恐灰尘飞扬，用衣袖挡帚，以礼迎贤士邹衍。《史记》："邹衍如燕，燕昭王拥篲先驱。"
[③] 剧辛乐毅：皆战国时人。燕昭王招贤者，剧辛自赵往任国政。乐毅为燕昭王卿，率五国兵伐齐，下齐七十余城。
[④] 黄金台：在易水东南，燕昭王置千金于台上，以招揽天下士。

Have you not heard of King of Yan in days gone by,

Who venerated talents and built Terrace high

On which he offered gold to gifted men

And stooped low and swept the floor to welcome them?

Grateful, Ju Xin and Yue Yi came then

And served him heart and soul, both full of stratagem.

The king's bones were now buried, who would sweep the foot

And the Gold Terrace any more?

Hard is the way. Go back without delay!

The poet shows the way of the world was hard for talents like Feng, Zhou, Han, Jia. Only the King of Yan built a terrace to offer gold to talents, but he is no more now. So the poet says it would be better to go back without delay.

日出入行 ①

李 白

日出东方隈 ②，

似从地底来。

历天又复入西海，

六龙 ③ 所舍安在哉?

其始与终古不息，

人非元气 ④，

安得与之久徘徊?

草不谢荣于春风 ⑤，

木不怨落于秋天。

---

① 这是一首以乐府旧题抒发自我感慨的古体诗。《日出入》是汉乐府《郊祀歌》旧题，原诗大意为：日之出入无有穷期，人命却很短促，故希望乘六龙升仙入天。李白此诗一反其意，指出日之无穷和人生短促都是自然规律，故主张顺应自然。

② 隈（wēi）：山或河转弯的地方。

③ 六龙：古代神话传说认为日乘车，以六龙驾之。

④ 元气：天地未分前的混沌之气。

⑤ 谢荣于春风：因为开花而向春风表示感谢。荣，草木开花。这两句诗，语出《庄子·内篇·大宗师》郭象注："故圣人之在天下，暖焉若阳春之自和，故蒙泽者不谢；凄乎若秋霜之自降，故凋落者不怨也。"

Song of Sunrise and Sunset

Li Bai

From the east the sun comes around;

It seems to rise from underground.

Crossing the sky, it sinks in the sea of the west.

Where could the six dragons driving it take their rest?

It never changes from beginning to end.

Man is not a spirit,

Could he accompany it

As a dear friend?

Grass will not for its growth thank the spring breeze;

Leaves won't complain of autumn when fallen from trees.

谁挥鞭策驱四运^①，

万物兴歇皆自然。

羲和^②！羲和!

汝奚汩没于荒淫之波^③？

鲁阳何德,

驻景挥戈?

逆道违天^④,

矫诬实多。

吾将囊括大块,

浩然与溟涬同科^⑤。

① 四运：指春、夏、秋、冬四时的运行。
② 羲和：神话传说中掌管太阳运行的神。
③ "汝奚"句：奚，疑问副词，为什么。汩没，沉没。荒淫，这里是广大无边的意
  思。相传太阳没入虞渊之中。
④ "逆道"句：道，指自然规律。天，指自然界。
⑤ "吾将"二句：囊括，包罗。这里用以形容胸怀的广阔。大块，宇宙。浩然，这
  里也是用来形容胸怀的广阔。溟涬（xíng），天地未形成前，自然之气混混沌沌
  的样子，泛指自然之气。同科，同类。

Who could drive summer and winter, autumn and spring?

Nature rules over rise and fall of everything.

O Driver of the Sun,

What on the boundless waves have you done?

O Herculean Son,

How could you wield your spear to stop the Driver's run?

You go against the law divine.

What you do is quite out of line.

I would embrace the universe

To be one with Nature for better or for worse.

许
渊
冲
译
唐
诗
三
百
首

The legend went that the Driver of the Sun rode on six dragons, but the poet doubts it and jeers at the legendary Driver and the Herculean son who could stop his run. At last the poet would become one with nature.

江上吟

李　白

木兰之枻沙棠舟 ①，玉箫金管 ② 坐两头。

美酒樽中置千斛 ③，载妓随波任去留。

仙人有待乘黄鹤 ④，海客无心随白鸥 ⑤。

屈平辞赋悬日月 ⑥，楚王台榭 ⑦ 空山丘。

兴酣落笔摇五岳 ⑧，诗成笑傲凌 ⑨ 沧洲 ⑩。

功名富贵若长在，汉水 ⑪ 亦应西北流。

① 木兰之枻（yì）沙棠舟：木兰，又名玉兰，落叶乔木，高丈余。枻，船桨。沙棠，树名，古代传说，人吃了它的果实，可入水不溺。木兰枻、沙棠舟，形容船和桨的名贵。
② 玉箫金管：指吹箫、笛等乐器的人。
③ 斛（hú）：旧量器，方形，口小底大。十斗为一斛。
④ "仙人"句：有待，语出《庄子·逍遥游》，意为等待外力的帮助。黄鹤，湖北武汉武昌区西有武昌山，山西北有黄鹤矶，峭立江中。传说仙人王子安乘黄鹤过此。本句是说：仙人骑黄鹤而飞行，还必须依靠外力（黄鹤）的帮助，并未得到真正的自由。
⑤ "海客"句：《列子·黄帝篇》中有则寓言说，古时海边有一个人非常喜欢鸥鸟，每天清晨到海边，与鸥鸟游戏，常有成百只白鸥飞到他身旁。这里诗人以海客自比。
⑥ "屈平"句：屈平，即屈原，平是名，原是字。悬日月，如日月高悬，光辉四照。
⑦ 楚王台榭（xiè）：指战国时楚王游憩的台榭。榭，建筑在台上的房屋。
⑧ 五岳：指东岳泰山、西岳华山、南岳衡山、北岳恒山、中岳嵩山，此处泛指山岳。
⑨ 凌：凌驾的意思。
⑩ 沧洲：泛指江海之地。
⑪ 汉水：汉江，源出陕西宁强，东流到襄阳与白河汇合，南流由汉阳入长江。

Song on the River

Li Bai

In a ship of spice-wood with unsinkable oars,

Musicians at both ends, we drift along the shores.

We have sweet wine with singing girls to drink our fill,

And so the waves may carry us wherever they will.

Immortals could not fly without their yellow crane;

Unselfish men might follow white gulls to the main.

The verse of Qu Yuan shines as bright as sun and moon,

While palaces of Chu vanish like dreams at noon.

Seeing my pen in verve, even mountains shake;

Hearing my laughter proud, the seaside hermits wake.

If worldly fame and wealth were things to last forever,

Then northwestward would turn the eastward flowing river.

许渊冲译唐诗三百首

The romantic poet thinks himself as happy as immortals while roaming on the river.

月下独酌[①]四首（其一）

李　白

花间一壶酒，
独酌无相亲。
举杯邀明月，
对影成三人[②]。
月既[③]不解[④]饮，
影徒随我身。
暂伴月将[⑤]影，
行乐须及春。
我歌月徘徊，
我舞影零乱。
醒时同交欢[⑥]，
醉后各分散。
永结无情[⑦]游，
相期[⑧]邈[⑨]云汉[⑩]。

① 独酌：一个人饮酒。
② 成三人：明月和我以及我的影子恰是三人。
③ 既：且。
④ 不解：不懂。
⑤ 将：和。
⑥ 交欢：一起欢乐。
⑦ 无情：忘却世情。
⑧ 相期：相约。
⑨ 邈：遥远。
⑩ 云汉：银河。

Drinking Alone under the Moon (I)

Li Bai

Among the flowers, from a pot of wine
I drink without a companion of mine.
I raise my cup to invite the Moon who blends
Her light with my Shadow and we're three friends.
The Moon does not know how to drink her share;
In vain my Shadow follows me here and there.
Together with them for the time I stay,
And make merry before spring's spent away.
I sing and the Moon lingers to hear my song;
My Shadow's a mess while I dance along.
Sober, we three remain cheerful and gay;
Drunken, we part and each may go his way.
Our friendship will outshine all earthly love;
Next time we'll meet beyond the stars above.

许渊冲译唐诗三百首

The lonely poet thinks it happy to drink with the moon and his own shadow. His loneliness reveals his discontent with his actual life.

拟古十二首（其九）

李　白

生者为过客，

死者为归人。

天地一逆旅^①，

同悲万古尘。

月兔空捣药，

扶桑^②已成薪。

白骨寂无言，

青松岂知春。

前后更叹息，

浮荣何足珍？

---

① 逆旅：旅舍。逆，迎。古人以生为寄，以死为归，如《尸子》："老莱子曰：人生于天地之间，寄也；寄者固归也。"又如《青青陵上柏》："人生天地间，忽如远行客。"此用其意。

② 扶桑：东方的一棵神树，此树位于东方大海一座山的温泉山谷中，太阳由此升腾而起。

Life and Death (IX)

Li Bai

The living are but passers-by,

And those are going home who die.

The sky and earth are hotels just

For all to grieve over age-old dust.

The Moon Goddess lives long in vain;

The sacred tree's cut down with pain.

The bleached bones can not speak nor sing.

Could green pines feel the warmth of spring?

Ancestors and posterity,

Don't prize but sigh for vanity!

This is a philosophical poem in which the poet equalizes life and death, imagines the sacred tree cut down, from which rose the sun, and sighs for the vanity of man.

曲江二首（其一）

杜 甫

一片花飞减却^①春，

风飘万点正愁人。

且看欲尽花经眼^②，

莫厌伤多酒^③入唇。

江上小堂巢翡翠^④，

苑边高冢卧麒麟^⑤。

细推^⑥物理^⑦须行乐，

何用浮荣绊此身？

① 却：去，掉。
② "且看"句：且看，但看。欲尽花，将要落尽的花。欲，将。经眼，打眼前经过。
③ 伤多酒：过量的酒。伤，过度、过量。这句说，不要腻烦过多的酒入口。
④ "江上"句：小堂，指曲江的楼堂建筑。巢，鸟做窝。翡翠，鸟名，喙长而直，有蓝色和绿色的羽毛，羽毛可做装饰品。
⑤ "苑边"句：苑，指唐代的宫苑芙蓉苑，又叫芙蓉园，在曲江西南。高冢，或指杜陵汉宣帝墓，墓近芙蓉苑。卧麒麟，古代帝王及贵族坟墓的墓道两旁，都立有石兽。这里说麒麟一类的石兽已经倒卧在地了。
⑥ 推：推究。
⑦ 物理：事物盛衰变化之理。

The Winding River (I)

Du Fu

Spring fades when petals on petals fly as they please;
It grieves me to see dots on dots waft in the breeze.
Enjoy the blooms passing away before your eyes;
Do not refuse to drown your grief in wine and sighs!
In the riverside halls kingfishers build their nest;
Before the tomb the stone animals lie at rest.
The law of Nature tells us to enjoy as we may.
Why spoil our joy by sheer vanity of the day?

The poet tells us to enjoy delight on the Winding River while we may.

曲江二首（其二）

杜　甫

朝回日日典春衣^①，

每日江头尽醉归。

酒债寻常行处有^②，

人生七十古来稀。

穿花蛱蝶深深见^③，

点水蜻蜓款款^④飞。

传语风光共流转^⑤，

暂时相赏莫相违^⑥。

① "朝回"句：朝回，去皇宫上朝后退朝回家。典，典当，即拿实物去当铺抵押现
金，对方收取利息。
② "酒债"句：寻常，随便。行处，走到的地方。这句说，随便到哪里都欠有酒债。
③ "穿花"句：穿花蛱蝶，在花丛中穿行的蝴蝶。深深见，忽隐忽现。深深，隐。
见，同"现"。蝴蝶飞落到花上时，身上的花纹与花的颜色混在一起，故若隐。
当它飞离花丛，又显现在眼前，故若现。蛱蝶，蝴蝶。
④ 款款：徐缓的样子。
⑤ "传语"句：传语，传话。风光，春光。共流转，在一起逗留盘桓。
⑥ "暂时"句：相赏，指与春光共同赏玩。相违，互相分开。

The Winding River (II)

Du Fu

Back from the court from day to day, I pawn spring gown

To get drunk by the riverside where I go down.

In every wine shop I have a debt to pay;

It's rare to live to seventy since olden day.

Deeper and deeper amid flowers go butterflies;

Slowly and slowly on water skim dragonflies.

I will enjoy the present with those on the wing.

Do not let pass away any delightful thing!

The poet tells us how he enjoys delight in poverty.

登高①

杜　甫

风急天高猿啸哀②，
渚③清沙白鸟飞回④。
无边落木萧萧下⑤，
不尽长江滚滚来。
万里悲秋常作客⑥，
百年⑦多病独登台。
艰难苦恨繁霜鬓⑧，
潦倒新停浊酒杯⑨。

① 登高：指农历九月九日重阳节登高。
② 猿啸哀：三峡多猿，啼声凄厉哀切。
③ 渚：水中沙洲。
④ 鸟飞回：因风急所以飞鸟盘旋。
⑤ "无边"句：无边，无边无际。落木，落叶。萧萧，落叶声。
⑥ 客：旅居在外的人，这里是诗人自指。
⑦ 百年：一生。
⑧ "艰难"句：艰难，指长期漂泊在外所经历的艰难困苦。苦恨，深恨。繁霜鬓，
　白发增多。
⑨ "潦倒"句：潦倒，失意、衰颓。新停浊酒杯，诗人因肺病而戒酒。

On the Height

Du Fu

The wind so swift, the sky so wide, apes wail and cry;

Water so clear and beach so white, birds wheel and fly.

The boundless forest sheds its leaves shower by shower;

The endless river rolls its waves hour after hour.

A thousand miles from home, I'm grieved at autumn's plight;

Ill now and then for years, alone I'm on this height.

Living in times so hard, at frosted hair I pine;

Cast down by poverty, I have to give up wine.

许渊冲译唐诗三百首

This is the most balanced verse in Tang poetry.

登科后

孟　郊

昔日龌龊[①]不足夸，
今朝放荡[②]思无涯。
春风得意马蹄疾，
一日看尽长安花。

① 龌龊：本指齿相近，这里指登科前处境不如意。
② 放荡：自由自在，不受拘束。与"旷荡""放达"义近。但不同于现代的"放浪"的意思。

Successful at the Civil Service Examinations

Meng Jiao

Gone are all my past woes! What more have I to say?
My body and my mind enjoy their fill today.
Successful, faster runs my horse in vernal breeze;
I've seen within one day all flowers on the trees.

This is the most balanced verse in Tang poetry.

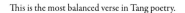

竹枝词九首（其七）

刘禹锡

瞿塘①嘈嘈②十二滩，

此中道路古来难。

长恨人心不如水，

等闲平地起波澜。

① 瞿塘：瞿塘峡，又名夔峡，西起奉节白帝城，东至巫山县大溪镇，全长八公里。瞿塘峡是三峡中最短、最窄、最险的峡谷。
② 嘈嘈：流水发出的嘈杂声。

Bamboo Branch Song (VII)

Liu Yuxi

From beach to beach the torrent splashes down its way;
It's hard to sail in the Three Gorges since olden day.
But human heart is more dangerous than a whirlpool;
You may be drowned in it though it seems calm and cool.

许渊冲译唐诗三百首

The poet compares human heart to a dangerous whirlpool.

琵琶行

白居易

浔阳江^①头夜送客，

枫叶荻花^②秋瑟瑟。

主人下马客在船，

举酒欲饮无管弦。

醉不成欢惨将别，

别时茫茫江浸月。

忽闻水上琵琶声，

主人忘归客不发。

寻声暗问弹者谁?

琵琶声停欲语迟^③。

移船相近邀相见，

添酒回灯重开宴。

千呼万唤始出来，

犹抱琵琶半遮面。

① 浔阳江：长江流经浔阳郡境内的一段。
② 荻（dí）花：荻是水生植物，秋天开草黄色花。
③ 欲语迟：想回答又有些迟疑。

Song of a Pipa Player

Bai Juyi

One night by riverside I bade a friend goodbye;

In maple leaves and rushes autumn seemed to sigh.

My friend and I dismounted and came into the boat;

We wished to drink but there was no music afloat.

Without flute songs we drank our cups with heavy heart;

The moonbeams blended with water when we were to part.

Suddenly o'er the stream we heard a pipa sound;

I forgot to go home and the guest stood spell-bound.

We followed where the music led to find the player,

But heard the pipa stop and no music in the air.

We moved our boat towards the one whence came the strain,

Brought back the lamp, asked for more wine and drank again.

Repeatedly we called for the fair player till

She came, her face half hidden behind a pipa still.

转轴拨弦三两声，

未成曲调先有情。

弦弦掩抑声声思，

似诉平生不得志。

低眉信手续续弹，

说尽心中无限事。

轻拢慢捻抹复挑[①]，

初为霓裳后六幺[②]。

大弦嘈嘈如急雨，

小弦切切如私语[③]。

嘈嘈切切[④]错杂弹，

大珠小珠落玉盘。

① "轻拢"句：弹奏的各种手法。
② 霓裳：《霓裳羽衣曲》，据说是开元时从印度传入的，原名"婆罗门"，经唐明
   皇润色并改此名。作者还有《霓裳羽衣舞歌》，对此有较详细的描写。六幺：琵
   琶曲名。也作《绿腰》，原名《录要》，以乐工进曲录其要点而得名，是当时流
   行的曲调。
③ "大弦"二句：大弦指琵琶四弦（或五弦）中最粗的弦，小弦指细弦。
④ 嘈嘈切切：嘈嘈，形容低重之音。切切，形容轻细之音。

She turned the pegs and tested twice or thrice each string;

Before a tune was played we heard her feelings sing.

Each string she plucked, each note she struck with pathos strong,

All seemed to say she'd missed her dreams all her life long.

Head bent, she played with unpremeditated art

On and on to pour out her overflowing heart.

She lightly plucked, slowly stroked and twanged loud

The song of "Green Waist" after that of "Rainbow Cloud".

The thick strings loudly thrummed like the pattering rain;

The fine strings softly tinkled in a murmuring strain.

When mingling loud and soft notes were together played,

You heard large and small pearls cascade on plate of jade.

许渊冲译唐诗三百首

许
渊
冲
译
唐
诗
三
百
首

间关莺语花底滑^①，

幽咽泉流冰下难^②。

冰泉冷涩弦凝绝，

凝绝不通声暂歇。

别有幽愁暗恨生，

此时无声胜有声。

银瓶乍破水浆迸^③，

铁骑突出刀枪鸣。

曲终收拨当心画^④，

四弦一声如裂帛。

东船西舫悄无言，

唯见江心秋月白。

沉吟放拨插弦中^⑤，

整顿衣裳起敛容。

① "间关"句：间关，鸟鸣声。滑，形容乐声婉转流畅。
② 冰下难：形容乐声艰涩低沉、呜咽断续。
③ "银瓶"二句：形容曲调暂歇之后，忽然急促高亢，又进入高潮。
④ "曲终"二句：描写演奏结束时，演奏者用拨子对着四弦的中心用力一划，琵琶
声像猛然撕开布帛时发出的声响。
⑤ "沉吟"二句：沉吟，沉思回味。敛容，整理情绪，从音乐意境中收回心来，表
现出严肃而又恭敬的神态。

Now you heard orioles warble in flowery land,

Then a sobbing stream run along a beach of sand.

But the stream seemed so cold as to tighten the string;

From tightened strings no more sound could be heard to sing.

Still we heard hidden grief and vague regret concealed;

Then music expressed far less than silence revealed.

Suddenly we heard water burst a silver jar,

And the clash of spears, and sabers come from afar.

She made a central sweep when the music was ending;

The four strings made one sound, as of silk one was rending.

Silence reigned left and right of the boat, east and west;

We saw but autumn moon white in the river's breast.

She slid the plectrum pensively between the strings,

Smoothed out her dress and rose with a composed mien.

自言本是京城女，

家在虾蟆陵^①下住。

十三学得琵琶成，

名属教坊第一部^②。

曲罢常教善才伏^③，

妆成每被秋娘^④妒。

五陵年少争缠头^⑤，

一曲红绡^⑥不知数。

钿头银篦击节碎^⑦，

血色罗裙翻酒污。

---

① 虾蟆陵：在长安城东南曲江附近，是歌女聚居的地方。旧说董仲舒葬此，门人经
过这里，都下马步行，所以叫下马陵。后人误传为虾蟆陵。

② "名属"句：教坊，唐高祖时设置的宫内教练歌舞的机构，唐玄宗又设内教坊和
左教坊、右教坊。这位弹琵琶的女子当是挂名教坊，临时入宫供奉的。第一部，
首席乐队。

③ 伏：敬佩。

④ 秋娘：当时的一位名妓。

⑤ "五陵"句：五陵年少，富贵人家子弟。五陵，指汉代的长陵、安陵、阳陵、茂
陵、平陵，都在长安城北，是汉朝王公贵族的聚居处。缠头，古代赏赠给歌人舞
女的丝织品。争缠头，争先恐后地送缠头。

⑥ 红绡：红色绫缎。

⑦ "钿头"句：钿，用金玉珠宝等制成的花朵形的首饰。银篦，银制的篦子，也是
一种首饰。击节碎，用贵重首饰打拍子，碎了也不可惜。

"I spent," she said, "in the capital my early springs,

Where at the foot of Mount of Toads my home had been.

At thirteen I learned on the pipa how to play,

And my name was among the primas of the day.

I won my master's admiration for my skill;

My beauty was envied by songstresses fair still.

The gallant young men vied to shower gifts on me;

One tune played, countless silk rolls were given with glee.

Beating time, I let silver comb and pin drop down,

And spilt-out wine oft stained my blood-red silken gown.

今年欢笑复明年，

秋月春风等闲度。

弟走从军阿姨死，

暮去朝来颜色故。

门前冷落鞍马稀，

老大嫁作商人妇。

商人重利轻别离，

前月浮梁①买茶去。

去来江口守空船，

绕船月明江水寒。

夜深忽梦少年事，

梦啼妆泪红阑干②。

我闻琵琶已叹息，

又闻此语重唧唧③。

---

① 浮梁：唐天宝年间改设的县，治所在今江西省景德镇市浮梁县。是个茶叶贸易
中心。

② "梦啼"句：妆泪，脂粉和眼泪混在一起。阑干，（泪水）纵横。

③ 重唧唧：重，更加。唧唧，叹息。

From year to year I laughed my joyous life away

On moonlit autumn night as windy vernal day.

My younger brother left for war, and died my maid;

Days passed, nights came, and my beauty began to fade.

Fewer and fewer were cabs and steeds at my door;

I married a smug merchant when my prime was o'er.

The merchant cared for money much more than for me;

One month ago he went away to purchase tea,

Leaving his lonely wife alone in empty boat;

Shrouded in moonlight, on the cold river I float.

Deep in the night I dreamed of happy bygone years,

And woke to find my rouged face crisscrossed with tears."

Listening to her sad music, I sighed with pain;

Hearing her story, I sighed again and again.

许
渊
冲
译
唐
诗
三
百
首

同是天涯沦落人，

相逢何必曾相识！

我从去年辞帝京，

谪居卧病浔阳城。

浔阳地僻无音乐，

终岁不闻丝竹声。

住近湓江地低湿，

黄芦苦竹绕宅生。

其间旦暮闻何物？

杜鹃①啼血猿哀鸣。

春江花朝秋月夜，

往往取酒还独倾。

岂无山歌与村笛？

呕哑嘲哳②难为听。

① 杜鹃：又名子规，鸣声凄切。相传古代蜀国的一位国君名叫杜宇，又称望帝，死后魂化杜鹃，鸣声凄切，常常啼叫得口角流血。
② 呕哑嘲哳：形容乐声杂乱难听。

Both of us in misfortune go from shore to shore.

Meeting now, need we have known each other before?

"I was banished from the capital last year

To live degraded and ill in this city here.

The city's too remote to know melodious song,

So I have never heard music all the year long.

I dwell by riverbank on a low and damp ground

In a house with wild reeds and stunted bamboos around.

What is here to be heard from daybreak till nightfall

But gibbon's cry and cuckoo's homeward-going call?

By blooming riverside and under autumn moon

I've often taken wine up and drunk it alone.

Though I have mountain songs and village pipes to hear,

Yet they are crude and strident and grate on the ear.

Listening to you playing on pipa tonight,

With your music divine e'en my hearing seems bright.

今夜闻君琵琶语,

如听仙乐耳暂明。

莫辞更坐弹一曲,

为君翻作①琵琶行。

感我此言良久立,

却坐②促弦弦转急。

凄凄不似向前声,

满座重闻皆掩泣。

座中泣下谁最多?

江州司马③青衫湿。

① 翻作:按曲填写歌词。
② 却坐:重新坐下。
③ 江州司马:作者自指。

Will you sit down and play for us a tune once more?

I'll write for you an ode to the pipa I adore."

Touched by what I said, the player stood for long,

Then sat down, tore at strings and played another song.

So sad, so drear, so different, it moved us deep;

Those who heard it hid their faces and began to weep.

Of all the company at table who wept most?

It was none other than the exiled blue-robed host.

许
渊
冲
译
唐
诗
三
百
首

This is one of the most popular songs of the Tang Dynasty in which the poet describes a musician and her music.

与梦得^①沽酒闲饮且约后期

白居易

少时犹不忧生计，

老后谁能惜酒钱？

共把十千沽一斗，

相看七十欠三年。

闲征雅令穷经史，

醉听清吟胜管弦。

更待菊黄家酝熟，

共君一醉一陶然^②。

---

① 梦得：刘禹锡，字梦得，与白居易同龄。开成二年（837年），白、刘（六十七岁，故云"相看七十欠三年"）同在洛阳。刘任太子宾客分司，白任太子少傅，都是闲职，故得"闲饮且约后期"。
② 陶然：舒畅快乐的样子。

Drinking Together with Liu Yuxi

Bai Juyi

While young, I was not worried about livelihood.
Old now, how could I grudge money for buying wine?
Let's spend ten thousand coins for a jarful of drink good!
Looking in face, two years more we'll be sixty-nine.
We read and play the drinkers' wager game at leisure;
Drunk, we listen to verse better than music light.
When chrysanthemums yellow, may I have the pleasure
To invite you to drink my home-brew with delight?

The poet expresses his delight in drinking together with an old friend.

官街鼓

李 贺

晓声隆隆催转日，
暮声隆隆呼月出。
汉城^①黄柳映新帘，
柏陵^②飞燕埋香骨。
碜碎千年日长白，
孝武秦王听不得。
从君翠发芦花色，
独共南山^③守中国。
几回天上葬神仙，
漏声^④相将无断绝。

① 汉城：指唐都城长安。
② 柏陵：指坟墓。
③ 南山：指终南山。西起甘肃省天水，东至河南省陕县，绵亘千余里。
④ 漏声：铜壶滴漏的声音。滴漏是古代计时的漏器，用铜壶盛水滴漏来计时刻。

Official Drums

Li He

At dawn official drumbeats hasten the sunrise;
At dusk the booming drums call the moon to the skies.
When yellow willows put forth new buds in the town,
In tomb is buried the favorite of the crown.
The drums have boomed a thousand years, still shines the sun,
But ancient emperors of Qin and Han have done.
Your hair once black may turn white as reed flowers stand,
The drums with southern hills will ever guard our land.
Even immortals were buried in the sky,
The drumbeats and the water-clock will never die.

许渊冲译唐诗三百首

The time-marking drumbeats, says the poet, will last longer than imperial dynasty and human life.

将进酒

李 贺

琉璃钟，琥珀浓，

小槽酒滴真珠红。

烹龙炮凤玉脂泣，

罗帏绣幕围香风。

吹龙笛，击鼍鼓[①]；

皓齿歌，细腰舞。

况是青春日将暮，

桃花乱落如红雨。

劝君终日酩酊醉，

酒不到刘伶[②]坟上土！

[①] 鼍（tuó）鼓：鼍，即扬子鳄，产于长江中下游，亦称鼍龙，俗称猪婆龙。鼍鼓即鼍皮制成的鼓。

[②] 刘伶：魏晋时期的文坛领袖、"竹林七贤"之一。他酷好饮酒，自诩为"天生刘伶，以酒为名"。其每每外出饮酒，必带一小童背铁锹相随，告之曰："死便埋我。"惊世骇俗，无出其右。

Drinking Song

Li He

A glazed cup full of amber wine,

The strong drink drips like red pearls fine.

The dragon boiled and phoenix roasted would weep;

The fragrant breeze blows into broidered curtains deep.

The dragon flute is played;

Beaten the drums covered with alligator's skin.

The songstress sings with teeth as bright as jade,

And dancers dance with waist as slender as hairpin.

The prime of your life like the sun on the decline,

Peach blossoms fall pell-mell like rain of petals pink.

So I advise you to get drunk with wine.

When buried in the grave, what could you take to drink?

This imaginative song is full of sensual beauty. The reader may see amber wine and red pearls, hear the drink drip and the phoenix weep, smell the fragrant breeze and touch the dancer's slender waist and taste boiled dragon and roasted phoenix.

锦瑟

李商隐

锦瑟^①无端^②五十弦，

一弦一柱思华年^③。

庄生晓梦迷蝴蝶^④，

望帝春心托杜鹃^⑤。

沧海月明珠有泪^⑥，

蓝田日暖玉生烟^⑦。

此情可待^⑧成追忆，

只是当时已惘然。

① 锦瑟：《周礼·乐器图》："雅瑟二十三弦，颂瑟二十五弦，饰以宝玉者曰宝瑟，绘文如锦者曰锦瑟。"《汉书·郊祀志上》："秦帝使素女鼓五十弦瑟，悲，帝禁不止，故破其瑟为二十五弦。"古瑟大小不等，弦数亦不同。一般说法，古瑟是五十条弦，后来有二十五弦或十七弦等不同的瑟。

② 无端：没来由；无缘无故。此隐有悲伤之感，乃全诗之情感基调。

③ "一弦"句：柱，是调整弦的音调高低的"支柱"，它把弦"架"住。"思"字应变读去声。律诗中不许有一连三个平声的出现。

④ "庄生"句：《庄子·齐物论》："昔者庄周梦为蝴蝶，栩栩然蝴蝶也；自喻适志与！不知周也。俄然觉，则蘧蘧然周也。不知周之梦为蝴蝶与，蝴蝶之梦为周与？"商隐此引庄周梦蝶故事，以言人生如梦，往事如烟之意。

⑤ "望帝"句：望帝，古代蜀国的君主，名杜宇，传说他让位死后，化为杜鹃鸟，悲啼不已。春心，伤春之心。

⑥ "沧海"句：相传珍珠是由南海鲛人（神话中的人鱼）的眼泪变成，古人还认为海里的蚌珠随月亮盈亏而有圆缺变化，这里糅合了以上的典故。

⑦ "蓝田"句：蓝田，即蓝田山，在今陕西蓝田县，为有名的产玉之地。日暖玉生烟，相传宝玉埋在地下，在阳光的照耀下，良玉上空会出现烟云。

⑧ 可待：岂待；何待。

The Sad Zither

Li Shangyin

Why should the sad zither have fifty strings?

Each string, each strain evokes but vanished springs:

Dim morning dream to be a butterfly;

Amorous heart poured out in cuckoo's cry.

In moonlit pearls see tears in mermaid's eyes;

From sunburnt jade in Blue Field let smoke rise.

Such feeling cannot be recalled again;

It seemed lost even when it was felt then.

许渊冲译唐诗三百首

The zither evokes vanished springs dim and free as the dream of a butterfly, amorous as the heart of a cuckoo, tearful as moonlit pearls and vaporous as the smoke rising from sunburnt jade in the Blue Field.

乐游原 ①

李商隐

向晚 ② 意不适 ③，
驱车登古原。
夕阳无限好，
只是近黄昏。

---

① 乐游原：在长安城南，地势较高。《长安志》："升平坊东北隅，汉乐游庙。"
注云："汉宣帝所立，因乐游苑为名。在高原上，余址尚有。……其地居京城之
最高，四望宽敞。京城之内，俯视指掌。每正月晦日，三月三日，九月九日。京
城士女咸就此登赏祓禊。"
② 向晚：傍晚。
③ 意不适：情绪不好。

On the Plain of Imperial Tombs

Li Shangyin

At dusk my heart is filled with gloom;
I drive my cab to ancient tomb.
The setting sun seems so sublime,
But it is near its dying time.

许渊冲译唐诗三百首

The Merry-making Plain was also called Plain of Imperial Tombs for emperors were buried there. The last two lines are proverbial as "He laughs best who laughs last."

叹花

杜 牧

自是寻春去校迟，
不须惆怅[①] 怨芳时。
狂风落尽深红色，
绿叶成阴子[②] 满枝。

① 惆怅：伤感；失意。
② 子：草木的果实，如《汉武故事》中有"因指谓上，王母种桃，三千年一结子"。

Sighing over Fallen Flowers

Du Mu

I regret to be late to seek for blooming spring;

The flowers not in full bloom in years past I've seen.

The strong wind blows down flowers which sway and swing,

The tree will be laden with red fruit and leaves green.

许渊冲译唐诗三百首

It was said that the poet met with a beautiful maiden and asked for her hand, but next year when he came she was married, so he compares the maiden to a tree with fruit.

图书在版编目（CIP）数据

许渊冲译唐诗三百首 ：汉文、英文 ／（唐）李白著 ；
许渊冲译注. — 北京 ： 中译出版社，2021.7（2024.4重印）
（许渊冲英译作品）
ISBN 978-7-5001-6441-8

Ⅰ．①许… Ⅱ．①李… ②许… Ⅲ．①唐诗－诗集－
汉、英 Ⅳ．①I222.742

中国版本图书馆CIP数据核字（2020）第242946号

出版发行　中译出版社
地　　址　北京市西城区新街口外大街28号普天德胜大厦主楼4层
电　　话　（010）68359719
邮　　编　100088
电子邮箱　book@ctph.com.cn
网　　址　http://www.ctph.com.cn

出 版 人　乔卫兵
总 策 划　刘永淳
责任编辑　刘香玲　张　旭
文字编辑　王秋璎　张莞嘉　赵浠彤
营销编辑　毕竟方

封面制作　刘　哲
内文制作　黄　浩　冯　兴
印　　刷　中煤（北京）印务有限公司
经　　销　新华书店

规　　格　840mm×1092mm　1/32
印　　张　24
字　　数　720千字
版　　次　2021年7月第1版
印　　次　2024年4月第5次

ISBN 978-7-5001-6441-8　定价：86.00元

中 译 出 版 社